THEY RODE PALE HORSES

BOOK ONE

A THATCHER EVANS NOVEL

BY GIDEON STONE

CHAPTER ONE

1877, Eastern Wyoming

Rain battered the windows of the train and Nadine thought of the wet cobblestone streets of London. Outside, the Wyoming terrain had changed from long stretching plains to rolling hills and then to rocky mountains. It wouldn't be much farther until they reached the town of Broken Stone. Part of Nadine would be thankful to finally arrive after the long journey by ship and now by train, but mostly it filled her with trepidation. She glanced at her sleeping fiancé, Earl, and released a heavy sigh.

London seemed very far away.

"Can I get you anything, Miss?"

Nadine smiled at one of the three stewards in the Pullman car. She leaned closer and spoke in a lowered voice as to not disturb Earl. "I would *love* a cup of hot tea."

"Milk and sugar?"

"There's simply no other way." Nadine smiled.

The steward nodded and smiled back. "You're from England."

"London, yes."

"I… I dream of going there some day." The steward glanced away shyly. "I ain't never met nobody who's from there, though."

Nadine smiled brightly, glanced at Earl, still sleeping, and then back to the steward. "If you find yourself able to pry away for a few moments, come sit and I'll tell you anything you would like to know."

"That'd be real nice of you." The steward smiled and nodded as she took a step backward. "I'll get your tea for your right away, Miss." She ushered off to the rear of the car.

Nadine nestled against the plush red-velvet seat and studied the details of the train car. She was both amused and filled with admiration at the decadent choices of fabric and wallpaper and the richly-grained wood trim. It seemed like the room of a fine hotel room and if not for the jostling against the tracks, it would be easy to forget they were on a train.

The train car rocked slightly as a powerful gust of wind hit them. There were low murmurs from several of the car's passengers and Nadine stared out the windows at the sheets of heavy rain beating against the panes of glass.

She turned to the snoring sounds of Earl, undisturbed by the buffeting of the train. Nadine's gaze focused on the older man's gray beard, full and long enough to conceal the collar of his shirt. There, in its center, entangled as if it was a bird's nest, Nadine saw a pea-sized crumb of the biscuit Earl had eaten for breakfast.

The longer she stared, the more Nadine imagined the head of a young starling popping its head up from the strands of beard hair and hungrily snatching at the dry morsel. The longer she imagined it, the funnier it became until laughter rose inside her like bubbles floating toward the surface of water.

Nadine's eyes grew glassy as she tried to contain herself. She shook her head, trying to stifle laughter, but her effort was futile. The combination of her imagination and the weariness of long travel got the best of her until Nadine had no choice but to cover her mouth and embrace the laughter shaking her body.

Earl snorted in his sleep and his beard rippled, making the crumb rise and fall. For the briefest of moments in her mind's eye, Nadine saw the baby starling come out of hiding. Its mouth gaped opened wide and reached for the crumb. The thought only increased her fit of humor and Nadine trembled in her seat with silent laughter. Tears flooded her eyes and Earl inhaled deeply, cleared his throat, and blinked his eyes open.

His gaze found Nadine. "Have we gone through Cheyenne yet?"

Nadine bit her lower lip and then exhaled slowly. She blinked her tears away and shook her head. "Not yet, but you rest your eyes and I'll wake you when we get close to Broken Stone. Not much longer." She wiped at her eyes and purposefully avoided looking at Earl's beard.

He grunted and mercifully turned away from her toward the window and resumed snoring not long after.

Nadine looked skyward, and her face filled with amusement once more, the sheer and utter ridiculousness of her life suddenly very clear.

"Here you are, Miss."

Nadine looked up at the steward who appeared with a mug of steaming hot tea. As Nadine reached for it, the door to the Pullman car slammed open and a man stepped through with a revolver held out in front of him.

CHAPTER TWO

"Good afternoon, *fiiine* people." The man leveled the barrel of his LeMat revolver so the passengers could see. There was amusement in his bright blue eyes as he studied the scared expressions of the passengers. "Anyone makes any sudden moves, and their journey on this train will come to an end."

"It even *smells* like money in here." Another man walked into the car behind the first.

The other man snickered as he held out an open leather satchel and stared out over the seats of passengers. "It might sting a little at first, but if you'll all be so kind as to hand over your valuables, you just might live through the afternoon."

Both of the men wore long duster coats, and held LeMat revolvers in their hands.

Nadine's heart raced in her chest. Beside her, Earl had woken up and glared at the first man as he walked the aisle with his leather bag, taking pocket watches and wallets from the passengers. The second man stood at the threshold, his gun ready.

"That's it, don't be shy, hand it on over." The blue-eyed man stepped closer, two seats away from Nadine, and she reached for the sapphire necklace around her throat, an engagement present from Earl.

He grunted at her action and she turned to see his disapproving expression.

"Hand it on over, whatever you got." The man with the revolver said.

Nadine looked up at the blue-eyed outlaw as she continued pulling the necklace. The thin gold chain snapped at the clasp and she held the jeweled necklace out and dropped it into the open satchel.

"The ring, too." He nodded at Nadine's hand.

She slid the diamond engagement ring from her finger and handed it over.

"This… this is *preposterous!*" Earl growled the words as

he stiffened in his seat.

The blue-eyed outlaw pointed his LeMat upward and fired. A hole blossomed in the ceiling and in the confines of the Pullman car, the sound was deafening. Several passengers screamed and the man lowered his pistol and aimed the barrel at Earl's face. "Does anyone *else* think this is preposterous?"

Silence from the passengers was the answer, and the outlaw grinned at Earl. "Hand over your valuables, ol' timer, or I'll show you what *preposterous* really is."

Nadine saw Earl's face blanch white and he slowly reached inside his suit jacket, withdrew a leather billfold, and handed it over to the other man.

Using his thumb to part the pieces of leather, the outlaw looked inside and fanned the money apart. His face changed from amusement to frustration and he glared at Earl.

English pound notes fell from the billfold and the outlaw's expression turned to rage. "Giving me grief and all you got is this? Can't even spend it here!" He cocked the hammer on the LeMat. "I ought to end your sorry—"

"Easy, Blaine, easy." The other man said. "Not just yet. Don't forget what we're here for."

The man spoke through clenched teeth. "I know *damned well* what we're here for, but ain't no reason to leave money on the table."

"There'll be enough money for a lifetime... for each one of us."

His blue eyes blazed with rage, and he tightened the grip on his LeMat. "Well we ain't exactly got cash in hand yet, now do we?"

A sound ticked against the train windows—a hard, patterned noise like pellets of ice. There was a low rumble outside, like distant thunder, and the outlaw's gaze shifted beyond the glass.

Nadine saw what looked like tiny chips of stone bouncing off of the rain-streaked windows, and when she looked beyond, she could see the train tracks curving to the right through a slice carved into a mountain. A bridge wasn't far ahead, along with the deep blue shimmer of water far below.

There was another deep rumble, and the entire train car shook. The two outlaws exchanged glances as the hard patter against the glass grew louder. A stone shattered a window several seats ahead of Nadine, and a woman screamed.

"What in the blue hell is—"

A roaring sound came from outside, cutting off the words of the outlaw standing at the threshold of the Pullman car. The entire train heaved and shuddered and Nadine watched through the window as massive boulders rolled down the mountain toward them.

Something massive slammed into the car behind them and passengers screamed as the entire train seemed to buck upward from the tracks and tilt sideways at an angle. The sound of luggage shifting and falling objects filled the car and Nadine slammed against Earl's side.

The horrible shriek of rending metal filled the air and Nadine grabbed onto the rear of the seat in front of her. For the briefest of moments, through the window, she saw a river far below, and then the train car shuddered in place.

It was dead silent as everyone seemed to be holding their breath. The entire compartment jolted at an angle, and the rear of the train car dropped down and slammed to a hard stop. Everyone screamed and then it grew deathly quiet.

"Dear God," Earl whispered under his breath as he stared out the window.

Past her fiancé, Nadine saw that their train car was hanging off of the railroad track over the bridge. She turned, slowly, to look at the blue-eyed outlaw, who crouched down and gripped one of the seats.

A loud groan of steel against steel cut through the air and the train car shimmied in place and whined against the weight and strain of the couplers holding it in place. The entire car dropped a foot and slammed to a stop and people screamed again.

"Blaine?"

The blue-eyed outlaw turned to look at the other man and there was fear in his expression.

The entire train car shifted and for an instant, Nadine floated as gravity left her. The Pullman car slammed to a stop, almost vertical in its angle and Earl screamed as he tumbled backward from his seat.

"Earl!" Nadine reached for him, but it happened too quickly and he slammed down against the rear of the car.

"Climb out! Get the hell out of here!" The blue-eyed outlaw yelled and tried to claw his way up against the seats. The other man pushed against the door and flipped it up and open. The steward was in a panic as she climbed over the seats after him. She clutched onto one of the man's ankles and the outlaw turned his LeMat and shot her in the chest.

The bullet went clean through and a chunk of mahogany blasted from the wall. Blood sprayed from the back of the steward, and she fell through the air, dead before she landed against the rear wall of the car beside Earl.

Nadine tucked herself forward, using the rear of the seat ahead to hold herself in place. The stink of coal smoke poured in from the open door at the top of the car, along with the sweet smell of rain.

The red velvet cushions were slippery to hold onto, and Nadine heard a low whine as she watched the thin wood trim on the rear of the seat begin to separate from the bench seat itself. She adjusted her hands, trying to gain purchase and hold herself in place.

Outside, there was a loud screech of metal against metal, and Nadine felt her stomach flip as the train coupler broke and the entire car fell loose from the tracks. The compartment was filled with screams as Nadine descended into darkness.

CHAPTER THREE

Someone groaned in pain, but Nadine heard it from someplace far away. Another person screamed and Nadine opened her eyes.

The heavy downpour had eased to a drizzle and the air was thick with smoke. Nadine tried to breathe and spikes of pain shot through her chest and ribs. She didn't remember crawling out of the train car, but she lay in the cold shallow water in the middle of the river. When Nadine tried to move, she felt smooth round rocks beneath her hands. She was weak, felt as if all the strength had leeched out of her entire body.

A deep whine of metal against metal echoed against the water and Nadine looked up. High above her, a single train car dangled from the tracks cross over the river. It shifted and dropped several feet, slammed to a stop, and the breath left Nadine's lungs. She clawed over the rocks, pulling herself forward through the shallow water. Her right shoulder screamed in protest as bolts of pain flowed through her body.

She heard a loud snapping sound, as if something heavy had given way, and as Nadine scrambled along the river, the air split apart behind her in a great rush as the train car fell. When it crashed against the rocks, the sound was deafening. Its end crumpled like a can of peaches.

Nadine stared, wide-eyed, at the vertical train car, and saw it tremor and begin to tilt toward her. She twisted away and clawed with both hands, mindless of the shrieking pain in her shoulder and ribs, and lunged away from the falling car.

It landed on its side several feet away behind her, and splashed water six feet high all around. Nadine crawled behind a boulder the size of a rain barrel. A long-dead twist of a Lodgepole pine draped above and around her, almost protectively, and Nadine reached out to grab the branch and pull herself up. Her heart slammed against her chest.

A gunshot thundered above the sound of the fast-moving water, and Nadine's gaze snapped to the right, farther up river. The outlaw from the train, the one with blue eyes—

Blaine, the other man called him Blaine.

—pointed a revolver at something in the water. Smoke curled from the barrel of his gun and the man walked a few steps and aimed his LeMat again.

Someone in the water reached up toward the outlaw and Nadine heard a voice pleading for mercy. Blaine squeezed the trigger and the LeMat blasted. The arm fell down into the dark waters and the outlaw walked away.

Nadine cupped a hand over her mouth and stifled a gasp. She bit her bottom lip, hid behind the large river rock and watched around the edge.

Blaine turned to look upstream and then yelled out. "Think Abram's got it hid yet?"

"Hell if I know." Another voice called back.

Slowly, Nadine turned to her right and saw another man walking along the river bank.

"Please… please don't." A woman's voice, begging him.

The man aimed and fired his revolver as casually as if he was target practicing and the woman's voice was no more.

The passengers… no, the witnesses… *they're killing all of the witnesses.*

Nadine bit down on her lip hard enough to taste her own blood. She stared and watched the surface of the water's current, as a thin stream of blood floated toward her. Nadine turned away and her gaze fell on the weeds growing in the soft mud of the river bank. She glanced back at the man searching for other survivors, and then Nadine reached beneath the water and grabbed a handful of mud. Bringing it back, she rubbed it over her face and then did it a second time, coating it thickly.

"*Awww* hell." The man from upstream said.

Two more gunshots echoed along the river banks and Nadine flinched. She sunk down up to her neck into the icy water and pressed herself close to the rock.

"What is it?" Blaine called from farther away.

"Luke's dead!"

There was a pause, and then Nadine heard the sound of someone running through the river, charging from downstream toward her direction. Nadine closed her eyes and felt her heart pounding in her ears.

The splashing sounds stopped and when Nadine heard a revolver's hammer cocking back, she opened her eyes and looked up at the blue-eyed outlaw.

"Howdy." Blaine glared at her with rage-filled eyes and took aim at her face.

A shot thundered and Nadine watched as a bullet punched a hole in the man's shoulder. The exit wound blew out a spray of blood and meat into the icy river. He screamed and the LeMat revolver flew from his hand and splashed into the river.

An exchange of gunfire erupted around her, and Nadine heard some bullets ricochet while others found a home, either in the damp earth of the river banks or when she heard someone scream. She heard men yelling and the sound of horse hooves.

More gunfire, a hail of it upstream from her, and Nadine tried to lift her head and peek around the rock, but she felt so weak and tired. Her legs and arms were stiff and numb from the freezing river water and shivers racked her body. She rested her head against the cold rock and when she closed her eyes, the world faded away.

CHAPTER FOUR

"Sheriff!"

Nadine heard the man's voice and the sound of someone rushing through water. She felt like a chunk of ice, broken and free, ready to float down river. The rain had eased to a soft drizzle and she was cloaked in the noise of the burbling river.

"I think there's one alive!"

The splashing grew closer, and closer still, and then Nadine felt strong hands beneath her arms, dragging her out of the river onto the muddy bank. Her eyes fluttered open and she saw flashes of images—a man in a black wool coat, his face close as she felt herself being lifted up from the damp ground and then carried. She saw the river rushing by, the twisted wreckage of train cars, luggage and cargo scattered about, some intact, others busted open with their contents spilling free. Nadine saw the carnage; the mangled bodies of passengers, some killed in the fall, others with bullet holes in their heads or hearts.

There's the steward who brought me tea. She dreamed of going to London.

There's the man who dropped his hat at the train station in Boston.

There's Earl.

Nadine saw her fiancé's corpse, open-eyed and staring at the sky. Soft rain pelted his face and gathered in his beard like drops of morning dew. A strange twist of pain rushed through her heart, not what she would call love, but closer to disappointment.

Or relief.

As the world spun, Nadine lay her head against the chest of the man carrying her. Her body was beyond numb, as if it simply didn't exist anymore. She floated on gossamer clouds as the man carried her up the hillside.

"You're alright now, we got you." His voice was rough,

but calming at the same time. Comforting.

The man set her down in the bed of a wagon and wrapped her in a heavy wool blanket. Nadine lay down, closed her eyes, and curled up as tightly as she could.

"Them sons o' bitches. Them *damned* sons o' bitches. Who the hell shoots women and…"

That was another man, his voice deeper than the other. She heard a heavy exhale and the sound of a man spitting.

"We've gone through three times, Sheriff. I think she's the only one, alive."

That was the voice of the man who had carried her from the icy waters.

Nadine felt a tingling in her fingers, an awareness that her hands even *existed* was an improvement.

"Have them search once more. Hellfire and damnation… it'll take four undertakers a whole week to make coffins for…" The man paused for a moment and spit again. "I ain't never in my whole damned life seen anything as horrible as this."

CHAPTER FIVE

The wagon jolted and Nadine's eyes snapped open. Overhead, the sky was a slate gray, threatening more rain any moment. As they began to roll forward, she looked around the and saw the wagon bed was empty, save for two rifles and a coil of rope.

"S-stop." Her voice rattled out in a whisper, and Nadine reached a hand up toward the bench seat of the wagon. She felt cloth against her fingertips, grabbed and pulled on it.

"Hey!"

The wagon came to a stop and Nadine looked up to see an older man turn around from the bench and look down at her. He had a short white beard and mustache, kind, pale eyes and he gave her a soft smile. "We got you, ma'am. It's going to be alright now."

"Lug…" She shook her head slightly and a full body shiver ran through her, making her limbs tremble. "Luggage."

The old man stared, snorted a laugh and then sat up and spoke to the passenger beside him. "She wants her luggage."

Nadine heard the other man sigh.

"Of course, she does."

"Well, I reckon she might need dresses or… womanly things, you know."

There was another sigh and she heard the sound of someone climbing down from the wagon. A man's face peered over the side panel and looked at her. "Which one is yours?"

"B-Bartlett," Nadine croaked.

He nodded and turned to the older man. "You got any water up there, Birdie?"

The old man shuffled a moment, and then handed a canteen down toward Nadine. She reached out, but her arm trembled and her cold fingers didn't want to work properly. Her insides still felt carved out of blocks of ice.

"Here, here." The other man took the canteen, uncapped

it, and held it to Nadine's lips so she could drink.

The water was good, but it only added to the cold she felt. Nadine put her head down and the man pulled the wool blanket up over her arm again. He tucked it around her neck to hold in warmth.

"I-I'm... Nadine Bartlett... of the L-London Bartletts." Her voice sounded weak, but at least steady.

"Well, I..." The man stared at her as he put the cap back on the canteen. "I'm Thatcher Evans of the Wyoming Evanses." He chuckled as he handed the water back to the man on the bench seat.

"L-luggage is... st-stamped with... Bartlett."

Thatcher glanced at the older man and then nodded at her. "Alright then."

She heard him march away from the wagon and she closed her eyes. It wasn't long before he returned, and Nadine watched as he slung two rectangular trunks up onto the wagon. The bed of the wagon shimmied with the weight. Mud caked the sides panels of the trunks, but they were intact. She nodded at Thatcher, gave him a thin smile. "M-more."

He stared at her, cleared his throat and sighed, then the man nodded, and walked away again. When he returned with the largest of the trunks, Nadine saw another, younger man, help Thatcher heave the trunk up onto the wagon. The bed shimmied in place with the weight.

"Ma'am, did you pack up most of London when you left?" Thatcher took off his hat and wiped his forehead with the sleeve of his coat.

"It's a... a w-whole other country, you know?" Nadine held the blanket around her and pushed herself up slightly. Her teeth still chattered as chills rippled through her. "I was... l-leaving it behind entirely, so..." She paused, slowly taking in a deep breath as her ribs ached. "So pardon me if I may have more than a bag or two to pack up the entirety of... my old life."

"Yeah, alright. My apologies, ma'am." Thatcher's

expression softened and he looked away. He nodded at the three pieces of luggage. "Is that all of them?"

"T-two more." Nadine said. "Smaller t-than this."

He nodded and trudged away.

The simple effort of sitting up slightly had taken all the strength Nadine had left, and she eased down flat again and closed her eyes. At one point, she heard and felt more weight loaded into the rear of the wagon, but she was too exhausted to look. On some level, Nadine felt the wagon jolt as they started moving ahead, but sleep embraced her tightly.

"The London Bartletts… that mean anything to you?"

"Can't say that it does, but then, I ain't very worldly either." The old man laughed.

"Well, I reckon I ain't too worldly either. The territory's big enough as it is. Besides, compared to Wyoming, I'm afraid the rest of the world might be a bit of a disappointment." Thatcher laughed as the wagon jostled along.

Nadine heard the sound of a horse, approaching fast, and then it slowed as it neared the wagon.

"They got 'em." The rider was breathless as he spoke.

"Got who?" The old man asked.

"Them," the rider smiled. "The Pale Horse gang. Well… three of 'em that're still alive, at least."

"The Marshals caught up to them?" Thatcher asked. "Where? I thought they skinned away from that river on a goose chase."

"They caught up to them at Crimson River. Marshals killed one of them and got the other three in a jail wagon."

"They brought a jail wagon?" Thatcher smiled and shook his head. "Well that was mighty confident of 'em, wasn't it?"

"You ain't wrong, Thatcher." The old man said. "Hell, this would make it the eleventh time them Pale Horse sons o' bitches… it don't matter. Got 'em now, and them Marshals should put a bullet in every last damned one of 'em."

"I reckon you're right, Sheriff." The rider shook his head and shrugged. "Hell, they might even run free before the end of it all."

"The hell you say?" The Sheriff scoffed and spat. "After what they done? They killed half the damned—"

"Ain't no one seen 'em do it, Sheriff." The rider cut him off. "Not robbing the train, nor any of that other mess... there ain't no one seen 'em do it. This, or anything else we know damned well that they've done in the past."

The old man gestured toward the rear of the wagon and after a moment, the rider spoke again. "Holy mother... is she still—"

"Yep."

Nadine listened and there was another stretch where the only sound was the wagon wheels and the rider's horse walking on the trail.

"Sheriff?"

"Yes, Williams?"

"She's alive, so—"

"I know, Williams. I know. We'll get her healed up and we'll see what comes next. But for now, you ride out and tell them Marshals to keep them men held tight, you hear? Tell them there's a witness. Tell them to expect a telegram or two when they get to Casper."

"Yes sir." The sounds of a horse breaking into a run faded as quickly as they had begun.

Nadine opened her eyes and for the briefest of moments, the last thing she saw before sleep pulled her under once again, was the face of Thatcher Evans looking back her with a worried expression on his face.

CHAPTER SIX
West of Broken Stone, Wyoming

Abram Foster looked at the leg irons around his ankles and the chains jangled against the wooden floorboards of the wagon as he drew his knees up. He rested his arms against his knees and stared at the handcuffs around his wrists.

The jail wagon was a flat-bedded cart with a square cage made of steel strapping. A Marshal rode on either side of them with two sitting on the bench seat. Abram would catch them glancing at them every so often.

They look awful proud of themselves, Abram thought. *Smug.*

Calhoun and Blaine sat on the other side of the cage, both of them with disgusted expressions. One of the Marshals had put a makeshift bandage around Blaine's shoulder, but it was soaked with blood and Blaine's face pale as birch bark. His eyes were red-rimmed and glassy and it was obvious he was in a lot of pain. Abram wished he could give the man at least a bottle of whiskey, but at the moment, they were far away from a welcoming saloon.

Calhoun glared at the trail behind them. Sometimes Abram thought the man was driven by pure hate and not much else. The death of his brother wouldn't go far for improving his disposition, but Abram knew he had to say something.

"I'm sorry about Luke." Abram shifted his position as the wagon jostled over rocks in the trail.

Calhoun glanced at him and gave a nod of acknowledgement. He opened his mouth as if to speak and then closed it again. Abram watched the muscles flex in the man's jaw as if he was clenching his teeth. He suddenly turned, as if he'd worked up the nerve to speak.

"You changed your tune real quick after Hobsen got shot by..." Calhoun nodded toward the Marshal on the right side of the wagon. "That son of a bitch up there with a badge. Did

Hobsen's death turn you into some kind of—"

"Don't say it, Calhoun." Abram shook his head and glared at him. "You say what you're thinking right now and I'll strangle you to death in this damned cage."

Calhoun's gaze never faltered, though for a moment, Abram thought he was going to keep running his mouth even after being warned. Calhoun let out a heavy sigh and gave a slight shake of his head. "Just saying… you put your gun down mighty damned quick."

Blaine turned his head to look at Calhoun and gave a shrug as he looked to Abram. He spoke in a breathless voice. "Well, he… he ain't wrong. You laid your irons down mighty fast."

"Hobsen was a good man, and he deserved a hell of a lot better than being put down like a dog by a Marshal, and yeah…" Abram nodded at the two men. "I reckon I did put my guns down 'cause there ain't no situation worth dying over, especially this one."

Now, Calhoun *did* clench his teeth. "I'd rather go down shooting lead at the law and at least *try* to get away, rather than die hanging from a noose."

"That's 'cause you don't think like I do." Abram glanced around at the Marshals, leaned forward and lowered his voice. "We ain't staying in this here cage, fellers. Help's on the way."

"What are you talking about, Abram?"

"I got some men on retainer."

"What's that?" Calhoun looked confused.

"*Re-tainnn-err.*" Abram drew it out slowly, as if he was teaching a child a new word. "It means I offer some money to men to be there in case we need them." Abram shrugged. "We don't need them, then they keep the money. But at the moment, we *do* need them, so they'll come take care of things and be paid more for their efforts." He leaned back against the steel cage and smiled. "It's taken care of."

"What men? Who is it?" Calhoun straightened his legs

out, glaring at the heavy chains against the wood.

"Horace Conway and his gang." Abram smiled. "After the train, we was supposed to meet up with them at Striped Rock Canyon. I was to pay them five hundred dollars to be there." Abram shrugged and gave a slight frown. "If we didn't show up, that meant things had gone wrong and Horace and his men were to come runnin' after us."

"And what'll that cost to get us out of this damned cage?" Blaine wheezed.

Abram sighed. He knew neither of the men were going to like his answer, but with high risk there came a cost, and attacking four Marshals to bust men out of a jail wagon most certainly came with high risk. "Four thousand."

Calhoun winced, gritted his teeth and turned away, looking down the trail of dust behind them. He let out a long slow breath and spoke to Abram without looking. "The whole damned haul only came to twelve thousand."

"It sure did, but it beats hell out of a hangman's noose, now don't it, Calhoun?" Abram smiled. "So instead of exchanging hot lead with four Marshals, we sit for a while until Horace and his men arrive."

Blaine put his head back against the wagon and started to laugh. A thin but constant drip of blood fell from the bandage around his shoulder. His eyes were glazed and wild.

"The hell are you laughing at?" Abram growled his whispered question.

"Luke and I… we, we weren't very sure about this from the start, so… so we… " Blaine sighed heavily as he strained to breathe. He glanced at the bloody bandages and then looked at Abram. "We hired someone… on a *re-tainnn-err* for a… a hell of a lot cheaper than four thousand dollars."

Abram stared at him, trying to read Blaine's expression. And then it hit him and he put his hand up over his forehead, already expecting the headache to rush in like the flood of a spring melt. "Please tell me… for the love of all that's holy… that you and Luke didn't hire Bonespur Bill."

Blaine shook with silent laughter and looked down at the small patch of blood beside him.

"That man," Abram rubbed his temples in frustration, "is an absolute lunatic. He'll end up putting a bullet in our heads by the time he saves us."

"He ain't that bad." Calhoun muttered.

"He's spent too much time in the hills off by himself." Abram glared at Calhoun. "Crazy bastard talks to piles of moss and runs around a fire a night, naked as a newborn child and shaking his—"

"Well Bonespur Bill is... coming after us, Abram." Blaine coughed, leaned forward and struggled for breath, and then eased back against the wagon panel.

Abram glared at him and then turned to Calhoun. "Well, when Bonespur Bill and Horace and his men get here, I reckon it'll just be one big ol' square dance, won't it?"

CHAPTER SEVEN

Broken Stone, Wyoming

Nadine felt warm beneath the weight of several blankets. The feather tick mattress was thick and soft and comforting. She didn't want to leave its soothing nest, but the buzzing thoughts in her mind roused her from sleep. The room was small, but clean, with a single window and curtains.

Her head felt swimmy, as if she had a glass too many of wine. She moved her left arm and pain raced down her side, but she felt detached from it, almost as if the sensation was happening to someone else. Moving slowly, Nadine pulled back the blankets and even though she had no memory of it, she saw she had been dressed in a clean nightgown. She pulled up the neckline to peek inside and saw almost the entire left side of her body was bruised black and purple.

She groaned and let the nightgown fall back in place. Her right hand was scuffed and scratched, and a bandage was wrapped around her wrist. A chair sat by the window and Nadine saw her dress draped over it, torn and splashed with mud from the ordeal at the river. On the floor below, she saw her boots in the same condition.

"Howdy, ma'am."

Nadine turned toward the door and saw the young man on horseback from the river. She pulled the blankets up over her again and he gave her an easy smile as he stepped into the room.

"Ma'am, I'm Deputy Williams. You're in the doc's office, so you…" He gestured with his hand. "You just rest for a bit. Take your time waking up." Williams nodded toward the doorway. "I was just on my way out, but Deputy Evans is taking over."

She nodded and watched as he slowly walked out of the room. Her mouth was dry as hardpacked dirt and Nadine felt like everything over the past day was a terrible dream. To the right of the bed, she saw a small stand with a pitcher and a glass of water. Nadine turned and inhaled sharply at the stabbing pain along her left side.

"Hey, hey... hang on a minute." Booted footsteps crossed the room and Thatcher Evans lifted the glass and leaned down closer to her. She reached for it with a shaking hand and he held onto the bottom as she drank. When she was done, she nodded and pulled away.

"There we go." Thatcher set the glass back down in place.

"Not sure what town I'm in, but..." Nadine nodded toward the door. "The lawmen seem awfully attentive around here to keep watch over an injured woman.

"Well..." Thatcher pursed his lips slightly. "It's a bit more than that."

"What do you—"

"*Naw, naw*." He took a step away from the bed. "Ma'am, you've been through a lot, a terrible thing, but you're safe now and you need healing." Thatcher gave a nod toward the doorway and lowered his voice to a whisper. "Doc McKenzie might smell like old cheese once in a while, but you could do a lot worse and he's good at what he does."

"My luggage—"

"Your luggage is just fine." Thatcher gestured toward a corner of the room and Nadine saw four pieces of luggage there. "I know you're missing one, but couldn't be helped. I reckon after that train wreck, homesteaders for miles down river will see clothes floating by. But there ain't nobody going to mess with your things in here." Thatcher smiled. "Convenient having your name plastered all over your luggage.

"Yes, I... my family is..." Nadine shook her head. "Earl Wistling, my fiancé was killed in the wreck and..."

"I'm... I'm sorry about that, ma'am." Thatcher took his hat off and his expression turned solemn. "It was... it was a terrible, awful thing." He sighed and picked at the brim of his hat. "You need some rest, but I'll be right here, just outside the door, so if you need anything, just call out."

"I'm... I'm quite knackered at the moment, but—"

"Eh... knackered, ma'am?"

Nadine blinked at him slowly. "Exhausted. Weary."

"*Ahh,* well alright then." He gave a soft pat over the blankets on her right foot, and Nadine thought his simple gesture was comforting, much like his voice.

"Thank you, Deputy."

He smiled at her and then walked from the room. Nadine heard the soft creaking sound of a well-used chair as he sat down. She had been told she was safe now, and though she didn't understand why, having Thatcher Evans close by *did* make her feel safe.

The thought ran though her mind like she was trying to solve a puzzle as she drifted off.

CHAPTER EIGHT

Thatcher eased back in the chair and crossed his arms. Doc McKenzie puttered about among his shelves and cabinets, checking jars and vials of medicines. He was a good man, if not prone to times of melancholy. His wife had died not long after they arrived in Wyoming, years ago. Like many others, it was supposed to be the start of a new life together, but also like many others, that start was marked with unexpected mourning.

He heard the Bartlett woman's breathing relax into a slow rhythm as she slept. Thatcher stretched his legs out in front of him and crossed his ankles. She was a beautiful woman, though she seemed a bit aloof and arrogant with her whole *from the London Bartletts* conversation. She had a funny way of talking that had crossed his mind more than a few times since he had carried her up out of that river. Not just the heavy English accent, but also the choice of words strung together.

Knackered, Thatcher thought, with a smile and a shake of his head.

It was easy to see she had lived a privileged life so far, which made Thatcher wonder if the misery of the past couple of days made it feel even worse than what it was.

There was no question the woman had been through a lot, and that wasn't even considering whatever else had taken place during the long journey, and on top of it all, to have her fiancé die in the train wreck.

Thatcher glanced at McKenzie and wondered if the doc had any coffee he could put on the stove. He thought he might buy a package of Arbuckles to bring back after his watch was finished and Deputy Williams took over again.

The Pale Horse gang, finally captured. He shook his head at the thought. They had done a string of robberies through Kansas, up through Nebraska and the Dakota territories, and then into Wyoming. The Marshals were fit to be tied over it all, because the gang of outlaws seemed to be shadows they couldn't even set eyes on, let alone catch up to.

They never left a single witness behind their robberies. The corpses of men, women, and children were all scattered behind their crimes. The only reason people knew of them at *all* was that as outlaws are often want to do, someone ran their mouth and boasted about their escapades. Word spread as they went from one dirty saloon to the next, knee deep in whiskey and women, and bragged about what they had gotten away with.

For the most part, it didn't matter what men said. Words were only words and if you listened to the drunkards in town, more than half would weave a yarn about how they were playing cards with Wild Bill Hickok when he was shot and killed.

But the Pale Horse gang kept on bragging as their escapades continued. There was no honor among thieves, and someone the gang had boasted to, told the tales to a Marshal. Once they got wind of who the gang was, they began to track them the best they could, always ending up a day late and a dollar short. The Marshals would arrive where the Pale Horse gang had *been*, finding dead bodies and bloodshed and tills empty of their money.

One Marshal had the clever forethought to get an article in the newspapers about a shipment of money headed through the territories and on to California to fund a bank. They made sure it was in every single newspaper they could pay to print it.

The bait had been set, and just as the Marshals had hoped, the newspaper article lured the Pale Horse gang right on in. Thatcher had to give credit where it was due on the idea, but then everything had gone to hell in a hand cart. He reckoned it would take a month, maybe two, to clean up the mess of the train wreck and the rock slide over the tracks.

"Mornin', Doc."

Thatcher looked up and saw Sheriff Birdie Mitchell walk inside the front of the office. He and McKenzie exchanged a few words and Birdie nodded and laughed. Glancing at

Thatcher, the Sheriff gestured for him to come closer and Thatcher rose from the chair and followed him outside onto the front porch.

"How's she doing?" Birdie leaned against a porch post and crossed his arms.

"Well," Thatcher shrugged. "She's resting, ain't talking very much. Doc says her left side is about as bruised as anyone could get before breaking everything inside."

"*Mmmmm.*" Birdie grunted acknowledgement and nodded as he looked over the main street.

"You send a telegram for the Marshals yet?"

"*Naw,*" the Sheriff shook his head. "They're probably only halfway to Bagger's Creek and well…" He winced and scratched the whiskers of his throat. "Something was telling me not to send such a message too early."

"You reckon the news would spread? Fall on the wrong ears?"

Birdie nodded. "I think the Pale Horse gang knows too many men on the wrong side of the law and they might come running."

Thatcher sighed. "The more time goes by—"

"I know." The Sheriff bit his bottom lip and shook his head. "I already know what you're going to say, and you ain't wrong." He pointed toward the doc's office. "Nadine Bartlett has got to get to Casper as close behind the Pale Horse gang as she can, because once word gets out that there's a witness, every drifter and outlaw in the territory is going to come gunning for her to keep her mouth closed for good."

"So, what then?"

"I've been chewing on this all damned night and I don't see any other way about it. We can't wait for the Marshals to come back and retrieve the Bartlett woman." Birdie took his hat off and let out a heavy sigh as he watched the townspeople walk along the street. He set his hat on the porch railing and dug in his coat pocket. "I exchanged telegrams this morning with the Governor." Birdie took a step forward, reached out and took off the Deputy badge on Thatcher's coat.

"Hey, what're you—"

Birdie held up another badge in his hand and pinned it in place of the old one on Thatcher's coat. "You have been appointed a US Marshal in accordance with—"

"*Nawww, naw.*" Thatcher shook his head, put his hands up and took a step back. "I ain't becoming a Marshal just so I can escort some—"

"Who else is there, Thatcher?" Birdie snapped, his voice a growl with a hard edge to it. "You want us to send Williams instead? Kid's barely old enough to stand at the bar, let alone guard a witness all the way to Casper." He clenched his teeth and sighed heavily, calming his voice. "I've had some good years as a lawman, Thatcher, but those are long behind me. I'm an old man and I can still shoot with the best of 'em." He gestured out over the hills. "But I ain't fast enough when I need to be."

Thatcher looked down at the Marshal's badge pinned to his coat and shook his head. There wasn't any use wasting words. Like it or not, Thatcher had to admit Birdie was right about everything. He sighed and nodded. "When do you want me to head out?"

"Tomorrow morning." Birdie settled his hat back on his head. "As soon as you leave town, I'll send a telegram for the Marshals, letting them know you're on your way, and—"

"*Naw,*" Thatcher shook his head. "I'll ride out in a few hours, travel by night when it's quiet and harder to see at a distance."

Birdie scratched his neck and considered it. "Alright then. Not a bad idea. I'll wait 'til morning to send the telegram." He nodded toward the doctor's office. "And *then* I'll let the Marshals know about her."

Thatcher leaned back against the building, considering the trip he was about to endure. "You really think men will come try to gun her down?"

"Once the Pale Horse gang finds out that a single woman

stands between them and getting a noose around their neck…" Birdie nervously scratched along his throat again. "I think it would be wise of you to keep your Peacemakers handy."

"That won't be *all* I'm taking with me."

"I reckon not. I'll get a scattergun and a Yellowboy ready for you. I'll have Williams load up one of the wagons and bring it over." Birdie sucked air against his front teeth and shook his head. "For the record, I'm sorry it has to be you, Thatcher, but I have faith in you." He stepped down from the porch into the street.

"I hope that faith of yours is enough to stop bullets." Thatcher replied as he walked back into the doctor's office. He glanced at McKenzie and then went back to sit in the chair outside of Nadine's room. Thatcher crossed his arms and stretched his legs out. He glanced down at the Marshal's badge pinned to his coat.

"Well ain't this a hell of a thing." Thatcher whispered to himself.

CHAPTER NINE
Plains north of Broken Stone, Wyoming

As he looked over the hillside and the stretch of rolling plains, Horace Conway puffed on a short stub of a cigar and considered what was next. The sun brushed the horizon line as dusk arrived.

"You sure they didn't cheat us?"

Horace clenched his teeth and ignored Ike's question. The jagged scar along the left side of Horace's face pulsed in his frustration. He had gotten the gruesome wound courtesy of a busted jug of whiskey from a barkeep in the Dakotas. Horace took the broken shard away from him and then carved up the man and left him on top of the bar counter for display. After he and his men took over the bar, any customers that remained got free drinks for the rest of the night. Few seemed to mind the corpse.

But ever since it had healed, the scar on Horace's face reddened whenever he was festering on something. It was a visible sign like a red flag for a bull, and everyone seemed to pay attention to it except Ike, who had asked Horace three times in the last hour if he thought Abram Byers and the Pale Horse gang had cheated them.

"Naww." He glanced at Ike, turned back toward the horizon, and exhaled a plume of smoke. "Abram is a killer, a robber, and a thief among other things. But he ain't a cheat." Horace took another drag from the cigar. "At least on things like this."

Ike nodded at his reply and then gestured toward the small camp behind them. "Degan has hot beans in the skillet, a few biscuits too."

Horace nodded and walked with Ike toward the fire. A rider barreled up on the other side of camp and reined his horse to a stop. When the Pale Horse gang hadn't shown up when and where they said they would, Horace had sent Skinner McGee to the town of Broken Stone to see if he could find out what happened.

Skinner stayed in the saddle as he spoke to Horace. "Well, they ain't in jail. At least not yet."

"What's that supposed to mean?" Horace took the stub of cigar from his mouth and tossed it to the ground.

"The train wreck's in the newspaper, but nothing else. No mention of it getting robbed, the Pale Horse gang, *nothing*." Skinner took in a deep breath and sighed. "But I asked around and found out US Marshals have them. There was a gunfight up at Crimson River and they killed Hobsen Jennings, but they got the three of 'em still above snakes, hauling them around in a jail wagon."

"Three of 'em? There was five to start with." Ike took a seat by the fire.

"Yeah, well…" Skinner turned and spit on the ground. "Luke died in the train wreck."

"*Ahh* hell. Calhoun's brother?" Horace shook his head. "I bet he's fit to be tied."

Horace reached inside his coat pocket and pulled out a fresh cigar, a skinny twist of dark tobacco. He fished around for a match, found one and set flame to the end of the cigar.

He considered the task he and his men had before them and the danger it brought going against a group of Marshals. For a while, he and his men had rustled cattle. There was good money in stealing them if you had men that could drive the herd fast enough. When ranchers started hiring crews of men with guns to protect their herds, Horace decided there were easier methods of making money. Protection sometimes, applying pressure on people other times, but what Horace liked was that *most* times, his revolver never even left its holster.

He drew a deep inhale from the cigar, thinking about what Skinner had told him. If the Marshals had the Pale Horse gang in a jail wagon, they weren't taking them north— the terrain would make most areas impassable. There wasn't any good reason to go south or west as the mountains nor the top of Colorado territory offered any towns big enough to keep them as prisoner. East made the most sense, take them to the bigger town of Casper maybe, and get them before a judge. Hell, they might even take the gang members back to Kansas, where their trail of hell all started.

"Break camp and do it fast." Horace gestured toward Degan, squatting by the campfire. "We'll ride east, through the night. Make sure your weapons are fully loaded."

Ike and Degan quickly shoveled spoonfuls of hot beans into their mouths to empty the skillet. Horace went to stand by his horse, a gray appaloosa he called Stormy. He gave the mare a few pats on the neck and then climbed up on the saddle.

The smoke from his cigar curled up around his face and Horace took it from his mouth and held it out in front of him. "Hey Skinner? You know how many Marshals have them?"

Skinner nodded. "Four of 'em."

"Four?" Ike looked up from packing his bedroll, shook his head and muttered to himself. "*Four* Marshals."

Horace ignored his muttering, but thought that rustling cattle and trading bullets with some hired hands sounded a hell of a lot better than going against four marshals.

Still, the payment at the end is worth the risk. I just hope I live to spend it.

CHAPTER TEN

Broken Stone, Wyoming

Nadine drank from the glass of water with a steady hand. When she was finished, she set it back on the bedside table and cautiously pushed herself to sit up. Though her left side ached, it was manageable. Nadine sighed as she turned and put her legs over the edge of the bed.

She looked at her dress on the back of the chair, the torn fabric and streaks of mud, patches of cloth stained with her blood or others. Easing herself up to stand, Nadine walked around to the luggage cases and opened one of the smaller boxes. She stared at the contents, and immediately remembered what the rest of the box contained. Fancy dresses, ball gowns and formal wear from back home. Nadine was under no illusions there would be such events out here in her new life, but bringing them with her was a small consolation to remember how extravagant they had been to attend.

Nadine held up a silk dress of the richest shade of deep green. Black lace had been sewn along the edges and neckline. Beneath it was another dress made of an elegant burgundy colored satin. She huffed and put the dress back into the trunk.

"That simply won't do. I'll bloody well stand out like a pig in a china shop."

She glanced at the other luggage and then slowly turned toward the torn dress.

That was the only normal clothing she had in the world.

No, this will not do at all.

Lifting her left shoulder felt like bits of broken glass grinding together in the socket, but Nadine clenched her teeth and kept going until she took off the nightgown. By the time she fitted on her own muddy dress and worked her feet into her boots—coated with river grit and grime—her shoulder pulsed with a heartbeat of its own.

She stood up, took a deep breath, and opened the largest

piece of luggage. After pulling back the canvas cloth to expose the contents, Nadine peeled off some paper bills from the money inside and folded them into her palm. She walked toward the door and paused after opening it. Nadine stared at the young deputy Williams, snoring lightly with his hat pulled down over his eyes. She smiled at him and walked down the hallway. Doc McKenzie slept on his work table, arms crossed and mouth open wide as he snorted in his sleep.

"Have a nice respite, boys." Nadine whispered and walked outside onto the main street of town. She looked left and then right, trying to decide. "Now then, let's see if we can find some proper attire."

She stepped off of the porch, felt a twinge of pain in her left hip, but continued down the street. Nadine ignored the looks of townspeople as she passed by in her filthy dress. There were many storefronts of all kinds—a butcher, a confectioner with displays of a hundred different kinds of sweets, two bakers, a gun smith—and Nadine stopped in front of a wide storefront with a sign across the front: MAXWELL'S GENERAL GOODS.

Nadine gave a slight nod and walked inside. There were only several other customers in the store, and an elderly man wearing suspenders and round spectacles behind the counter. She ignored his study of her muddy clothing and boots and smiled as she approached him.

"Good sir, I find myself in need of some new attire and some new boots, among other things."

He eyed up the torn shoulder of her dress, glanced around at the other customers, and lowered his voice. "Ma'am, I certainly mean no offense, but do you—"

Nadine withdrew the cash from her hand and showed it to the old man.

He stared at it and then looked back up to her with a smile on his face. "Let me show you our fine selection of clothing."

The old man shuffled from behind the counter with a

slight limp in his right leg. Nadine wondered if he had been injured in the war or if it was simply old age that had caught up with him. Now ignoring the mud on her dress, he offered his arm to her and she took it with a smile, slowly walking with him toward the rear of the store.

"There you are, Ma'am. We've got a few things that might be to your liking." He nodded to some shelves not far away. "Boots of all kinds are over there and if you can't find a pair on the shelves that fit, then we don't have it at the moment." He looked around the store as if he was studying anything else that might be of interest, and then his gaze returned to her. "My name's Max by the way. You take your time and if you need anything you don't see, just yell for me."

"Thank you kindly." Nadine watched as he shuffled away toward the counter once again.

It didn't take long to find two dresses and a pair of new boots that were slightly too big for her but would work well enough. As Nadine held her items, she opened a closed door near the right rear corner of the store and saw a small supply room. She glanced around the shop and then stepped inside and changed into one of the new dresses. Slowly, Nadine sat down on the floor and swapped her muddy boots for the new pair. The dress was a beautiful shade of the palest violet, and the fabric shimmered whenever she made the slightest movement. It wasn't a ballroom gown to be certain, nor was it as fancy as the dress she had been wearing, but it was beautiful and simple and would suffice.

Nadine walked from the room and strolled along the aisles. She paused and picked up a bristle hairbrush and a small bottle of lilac water. When she brought everything to the counter, she pointed to a tray of fine chocolates behind the glass. "And one of those please."

Max looked up at her with a grin as he drew the case of sweets from the counter. "Only one?"

Nadine smiled back and nodded. "I've found that

enjoying a single chocolate is enough to fulfil a desire and yet still leave cravings. More than one and somehow it feels like… gluttony."

"You're a rare one then, Ma'am." Max laughed and shook his head. "Most around these parts would eat the whole damned tray if they could. But then, I can tell from that lovely accent, you ain't exactly from around these parts." He used a pair of tiny metal tongs to lift one of the chocolates and set it on a sheet of paper lace, then held it out to Nadine.

"London." She accepted the candy gratefully, studying the delicate swirls and attention to detail. "A far way from home."

"Well," Max leaned on the counter. "Consider that sweet a welcome gift, Ma'am." He winked at her. "And may I say, that dress and the new shoes looks quite a bit better."

"That's very kind of you, and appreciated. Thank you, sir." Nadine held up the muddy dress as if it was a dead rat. "Might you have a… a rubbish heap to throw this on?"

Max held his hands out to take the dress and the boots from her. "I'll be more than happy to take care of these for you." He sat them down on the floor behind the counter and then used a pencil to tally up the items.

After telling her the total, Nadine handed over enough money to pay and then took the change from him.

"Thank you, Ma'am, and I hope you'll come back again."

"I hope I do too, Max." She gathered the thin canvas sack the old man had gathered the other dress and items into. "And I'm Nadine Bartlett."

He smiled and gave her a nod and then Nadine carried the sack in one hand and the chocolate in her other. She bit into it as she stepped outside onto the boardwalk and smiled at the rich flavors of powdered chocolate and truffle. A single small indulgence among the chaos of the last days.

Now, Nadine noticed townspeople tip their hat and nod. Some women smiled sweetly at her as she walked by. Nadine was slightly amused at the change in people's reactions over the difference of a muddy dress, but she forgave them their judgements as she walked onto the boardwalk and returned to the doctor's office.

As she closed the door and turned around, Nadine saw Deputy Williams standing near the door to her empty room. His face was as pale as driftwood and he marched down the hall right toward her. When he spoke, it was in an aggravated, scolding tone.

"Where *were* you?" He pointed at the street. "You can't just go off out there—"

"I beg your pardon, Deputy, but I was under the impression America was free."

"It *is* free, but right now, you can't—"

"Why?" She adjusted the canvas sack in her hand. "Why can I not bloody well go where I want to? Am I being—"

"Alright, alright!"

Thatcher's voice drew the attention of both Nadine and Deputy Williams. He closed the front door of the office behind him as he slowly walked down the hallway toward them. "My head feels like it's got a tiny little blacksmith in there and he's shoeing the horses of the entire 8th Calvary." He gestured between them. "So whatever this is, there's no need to be airin' your lungs about it."

Deputy Williams gestured toward Nadine and picked up his complaints right where he had left off. "She was in town, right out in the street, shopping for—"

"And why is that such a *bad* thing, you twit?" Nadine's eyes blazed as she turned toward Williams.

"Because it is! Every damned—"

Thatcher slammed his hand down against the doc's table and the sound snapped both of them to attention. He glared at Williams. "You…" Thatcher pointed a finger at the deputy. "If she was out walking around town, then that means you fell asleep during your watch. So you and I'll be talking later, but for now, keep your lip buttoned."

"And you." He turned toward Nadine. "Sit down."

"I will *not* be—"

"I *said* sit down." Thatcher glared back at her fiercely. "I carried you up out of that canyon and then drug those boulders you call luggage up for you. So, don't make the mistake of thinking I can't sit you down if I want to." Thatcher's expression eased and his voice softened as he went on. "But I'm *not* forcing you… I'm *asking* you… sit down."

Nadine glanced at Deputy Williams, who seemed ready to sulk over getting scolded. She stepped into her room, lay the canvas bag on the bed and sat down.

Thatcher walked in after her and leaned against the wall. "Miss Bartlett, though Deputy Williams approached the topic a bit roughly, he ain't wrong. Right now, you can't be walking around in the open like that. It ain't safe."

Nadine shook her head and stared at him. "I don't understand why. What's so *unsafe* for me?"

Thatcher crossed his arms and let out a heavy exhale. "Because there's an awful lot of men that are going to want to kill you real soon, if they ain't already on their way."

Thatcher stared at Nadine while she absorbed everything he had just explained to her. Williams kept quiet and leaned against the wall.

"I'm… I'm…" Nadine took a deep breath and shook her head. She looked up at Thatcher with tears in her eyes. "I'm the only one still alive?"

"I'm afraid so, ma'am." Thatcher knew this was a harsh truth, a jolt of reality for a terrible situation that only seemed to be getting worse for Nadine Bartlett. "Once these men, or… other men they know, get wind that you're alive and can testify as a witness, people are going to come after you. They'll want you dead."

Nadine swallowed hard and shook her head again. "Then don't say anything. No one needs to know I'm… I'm…" She wiped angrily at the tears in her eyes.

"The Marshals have the Pale Horse gang, the ones still alive, at least. If you come with me to the courts up in Casper and testify to what you saw, these men will go to prison, probably hanged, but it'll be over for good."

Thatcher took a step closer and looked into the beautiful woman's face. "These men have been doing this for a while now, killing, spilling blood and robbing. If you do this, you'll save lives, stop an awful lot of pain." Thatcher nodded toward the window. "And them dead passengers on the train, including your fiancé, at least they can rest in peace."

He released a heavy sigh as he watched Nadine stare at her lap and fuss with the fabric of her dress. "But if you want to leave, you go right ahead." Thatcher took a step back and let his gaze run over her from the crown of her head to the tips of her new boots.

She looked at him, confused. "What're you... what're you doing?"

"You're about... five-foot-four, yeah?"

"Five-foot-five, yes, but..." Nadine huffed. "Why are you asking?"

"Just want to make a note of it for later. The undertakers around here are a might busy and I reckon it'll make their job easier if I tell him your height ahead of time."

Nadine stared at him and her eyes were glassy, brimming with tears. She swallowed hard, glanced at the luggage cases in the corner of the room, and then looked up at Thatcher. Her helpless expression pained him, and part of Thatcher felt bad for being so blunt with his words and talking about the undertakers in such a cavalier way. But he needed her to understand the gravity of the situation.

"Alright then," she nodded. "Yes, I'll... I'll go tell a judge what I saw."

Thatcher let out a sigh of relief. "Okay, good. Then come on with me."

Nadine's eyes grew wide. "We're leaving? Right now?"

"*Naw*," Thatcher shook his head. "Not just yet. We just need to… make a little stop first and remedy some things."

Thatcher led Nadine down main street right back to Maxwell's. The old man looked up at the deputy and smiled. "Deputy Thatcher, anything I can help you—"

"Max, I know these things were only just purchased moments ago… so let's say we just exchange them for…" Thatcher looked at the rear of the store and held up a finger to Max. "I'll be right back."

Max glanced at Nadine without a word, and watched as Thatcher searched the clothing at the rear of the store. He grabbed items from the shelves and brought them to the counter. A men's work shirt, suspenders and a pair of heavy brown trousers, wide-brimmed hat and a pair of boy's boots all lay out in front of him. Thatcher looked at it and then ran back to return with a black wool coat to add. He looked at Nadine. "Go on… give them a try."

Biting her bottom lip, Nadine stared at the clothes and then gathered up the pile and went off to the small room at the rear of the store.

Thatcher turned to Max. "I reckon these items will be a might less expensive than them fancy stitches she purchased earlier."

The old man nodded and sighed. "Sadly, yes. I knew that flurry of shopping was too good to be true."

Nadine stepped out of the room, crossed her arms, and stared at Thatcher. "I look bloody ridiculous."

The shirt was slightly too big for her, and the trousers a might baggy, but the suspenders kept them in place. The trousers were a bit too long, with the ends bunched up against the small pair of boots. Even though Nadine's hair was past her shoulders, the wide-brimmed hat completed the appearance.

"Thatcher nodded and smiled. You look perfect."

She walked toward him and shook her head. "If this is what the women in America wear, then I—"

"Oh, they don't." Thatcher shrugged. "Well, mostly don't. This is what a man wears. A field hand, rancher... there's an awful lot of them out here and if you dress like them, most won't give you a second glance."

Nadine blinked at him with a thin-lipped expression.

Thatcher could see he needed to explain a bit more. "If you blend in, instead of wearing fancy things like you did in London, there's less of a chance of you getting a bullet put in your head." Thatcher said softly, and then smiled.

"Oh." Nadine's expression eased and she tugged on part of the shirt. "These will be fine, then. Are they..." She looked from Thatcher to Max and back again. "Are men's clothes always this itchy? Is that why they're scratching all the time?"

Thatcher smirked and spoke to Max in a whisper. "Keep the difference on the purchase, Max."

Williams brought a wagon around in front of the doctor's office. It had the weapons Thatcher had asked for, the Yellowboy rifle and a scattergun, with a wooden box of ammunition. The saddles for both horses on the team were also in the wagon, slid up against the side panel.

Thatcher noticed that somehow, the skinny little runt had loaded Nadine's heavy luggage onto the rear of the wagon. He shook his head and stopped by the two-horse team. His buckskin horse, a beautiful mare named Ginger, didn't seem pleased about being harnessed alongside the Sheriff's ornery older mare, Sadie. Birdie's horse tended to nip at anything within reach, and Thatcher figured it was a matter of time before Ginger had enough and bit her back.

"You uh... be careful out there." Williams put his hand out and shook Thatcher's.

"I will. This ain't nothing but a leisure trip." Thatcher grinned at him and started to climb up onto the wagon seat, but stopped and offered his hand to Nadine. "Ma'am."

"Thank you." She held onto it and climbed up, paused on the first step and let out a heavy breath that Thatcher knew was from pain. Nadine stepped up onto the wagon and sat down on the spring seat. Thatcher watched her for a moment longer before climbing up himself.

Williams stared at the sight of her dressed in men's clothing, but never uttered a single word. The man might be young, but he was observant and curious without questioning often, preferring to figure things out on his own. It was a rare quality Thatcher admired.

"You and Birdie hold things down while I'm gone." Thatcher told the young Deputy. "Who knows, you might even pop a few whiskers on that babyface of yours before I get back."

Williams snickered and shook his head. "Go on, get out of here."

Thatcher released the wagon brake and snapped the reins just as Sadie turned her head to nip at Ginger's right ear. Both horses gave a slight jolt and started forward. Thatcher glanced at Nadine Bartlett and then looked ahead as they drove down the street.

She might be in a man's clothes, but even so, Thatcher had to admit she was beautiful. "Pull your hat down a bit, lower over your eyes."

Nadine did as he asked and turned toward him. The brim covered the upper half of her face.

"Better." Thatcher nodded at her and they rode east with the setting sun behind them.

CHAPTER ELEVEN
Broken Stone, Wyoming

The man known as Bonespur Bill sat on the edge of the boardwalk in front of Macie's Saloon. He sipped from a small jug of blackberry whiskey and eased back against the thick porch post. It wasn't the first time he had been to Broken Stone, but the first time he had a reason to be here. The townspeople seemed friendly enough, which was unusual in its own right. He watched as they walked about or drove away, their wagons heavy with supplies.

He adjusted his fox-pelt hat and the thick leather belt around his waist. The belt held two Colt Walkers in custom holsters, a tomahawk tucked beneath the leather on his left side by a massive Bowie knife, and a long-barreled Kentucky pistol stuffed in front—just to the left so everyone could see it as he approached. Around his neck, he wore a necklace of bright turquoise stone and bison teeth strung on a length of sinew.

Bill glanced at his horse tethered up to the hitching post in front of the saloon. Patches was starting to get some age on her, sprinkles of gray along her mane and nose, but she was still a fine horse and he was thankful for her.

The Sheriff passed by earlier, a heavyset kindly looking man who seemed more fitted to sitting in a rocking chair on a porch rather than being a lawman. Bill watched him stop and talk with a few townspeople and then he walked inside the Sheriff's office.

Considering the size of Broken Rock, Bill knew there was no way a single man could enforce the law, even with townspeople as friendly as they all seemed to be. Bill had sat there most of the afternoon and evening, watching and waiting, but he hadn't seen a single deputy.

He took a drink of the blackberry whiskey and swirled it around his mouth, enjoying the flavor of the strong liquor. The two men from the Pale Horse gang, Luke Sullivan and

Blaine Johnson, had offered him a thousand dollars to track them down if they didn't show up at Macie's Saloon in Broken Stone. That was a day ago and he hadn't seen either of their ugly faces since they had first offered.

Normally, Bill would have already moved on, reckoning the men went about their way and he wasn't needed. Except they had already paid him five-hundred dollars on good faith.

He could take the money and ride, go back to what he had already been doing—trapping and selling the pelts—but that didn't sit right with Bill.

They already paid me half.

After reading the newspaper, Bill had ridden out along the tracks and seen the wreckage of the train. Buzzards circled around the skies while a few others pecked at bits of what looked like human limbs. A single train car lay in the river, its end smashed like a tin can. He eyed the group of men trying to clear the rock slide from the tracks and Bill didn't envy their task. Several boulders, taller than the train itself, had settled in place along the path and Bill reckoned it might take explosives to break them down.

But the entire thing didn't feel right to him. He knew the Pale Horse gang had been involved here, but the newspaper hadn't mentioned them at all. And then Luke and Blaine hadn't shown up like they had said they would.

After paying me five-hundred dollars.

Bill scratched along his whiskered throat and his thick beard along the sides of his face. As the sun began to set, the townspeople along the street thinned, heading home for a hot supper and rest. He stared at the window of the Sheriff's office and then glanced left and right.

Not a single deputy around.

Bill tilted the jug and took another drink, then stuffed the cork back in place. He groaned as he stood up, feeling as well as hearing the popping sounds in his knees, and put the liquor jug back into a saddlebag on Patches. He scratched his nose and ran a hand over his face and beard. Bonespur Bill pulled out the Kentucky pistol from his belt and marched toward the Sheriff's office.

As he opened the door, Bill moved his hand with the pistol behind his right leg. He turned toward the Sheriff with a smile and walked closer.

"What can I do for you, stranger?"

"Well, Sheriff, I..." Bill shook his head as if he was at his wit's end. "I'm hoping you can help me out."

The front door swung open and a young man wearing a Deputy badge stepped inside. "Well, he's off and..." The man let his words fade as he saw Bill and the Sheriff. He closed the door and shook his head apologetically. "I'm sorry, didn't realize you weren't alone in—"

"No apologies, son. Come on in. I was just trying to get a bit of help." Bill gestured with his free hand for the Deputy to come in further. He stepped back, closer to the Sheriff's desk. "I've been tracking some low-life snake raping sons o' bitches that stole three of my horses." Bill shook his head again and frowned, playing up his story. "I lost scent of 'em north of here, bunch that call themselves the Pale Horse gang."

Bill watched the Sheriff's expression, the slight flicker of his eyes. He raised the Kentucky pistol up and aimed the massive barrel at the old lawman's face.

The Deputy shifted and Bill glanced at him. "*Naw*, I wouldn't if I were you."

Raising his hands slowly, the Sheriff looked at the young man. "Take your Peacemakers out and lay them down, Williams. You ain't that fast."

Deputy Williams went white as a sheet, but eased his revolvers out of the holsters and started to put them on the floor at his feet.

"*Naw*. Slide them inside the jail cell over there." Bill nodded toward the high steel bars and watched as the Deputy walked slowly across the room and slid his revolvers inside the cell.

"Now then," Bill turned back toward the old lawman. "I used to play a lot of cards, Sheriff. Wasn't much good at it though. I can read a man just fine, easier than others, I reckon. It's all in the eyes, you know? You look hard enough, you can see it in there, the truth wrapped up in the lies."

Bill pressed the barrel of the Deringer right against the Sheriff's skull. "Where is the Pale Horse gang?"

"I-I ain't never—"

"Sheriff…" Bill scoffed and shook his head. "How about you? You play cards much?"

Birdie Mitchel swallowed hard and gave a slight shake of his head. "Sometimes."

Bill leaned closer. "I reckon you ain't never won a bluff though, have you?" He snickered. "That's alright, it's one of the reasons I stopped playing cards myself. I can't bluff worth a damn."

He cocked the hammer back on the gun and pressed it harder against the Sheriff's head. "But take a look in my eyes, Sheriff. If you don't tell me where the Pale Horse gang is, I'm going to paint that young deputy's coat with your brains." He tilted his head and smiled at Birdie. "Am I *bluffing*, or can you only see *truth* in my eyes?"

Birdie flicked his tongue out over parched lips and swallowed hard. "The M-Marshals got 'em—"

"How many Marshals?"

"Four Marshals." Sheriff Birdie looked pained as he spoke. "I'm not… not sure exactly where they are, but… they're taking them east to Casper, I think."

"*Mmmmhmm*. You think." Bill nodded at him and smiled. "What else?"

Sheriff Birdie closed his mouth and breathed heavily through his nose as if he was trying to hold back, but the massive gun barrel against his temple was a great persuader. "They… they're headed through… Bagger's Creek first, probably stop there for the night."

Bill smiled again and spoke to Deputy Williams without

looking at him. "Son, you lock up that jail cell and bring me the keys." Bill nudged the barrel against the Sheriff's head. "And you stand up real damned slow… set them Colt Navys on the desk."

Birdie did as the man asked and Bill took the revolvers. After he tossed them into the jail cell, he took the keys from Williams. He stared at the two of them and gestured with his Kentucky pistol. "Strip down."

"Sir?" Williams looked at him, glanced at the Sheriff, and then turned back.

"You heard me, boys. Strip down to what the good Lord brought you into the world with." Bill leaned back against the bars of the jail cell and smirked.

The two lawmen took off the clothes, down to their union suits beneath.

"I *said*…" Bill gestured at the undergarments and Birdie's face flushed with color, though it seemed to be more anger than embarrassment.

When they were done and standing naked in front of him, Bill gestured with his gun. "Step on back now." He walked forward and scooped up their clothes in one arm. "Thank you kindly. You've both been… very helpful." Bill looked over at the small wood stove in the corner of the room. "Might want to throw another hunk of wood on the fire, Sheriff. It's a might cold in here."

Bill laughed, used the long barrel of the Kentucky pistol to tip his hat, and walked outside to the street.

"Williams?"

"Yeah, Sheriff?"

"If I hear so much as a mouse fart in town about what just happened, I'll throw you in that jail cell along with those revolvers for the rest of your damned life." Birdie walked toward a cabinet in the corner of the office and took out a rag of cloth he used to clean the rifles.

"I reckon I could go the rest of my life never saying a word about this, Sheriff." Williams took his hat off and held it in front of him for modesty. "He… he's right though."

"About what?"

Williams cleared his throat and shook his head. "It's… it's damned cold in here."

"Deputy…" Birdie sat down behind the desk and shook his head. "I guess it's a good thing it'll be dark soon, ain't it?" He growled the words and let out a long exhale. "See if there's some horse blankets or something in the back room."

Williams turned and Sheriff Mitchel winced at the sight of the man's pale buttocks as he walked into the rear storage room and rummaged around.

Birdie thought of Thatcher riding out into the darkness. There was no question now that the Pale Horse gang was going to have men coming in after them. But there was no way to warn the Marshals for what was heading their way, either.

Birdie clenched his teeth, reached inside his desk and pulled out a bottle of Thistle Dew whiskey. The night and next few days were shaping up to be long ones.

CHAPTER TWELVE

East of Broken Stone, Wyoming

"If you're able to get some sleep, go ahead." Thatcher glanced at Nadine as he drove the wagon.

"It sure isn't a Pullman car, but I'll manage sleep at some point." She crossed her arms and rubbed the shoulders of her wool coat as if she was chilled.

"Well then, as long as you're going to stay awake a while." He glanced at her again and then looked at the sky overhead. It was a clear, deep indigo, speckled with stars as far as he could see. "It's been on my mind since you said it, and normally my… curiosity dies down."

"Go on." Nadine turned and looked at him.

"Well, this whole Bartletts of London thing. Should that mean something to me?"

Nadine gave a soft grunt and smiled. "I suppose it's unusual to *me*, though it shouldn't be. Not here in America." She rubbed her arms again and then stuffed her hands into the coat pockets. "In London, most of England, really, the Bartlett family is widely known."

"Known for what?" Thatcher smiled at her. "There's lots of people widely known out here, but it ain't always for something good."

"Fair point, Deputy."

"It ain't Deputy no more. I was made a Marshal so I could take you on this ride out of the territory." Thatcher tapped the badge on his coat and realized Nadine couldn't see it anyway.

"Well then, congratulations on the promotion." Nadine replied. "And I suppose every wealthy family has its share of…" Nadine sighed and shook her head. "Dark stains on the tapestries, so to speak. But the Bartletts were known for their business of import and export. Everything from lumber to tea, spices, silver and lead to… well, almost everything."

"That's all?"

"Well…" Nadine seemed flustered at Thatcher's reaction. "It… it's made my father and his father before him a tremendous amount of wealth." She waited a moment and when Thatcher remained silent, Nadine went on. "My father has a good heart, he seldom knows how to use it, however."

"*Hmmm*." Thatcher nodded. "So what brought you here, away from the luxuries of London?"

Nadine sighed, withdrew her hands from her pockets and crossed her arms again. "My fiancé was a business associate of my father's. After much discussion, Earl convinced my father to invest in opening a vast hotel in America, the new world."

"Sounds *exciting*."

She turned toward him and in the dim light of the stars, Thatcher thought he saw a smirk on her face.

"It was what was best."

"The hotel out here?"

"Ehh… no, I mean Earl and I."

"Your fiancé?"

"Yes, my…" Nadine let her words fade off and she sighed. "And what about you, *Marshal* Evans, of the Wyoming Evanses?"

"*Ohhhh*, I… I come from back east, Virginia. Came out to Wyoming when I was three or four. O' course, I don't remember any of that. Wyoming's all I know." Thatcher shifted on the seat and stretched his back. "I didn't see Pa much. He was always riding off and… providing for us somehow. Things were good, at least I thought they were." Thatcher gave her a thin-lipped smile and shook his head. "My Pa up and left when I was young, four or five maybe. Rode off one day and just never came riding back."

Thatcher glanced at her in the low light. "For years Ma wondered to herself why, but guess that was a question to remain unanswered. She passed on when I was fourteen and after that, it was just me. No kin back in Virginia, just me."

"Oh… that's absolutely dreadful." Nadine's voice was

soft. "I'm so sorry."

"It's alright. I thank you, but it's alright. I did what I could here and there, working as a ranch or field hand. I was a cheese maker for a while."

"A cheese maker? *You* were a cheese maker?"

Nadine laughed lightly and the sound made a warmth inside Thatcher.

"*Mmmmhmm*. I was... *awful* at it. Just terrible." Thatcher laughed. "But when I rode through Broken Rock, Sheriff Birdie Mitchell took a liking to me and eventually brought me on as Deputy. I've been there ever since, going on... *ohhh*, thirteen years now."

"No wife?"

"*Naw*, I..." Thatcher glanced at her. "Ain't that I'm against it or anything. I just ain't..."

"Found the right one yet?"

"Something like that, yeah."

"Understandable. Earl and I..." Nadine sighed. "It wasn't to be a marriage out of passion. More like a *business agreement* of sorts."

"So, it was what was best for *business*. Your father's as well as Earl's business."

"Well, as absolutely horrid as that sounds, yes."

Thatcher looked at her. "I reckon that kind of thing might sound reasonable over in London."

"But you don't agree?"

"O' course I don't agree. What the hell good's a husband and wife together without passion? *Love* at the very least." He glanced at her again. "*Naw*, Miss Bartlett, I'm... I'm awful sorry things have gone to hell for you since you come to Wyoming. I truly am. But considering the end to such a *business agreement*... as dark a thought as it might sound, it all might be a blessing in disguise."

For a while, she kept quiet and Thatcher began to think his directness had upset her, but then she spoke up again. "As macabre as your thoughts are, perhaps there is some truth.

And call me Nadine. I insist that anyone delivering me to a trial for murderous outlaws dispense with formalities and call me by my given name."

He stared at her a moment and did his best impression of her London accent. "Well then, you simply *musssst* call me Thatcher. I *insist.*"

Nadine snickered and then began to laugh. "Your imitation of a London accent is… it's bloody dreadful. It really is."

Thatcher joined her laughter and the two of them rode on through the night as their amusement burned itself out. It was a comfortable silence, and Nadine stretched her legs in front of her as far as she could, and eased herself down on the wagon seat. She crossed her arms and leaned her head forward.

The jostling wagon aside, it wasn't very long before Thatcher heard her breathing ease into a gentle rhythm. Riding along in the darkness, he thought he smelled lilacs.

CHAPTER THIRTEEN
Crow's Call Trail, Wyoming

Horace Conway placed his men on the low ground of the Crow's Call Trail. He reckoned the four Marshals would be as jumpy as cats on a porch full of rocking chairs, but riding along on high ground might give them the idea they were at an advantage for a while.

They did not.

Horace had studied how the trail narrowed as it angled downhill through the mountain pass, and knew there was no way for the Marshals to turn the jail wagon around once shooting started. He only hoped the rising sun would arrive and the bright glare would blind the Marshals as they approached.

Ike and Degan were on the left side of the trail, crouched down behind a thick grove of Lodgepole pines. Horace had brought Skinner with him on the other side, and they took cover behind a group of boulders, one of them as big as a Conestoga wagon.

Horace and his men had driven their horses hard through the night to get a jump on the Marshals. The Crow's Call Trail was the only route clear cut enough to drive a wagon toward Bagger's Creek. It wasn't enough to only *catch up* to them, they had to get *in front* of the group of Marshals and the jail wagon to cut them off.

Horace used a dirty index finger to claw the wad of old tobacco out of his cheek. He slung the damp gob on the ground and wiped his finger on his trousers. To the east, the sky was starting to lighten. Horace ran his tongue over the bits of tobacco in his mouth and spit.

"Reckon they'll be along soon?" Skinner sat on the ground and leaned back against the boulder.

"The faster they get to town, the faster they'll be celebrated for bringing in the Pale Horse gang, and I ain't never met a Marshal who didn't love rolling around in the public's adoration like pigs in shit." Horace peered around the big rock and stared at the empty trail. "We'll give them bullets before they get cheers."

Skinner snickered and nodded. "Damned right we will."

Four of them, though. Four damned Marshals, Horace thought. *They ain't simple-living ranch hands with guns. They're seasoned men, handy with shooting irons. If we don't hit them fast and hard, there'll be hell to pay for it.*

"Damned right we will." Horace repeated the man's words, though he wasn't sure if he was saying it for Skinner's benefit or for his own.

Abram woke up every hour, from either the jostling of the wheels as they drove over rocks in the trail, or from the sheer situation of being chained up in a jail wagon. Calhoun had pulled his coat as tightly as he could and crossed his arms before nodding off. Blaine groaned in his sleep occasionally, and the man's face was slick with sweat. The bleeding had stopped, but if they didn't soon get him to a doc's for the bullet wound, Blaine would never see a judge, let alone a hangman's noose.

For a while, the two Marshals on the wagon seat had chattered, talked about having some whiskey or what kind of hot meal they were going to enjoy when they reached Bagger's Creek. Abram had closed his eyes and listened, paying attention to see if he heard anything useful, but it was all just mindless tongue-wagging and nothing more.

As the sky began to brighten up, Abram heard the soft chirps of birds. He reckoned they had almost a full day's ride left, maybe a little more. Abram twisted his neck and felt the bones pop.

Where the hell are you, Horace?

At the thought of it, he looked at Blaine and thought about how he and Luke had hired Bonespur Bill. Part of Horace was angered they had done it without telling him, but mostly Abram was pleased, no matter how crazy the old bastard was. Abram had heard plenty of tales about the man, some harder to believe than others, but he thought there was a kernel of truth to most. He had only seen Bonespur Bill in person once, outside a saloon that was little more than a shack along the Chisholm Trail. Bill and a Pawnee brave were in front of the saloon, both of them swinging war clubs at one another like savages. The Indian was tall and lanky, and kept moving out of Bill's reach, so the old man stopped trying and only blocked or moved away from the Pawnee's attempts.

Try as he might, the Pawnee couldn't land a hit on Bill from either side, as the old man twisted and dodged away. Bonespur took his time and let the brave wear himself down with the repeated attempts to club him. When the frustration got too much, the Pawnee screamed out loud in a rage and swung his weapon straight down at Bill's head.

The old man crouched down, held up his war club with both hands to block the strike, and his weapon broke in half under the brutal assault. For the briefest of moments, the Pawnee smiled at the busted war club, and then Bonespur Bill lunged forward and drove one of the sharpened ends straight into the Indian's chest, killed him right where he stood.

Abram remembered the expression of surprise on the Pawnee's face, as if death had snuck up on him without warning. He also remembered Bonespur Bill slinging blood from his hands into the dirt and walking back inside the saloon.

The old man wasn't even breathing hard.

The jail wagon ran over a rock and shook Abram. It was getting brighter out and he expected to see a sliver of sunrise any minute. He looked over at Blaine and saw the man's chest still moving. A line of spittle hung from Calhoun's bottom lip.

Abram sighed and listened to the songbirds greet the morning.

Bonespur Bill is about as crazy as an outhouse rat, but

the more guns after the Marshals, the better.

Horace saw the wagon from a distance, not traveling slow and lackadaisical, but they weren't exactly rushing either. The Marshals wouldn't want to risk busting a wheel out here on the trail, not while transporting outlaws in the jail cage. Half of the morning sun had broken over the horizon and it was a white-hot blaze shining toward the jail wagon. Two men were on the wagon seat with a man on horseback on each side. They were the ones to take down first.

"*Ssssst!*" Horace whispered and saw Ike and Degan look his way. He nodded at them and they turned toward the distant trail. He saw Skinner had already turned around into a crouch behind the boulder, his Henry Repeater rifle aimed and ready.

"Don't fire until I say so." Horace took out his pair of Colt Navys and thumbed the hammers back. "The Marshals on horseback first. Put your sights on the one on the right side."

Skinner cocked the rifle and replied without looking back. "You got it, boss."

The wagon rolled closer and Horace watched the riders adjust the brims of their hats against the sun. The coats of the riders were pulled back from their sides, revolvers handy for a draw. In the rear of the wagon, Horace saw a tall steel cage and three men sitting inside.

"Get ready, Skinner," Horace whispered. He looked at Ike and Degan, saw the two men with their revolvers out and ready. Degan's palomino, behind the line of trees, snorted.

Horace glanced at the horse, then snapped his attention back to the wagon and saw the driver rein the two-horse team to a sudden stop. He was too far away to make out the words, but the Marshals spoke to each other and studied the terrain around them. Horace clenched his teeth and growled at Skinner. "Now."

The Henry rifle cracked and the Marshal to the right of the wagon was blown off his horse as a bullet punched into his chest. Horace took aim on the Marshal to the left as Degan and Ike opened fire toward the wagon drivers. The air was filled with smoke and hot lead.

One of Horace's bullets clipped the Marshal's leg and the man screamed as blood spurted from his thigh. A man on the wagon lifted a Yellowboy rifle and fired a shot.

Horace felt something soft spatter against his right leg and he looked down, saw his trousers splattered with blood and Skinner with the back of his head blown off.

"Damn it to hell!" Horace turned his Colt Navys and started firing one after the other, saw a bullet catch the Marshal in the neck and the man fell sideways from his horse, with one boot caught in the stirrup. The horse jolted forward, spooked, and dragged the Marshal behind as it raced along the trail past them.

The Yellowboy fired quickly—the Marshal had a practiced hand at cocking the rifle and shooting. Horace shot at the man and felt return fire buzz past his face a moment later. He pulled behind the large boulder and heard Degan scream. Horace looked over and saw half the man's face had been blown off. Ike clutched at Degan as he stood up and staggered away from the line of woods, right out in the open. Bullets blasted the man's body, blowing massive exit wounds through his back, and putting him out of his misery as he collapsed on the trail.

Horace clenched his teeth and reached for Skinner's Henry rifle. A bullet punched into the ground by the stock and he jerked his hand back behind cover.

He heard men yelling from the wagon and recognized Abram's voice. Horace tightened his grip on his Colt Navy revolvers and went to the left side of the boulder. He peered out and opened fire again, trying to take down the two men on the wagon, who had jumped into the rear behind the bench seat.

"Ike!" Horace called out.

"I-I'm here!"

"Let's fill these bastards full of lead!" Horace watched the wagon seat and saw a shift of movement. A rifle barrel pointed in his direction and Horace pulled back just as a bullet ricocheted off of the boulder. Ike opened fire from his position and several gunshots thundered from the wagon.

"Ike!" Horace called out and there was nothing but silence for a response. An icy chill raced up his spine and he glanced at his appaloosa and wondered if he could get on the saddle and ride without getting shot in the back. He bared his teeth like a rabid dog and gripped his Colt Navys, ready to charge around the boulder.

A single gunshot cracked through the air and it felt as if someone had driven a branding iron through his back. Horace saw a spatter of blood on the boulder in front of him and looked down at the gaping exit wound on his chest. The muscles of his legs turned to water and Horace dropped to his knees. The revolver in his left hand fell to the ground and he put his hand out against the rock to steady himself. Horace gasped for breath that didn't come and looked behind him.

The Marshal that had been shot in the throat and dragged by his own horse was standing there. His shirt was drenched in blood and he held his left hand against the side of his neck. In his right hand, the Marshal held a Colt Dragoon with smoke curling from its barrel.

Horace fell back against the boulder and wheezed to draw air in his lungs.

He knew the risk was high going up against four Marshals.

He wasn't angry about getting shot, not even about his three men getting killed.

Horace Conway died being angry that he was going

to die before the Marshal he had shot in the throat. Blood rose up inside him and Horace coughed, watched the spray land on the dry dirt and sparkle like freshly cut gems. The cold he had felt earlier along his spine spread and coursed through his limbs like the fast-moving current of a river.

He had time to take two shallow breaths and Horace died.

Two heartbeats later, the Marshal did the same.

CHAPTER FOURTEEN
Broken Stone, Wyoming

Abram watched the Marshals lift the two corpses up onto the bed of the wagon and close the gate. One with a length of bloody cloth tied around his arm glared at him. Abram leaned back against the bars of the cage and closed his eyes.

"You take the rifle and I'll take the reins. I won't be able to shoot worth a damn with my arm like this."

"Well let's hope I won't need to either. I've always been rubbish with a rifle."

The two men climbed up onto the wagon, snapped the reins and they began moving forward again.

Blaine hadn't moved an inch during the gunfight, only remained leaning against the cage, his face beaded with pain-sweat. He had his eyes closed and Abram looked on the floorboards beneath him. The puddle of blood there hadn't grown but Abram wasn't sure if that was a good or bad thing. Somehow, Blaine seemed even paler than he had in the daylight of yesterday and Abram wondered again if the man would live through the journey.

At some point during the shoot out, Calhoun got a bullet graze along his right cheekbone, not a serious wound, but it would leave one hell of a scar for a memory. Abram stared at the faces of the two dead Marshals, an expression of amusement on his face.

"I think my coat's the only thing holding my arm together." The wounded Marshal muttered to the other man.

Abram grabbed onto the steel bars and pulled himself to stand, though he had to crouch slightly from the height of the cage. "You've got to tie that rag tighter."

The Marshal turned toward him and glared. "Look at this, Virgil. Got a doctor in the wagon with us, you know that?"

"Sit down." The man with the rifle growled at him.

"You've got to tie that rag better or else you'll bleed to

death right there on the wagon bench." Abram kept his gaze locked on the wounded man. "You ain't never been shot before, have you?"

The man glared at him for a moment without saying a word, then he turned away from Abram and put the reins beneath his legs. He started undoing the knot of the cloth around his arm.

"It's not a bad wound, ain't like getting shot in the lungs or nothing, but if you don't stop it bleeding, you'll be back here with the others, stacked up like cord wood."

"I said sit down!" The other Marshal's voice rose.

"My legs are cramping up sitting like this for so long."

The Marshal raised the rifle in his hands, not aiming it yet. "Your damned skull's gonna cramp if you don't sit down."

Abram stared at the older of the two men. He glanced at the rifle in his hands and then back to the man's eyes.

"Two men, good men, were gunned down today by those sons o' bitches trying to get you out of there." The Marshal's eyes blazed as he glared at Abram.

"Yeah," Abram nodded, speaking in a sad tone. "A terrible thing, truly."

"Too bad those men will be rotting to dust out here, forgotten." The Marshal's eyes twitched. "Any more of your friends we should be out looking for?"

"Friends?" Abram frowned and shook his head. "I've never seen those men before in my life."

The old Marshal clenched his teeth as anger colored his face. "Y'all are gonna hang for what you done."

"What we've done?" Abram scoffed. "Why, Marshal, we were only passengers on that train. Not even sure what all this fuss is about." He shook his head and grabbed onto the steel cage as the wagon jostled. "That whole thing up at Crimson River was just a... a big misunderstanding. We thought you all were trying to steal our horses."

"Steal your horses?" The Marshal slammed the butt of the rifle stock against Abram's fingers holding onto the cage. "Sit down as you are… or you can sit down with a bullet in you."

Abram's ring finger went numb. He wasn't sure yet if it was knocked out of joint or broken, but he smiled wide through the pain, stared at the old Marshal and then eased himself down to sit once again.

The Marshal turned to speak to the driver. "Lyin' sons o' bitches." He turned to glare at Abram. "I'll be there, smoking a cigar, when the rope's put around your necks."

"Well, Marshal, I'll be sure and request a seat up front for you, close enough for you to smell my soiled britches afterward." Abram laughed at the man's expression.

The muscles in the lawman's face pulsed as he clenched his teeth, but he turned around away from Abram.

"Do you think," Calhoun leaned closer and whispered. "It's a wise thing to rile them up like that?"

"I think angry men let their guard down. Hot blood leads to one-track minds." Abram smiled and tenderly touched the knuckle of his ring finger. It felt like a piece of twisted root beneath his skin. He sighed heavily, lay the finger against the palm of his left hand and squeezed. The finger realigned with an odd snapping sensation and Abram grunted with the jolt of pain. He hissed through his clenched teeth and rested his hand on his leg.

"D-did you happen to… pay them men anything… ahead of time?" Blaine's voice wheezed, struggling with each word, but the man still had light in his eyes.

"*Naw.*" Abram shook his head.

"Well let's hope Bonespur Bill honors the five hundred you and Luke gave him." Calhoun spoke in a low voice.

Abram shook his head and whispered. "That crazy old bastard's probably halfway to Mexico by now." Pain radiated in pulses from his finger and Abram leaned back. "I never thought I'd say this but I hope to hell that ol' son of a bitch shows up."

CHAPTER FIFTEEN

Broken Stone, Wyoming

Thatcher drove the wagon onward until he saw the first signs of sunrise along the horizon. To stay awake, he had sung every song he could remember in his mind. The territory here wasn't a difficult one for a wagon, but it made for one long journey.

For the most part, Nadine slept, though several times she murmured in her sleep. When she shifted on the bench and leaned against him, Thatcher smiled, amused, but made no moves to stop her. He smelled the delicate scent of lilacs again and his mind went through their discussion from earlier.

He couldn't imagine taking a wife for the sake of business or money. It didn't seem right, and the more Thatcher turned it over in his thoughts, the more it seemed outright terrible to do such a thing. He looked down at Nadine, saw the wide-brimmed hat had shifted some and revealed her face. Thatcher shook his head and sighed.

She is a truly beautiful woman.

The front wagon wheel lifted and jolted back down as he ran over a rock. Nadine inhaled sharply, startled, and opened her eyes. She looked around, realizing she was leaning against Thatcher, and then sat up quickly, a look of embarrassment on her face.

Thatcher cursed himself for not keeping his eyes on the trail and avoiding the stone. He would have been perfectly happy with her sleeping there against him until they reached Bagger's Creek.

"I'm… I'm sorry, I was—"

"I'm glad you got some sleep in. It'll help you heal faster." Thatcher smiled at her. "How you feeling?"

Nadine stretched her arms in front of her, and then shifted her hat back in place. "Like I've been dragged along the cobblestones of downtown London." She gave a soft yawn and rubbed her eyes. "But… better than yesterday. Not as good as tomorrow."

"Can't ask for more than that, then." He nodded toward the rear of the wagon. "There's a canteen of water there right behind us and we'll stop in just a bit, let the horses take a rest."

"Splendid." Nadine twisted around and reached for the water.

Thatcher turned away from her so she wouldn't see him smiling.

Her way of speaking is a dangerous thing for me to listen to.

He looked out to the left of the wagon as the clusters of Lodgepole pines grew denser. The sky along the eastern horizon brightened as the sun rose. Thatcher was able to see the trail better as the horses went on. He started to say something to Nadine, but something felt wrong.

Not a single bird was chirping to greet the morning.

Thatcher shifted his arm from the side of the wagon and grabbed the reins.

An arrow sunk into the wood panel right where his arm had been a moment before.

"*Awww* hell." Thatcher snapped the reins and the horses bucked forward. He drew a Peacemaker and looked toward the thick growth of pines but saw nothing.

Nadine held onto the back of the seat, a scared expression on her face.

Thatcher aimed the pistol in the air, fired a shot, and another arrow whistled past in front of them. "*Heeyah!*" He yelled and the horses broke into a run, barreling along the trail. Another arrow sunk into the side of the wagon and Thatcher glanced at it, saw the fletching.

Cheyenne.

At the thought, Thatcher heard the yips and cries of Cheyenne braves riding in a group behind them. He gripped the Peacemaker tightly and thumbed back the hammer.

As the horses charged ahead, the left side of the wagon lifted up and when it slammed back down, something broke with a loud cracking sound and the right front corner canted at a sharp angle. Nadine flew from the bench and landed on her side in the dirt. Thatcher slid across the floorboards and when his boots caught the side of the wagon, he jumped out and landed beside her.

Nadine stood up from the ground and Thatcher saw the expression on her face, slack-jawed and shocked.

He shoved himself to his feet and moved in front of her as an arrow whistled through the air and sliced his left shoulder. "Get down!" He growled at her and drew his other Peacemaker, firing both of them into the air as the group of Cheyenne charged toward them.

Thatcher glared at them and yelled loudly in Cheyenne. *"Nótaxeo'o, nóxa'e! Hena'háanehe! Hena'háanehe!"*

The Cheyenne braves had faces painted red, with vertical white streaks like the swipe of a bear's claws down from their forehead. Their eyes widened at hearing Thatcher speak in their native tongue.

"Éneoestese! Né'áahtove!" Thatcher held his revolvers up, showing that their barrels pointed toward the sky. Two of the six warriors kept their bows held up in front of them, arrows notched and ready. Thatcher moved slowly around the wagon, watching as the men tracked him with razor sharp arrowheads aimed in his direction.

Thatcher took several steps closer, continuing to speak in Cheyenne. He glared as he talked in a raised voice and pointed back at Nadine. He gestured wildly and at her and continued talking to them in their native tongue.

"Stand up," he growled to Nadine.

"You told me to get down."

"Stand up!" Thatcher growl whispered and watched as Nadine rose to her feet. "Take your hat off."

She did as he told her and her dark hair flowed down around her shoulders.

The Cheyenne in the front of the group raised one hand in front of him and then lowered it quickly. Immediately, the two braves lowered their bows and arrows, though their angry expressions remained in place. The leader nudged his palomino horse and slowly walked along the side of the wagon. The Indian stopped and stared at Nadine for a moment, huffed, then let out a high-pitched yell at the sky. He kicked his horse into a fast run in the other direction away from them.

Thatcher smiled wide and nodded. "Étahéoo'kóhtaxe mo'éhno'ha!"

One of the braves narrowed his eyes and shook his head, confused, and then the group cut their horses around and followed the leader, leaving a trail of dust in their wake.

Thatcher let his head fall and released a heavy sigh of relief. He heard soft footsteps as Nadine walked closer, and he turned toward her. "This ain't no stage play in London, you understand? Out here, you can't just stand around watching things happen like you did when them Cheyenne were charging at us." Thatcher shook his head and glanced at the arrows stuck in the wooden planks of the wagon. "You need to take action and that means get *away* from danger or *be* the danger."

She stood there without responding and Thatcher noticed her eyes were glassy as if she had been scolded, even though he hadn't raised his voice. Nadine swallowed and nodded.

"It was a bit dodgy. I'm not exactly used to having people try to kill me. It's rather unusual in London."

"Well, you ain't in London anymore."

Her gaze focused on Thatcher's shoulder. She reached out for him and spoke in a gentle voice. "Are you alright?"

"Yeah, I'm… it only skinned me." Thatcher glanced down at the small patch of blood-soaked wool coat and he clenched his teeth. He took a few steps away from the wagon, looking around in the dry weeds until he saw the arrow that had sliced him. Thatcher picked it up and walked back beside Nadine. He lifted the weapon and smelled the arrowhead, winced and then snapped the arrow shaft over his knee and threw it away from him.

Thatcher shrugged off his wool coat and tossed it into the

wagon, then removed his shirt beneath.

"Why in the Dickens did you smell the-"

"The Cheyenne sometimes dip their arrows in buffalo chips so they—"

"Pardon?"

"Dung." Thatcher looked at the bloody area on the shoulder of his shirt and lay it on top of his coat. "Buffalo dung."

"Oh." Nadine took off her hat and wiped her face. "That's rather... horrid. What savages."

Thatcher's gaze snapped up and he shook his head. "Don't call them that. I understand why you would, I do. I've met a lot of Indians, but not a single savage. They're just doing what they need to do to survive. Most of 'em wouldn't do the savage things they're known for if we'd just leave them alone."

"It sounds as if you respect them."

"I do." Thatcher nodded. "Living like they live. Sharing, raiding... not fueled by greed over money. Yeah, I respect them, alright, but more than that, I feel sorry for them. And ashamed."

He looked down at his wound and pressed his fingertips close to the slice. "I ain't done a thing wrong to any one of them, but I still feel shame. I reckon they've got every right to be angry at anyone with a pale face." Thatcher shook his head and sighed. His voice softened. "I reckon if I was in their shoes, I'd want to wipe out most of the white man, too."

Nadine was quiet.

Thatcher glanced at her. "Sorry about that... I tend to prattle on a bit when I feel strongly about something."

"Passionate." Nadine said softly.

"Ma'am?"

She blinked as if she was coming out of a deep thought and smiled at Thatcher. "When you feel *passionate* about something. It's... refreshing to hear someone speak so strongly about anything that doesn't involve money or business or commodity prices or…" Nadine looked away and then her gaze returned directly to Thatcher's face. "It's refreshing."

That look on Thatcher made a warmth flow through his veins and he studied the arrow wound again.

"Yeah, well." Thatcher studied the slice in his flesh. It wasn't deep, but it didn't need to be. "Anyway, the dung causes a poison in the blood, an infection. If you don't take to some healing on it, the fever or the poison might kill you."

Nadine's face paled. "Are you—"

"*Naw, naw*. I'll be alright. The arrowhead was smeared with it, but wasn't more than a scratch." Thatcher dug around in the wagon bed, inside the canvas sack, and pulled out a bottle of Thistle Dew whiskey he had packed in his own bag. He yanked the cork and doused the wound liberally, grunting with the burning sensation. He took a drink from the bottle and offered it to Nadine. "Care for a bite?"

"I…" She looked at it and gave him a soft smile as she took it. "Only to… be polite."

"Oh, of course. Politeness." Thatcher smiled, suddenly very aware he was bare chested in front of a beautiful woman. He studied his wound, saw the line of fresh blood pooling along the lower edge of the sliced skin. "I'll be back."

Thatcher walked straight from the trail until he reached a thick Lodgepole pine. He drew out his Bowie knife and scraped a walnut-sized morsel of sap from the tree and then walked back to the wagon. "They didn't want to kill us. Only to get us out of the territory."

"How do you know?"

"I've seen Cheyenne braves do things with bows and arrows that just…" He shook his head. "It defies explanation." Thatcher used the blade of the Bowie to smear the tree sap over the slice on his shoulder. "If they wanted us dead, we would be, and them arrows they sent our way would be sticking in *us* instead of in the wagon."

"What did you say to them?"

Thatcher sheathed his Bowie knife and picked up his shirt. "Well, I told them to stop and listen to me." He looked up at Nadine. "I figured a white man speaking in Cheyenne would get their attention." Thatcher pulled his shirt back on and buttoned it as he continued. "Then I told them you were an important woman and I was escorting you." He smirked and Nadine saw his expression.

"That's an interesting tactic." She smiled and fixed the collar of Thatcher's shirt for him. "What else?"

"I told them they were embarrassing me and that you…" Thatcher snickered. "That you were the Queen of London, a place over the great waters, very far away."

"The Queen of…" Nadine's mouth dropped open in amusement. "Well first, there is no Queen of *London*, but… you essentially told them I'm the Queen of England?" She put a hand up over her mouth and her eyes sparkled with amusement. "And later? Right before they left?"

"Oh I…" Thatcher cleared his throat and pulled his coat back on. "I think I told them to… go give their horses a haircut. Maybe."

Nadine shook her head and looked at him questioningly.

"I wasn't around the Cheyenne much. I picked up what words I could." He grinned at her, turned around to look at the wagon wheel, and then let out a hiss of breath. "I knew it. I damned well *knew* it and I told Williams…"

Thatcher looked at Nadine. "Hell, I told *Birdie* that this pin was gonna…" He clenched his teeth and nodded to himself and then took the bottle of whiskey from Nadine. He took a swallow and corked it again. "Well alright then."

It took him less than five minutes to unharness the horses from the wagon rig, and then Thatcher lifted out the saddle for Ginger and fitted it on the buckskin, who seemed a lot more excited about getting away from the wagon.

"Are we going to leave the wagon behind?" Nadine watched Thatcher as he finished with Ginger and saddled up Sadie.

"Ain't got no choice at the moment." He tightened the

girth strap around Sadie's belly and stood up to look at Nadine. "We'll have to go on horseback. You can do it."

"Well I... yes, I can do it." She glanced at the luggage on the wagon.

Thatcher caught her gaze. "We can't take those with us. We'll come on back through this way and retrieve them, but you'll have to go for a few days without fancy things."

"It's not... there's not fancy..." Nadine bit her bottom lip and nodded. "Alright then." She yanked on the closest luggage box, heaved it away from the wagon, and drug it off the side of the trail beside a small Lodgepole pine.

Thatcher watched her, admiring her determination as she returned and took a second box off to the line of trees. When she came back again, only the large container remained and she put her hands on her hips and stared at it as if she was trying to figure out how to handle it by herself.

Shaking his head, Thatcher walked over to the rear of the wagon. "Come on." He grabbed a handle and dragged it toward the edge of the wagon, and then, together, they carried it through the weeds. Thatcher grabbed some dead brush and piled it around to hide the luggage and marched back to the wagon.

"I'll be right there." Nadine said softly.

Thatcher walked ahead without looking back and gathered up the shotgun and rifle from the back of the wagon. The ammunition came next and Thatcher stuffed the bottle of whiskey into Ginger's left saddlebag. When he buckled it shut, he turned and saw Nadine stuffing things into Sadie's saddlebags as well. From the other side of the horse, she looked at him over the saddle and smiled.

"Happy now?"

Nadine walked around the front of Sadie and stood with her arms crossed. "Why wouldn't I be happy? I'm dressed as a farmer in the bloody middle of... nowhere. We just survived an attack by sav... by Cheyenne Indians. I'm about to ride a horse without a proper saddle and—"

"They've got proper saddles on them."

Nadine glanced at the worn leather saddle on Ginger. "They're not... English."

Thatcher laughed and shook his head. "Just cause they ain't *English*... don't mean they ain't *proper*. Years ago, a whole bunch of people thought England wasn't very proper at all. They came over here on some big ol' boats to start something new. You might have read about it over there in some books or something."

Nadine gave him a lopsided smile. "*Yes*... I know about the pilgrims. A Bartlett was among the first to—"

"Climb on up in that saddle and you can tell me *allllll* about it." Thatcher got up on Ginger and took up the reins. The mare snorted and shook her head.

Nadine climbed up on Sadie, settled herself on the saddle and sighed as she held the reins.

"Ready?"

"The Queen of England is *always* ready." Nadine smiled as she snapped the reins and Sadie broke into a fast canter along the trail.

CHAPTER SIXTEEN

Little Branch, Wyoming

It had been almost five years since Ike had ridden out to his cousin's ranch. It was little more than a long shack and a big barn where most of Sullivan's gang slept when they weren't out robbing stage coaches or tearing up a town's gambling halls and saloons.

Ike reined his horse to a stop at the base of the path leading up to Sullivan Worth's place. Ike was a mess of bloody bandages — cloth he had cut from Horace and Degan's shirts and used as best he could.

A bullet had blown through his forearm, thankfully missing bones for the most part. Another had caught the outside of his left thigh, and every jostle of the horse sent fresh ripples of pain through it. The cloth of his shirt was stiff and tacky with his own dried blood. Ike had taken a bullet to the upper left of his chest and though he was sure it hadn't clipped a lung because he wasn't wheezing or coughing up blood, there was no exit wound and the lead was somewhere deep inside. He wasn't sure at the moment if that was a good thing or a bad one. But the wound that was driving Ike right out of his mind was his left little toe that had been completely blown off. He glanced down at the end of his boot and the perfectly round bullet hole caked with dried blood around the opening.

When he crawled out of the underbrush on the trail, Ike had bumped his foot against the root of a Lodgepole pine and he bit down on a mouthful of his coat sleeve to keep from screaming. The fabric had smelled like gunpowder smoke and tasted of Degan's blood.

Degan had died quickly and the thought of seeing the back of the man's head blown off made a shudder run through Ike's body. Horace had been shot in the back by the dead Marshal on the ground close by. The lawman's throat had taken a bullet, just enough to the side to let him live a might longer than Horace.

Ike had gathered up what he could, gotten onto his horse and ridden toward Sullivan's place. He couldn't think of where else to go for help, but the thought of seeing Sullivan face to face again didn't fill him with ease. Ike looked at the side of his horse at the scabbard for Skinner's Henry rifle and wondered if he should take it out before he rode closer.

Probably not. Sullivan's liable to pick me off from a distance if he sees me holding a rifle.

He let out a heavy sigh, urged the horse up the rocky trail, and clenched his teeth as the wound in his foot throbbed. Ike saw Sullivan on the front porch, sitting on a chair and leaning back against the logs of the building. Five or six men stepped out of the barn and watched Ike approach.

With one hand, Sullivan casually swung a double-barreled shotgun toward him. He lifted a jug of whiskey, took a drink, and then set it back down on the porch beside him. "That's far enough, you gib-faced son of a bitch."

"N-now Sullivan—"

"Where's Horace and that little shit weasel Skinner at?" Sullivan cocked the shotgun and looked around behind Ike.

The large double-barrels held Ike's attention but he forced his gaze up at the man. "They're dead. All of 'em."

Sullivan spit into the weeds at the edge of the porch. "By whose hand?"

"US Marshals."

Sullivan's bloodshot eyes stared at him and Ike wondered how long the man had been drinking today. Ike gestured with his hands a bit too quickly and three of the men to his left flinched, reaching for their weapons.

"Easy… *eeeeasy* fellers." Ike held his hands up in front of him and turned to Sullivan. "I know we're kin, but I also know we ain't… ain't always seen eye to eye on—"

"You slept with my wife, Ike." Sullivan growled and sat forward from his chair.

"Well now, yeah… yeah, I-I did, but uh…" Ike cleared

his throat and swallowed hard. "I-I wasn't the one that started that uh… y-your wife was the one who—"

"Shut the hell up, Ike. I know how she was. Not that it matters one damned sight right now." Sullivan raised the bottle and took another deep swig. "She done run off with some gambler down to Abilene. If that wagtail would've taken up work at a brothel, she'd be wealthy by now instead of giving it out for free to every wet noodle that came along."

Color rose in Sullivan's face and he glared out over the hillside for a moment, then turned back. "Why are you here, Ike? I got plenty of men… more than enough some days."

"Well… Horace and Skinner, Degan too… they were put down from Marshals but uh… we were trying to help some men, break them out of a jail wagon." Ike glanced at the group of Sullivan's men and then slowly eased his hands down. "Things went to hell on us pretty fast and I-I was hoping you and your fellers… might consider lending a hand."

Sullivan stared at him with his red-rimmed eyes. "What men were you breaking out? Who the hell's worth going gun to gun against some Marshals?"

"The uh…" Ike lowered his voice even though he knew it wouldn't matter. "The Pale Horse gang."

"*Awwww* hell." Sullivan grimaced and shook his head as he pointed with the shotgun barrels down the hillside. "Get the hell out of here while your guts are still inside your body. You already know I don't like that son of a bitch, Abram. I should've put a bullet in his heart years ago when I had the chance. Go on and get."

"There's pay for it." Ike looked around, knew it was a bold action to take next, but he shook his head and laughed. "From the looks of things, you all ain't got a whole lot of things going on at the moment."

Sullivan shook his head. "Ain't *no* amount of money—"

"Five thousand dollars." Ike locked his gaze on Sullivan's face and watched him.

The big man let out a heavy sigh as he stared back. He

tapped a finger against the trigger guard of the shotgun, and then shook his head. "*Naw*... five thousand dollars, my ass. You ain't got five thousand dollars to—"

"I don't, no sir." Ike nodded at him. "But Abram does. The Pale Horse gang robbed a train down near Broken Stone."

"I *knew* it." Sullivan sighed and nodded toward the group of men. "One of them heard about that mess and I..." He leaned back in his chair and took another slug from of whiskey. "Where are they?"

"Horace figured the Marshals were heading toward Casper to get 'em in front of a judge."

"Casper is a long ride from Broken Stone."

"I reckon. We wasn't sure, but Horace reckoned the Marshals might get a hot meal in Bagger's Creek on their way, maybe find a bed for the night." Ike felt his foot suddenly erupt with pain so bad it made his ears ring. He hadn't even taken his boot off yet and the thought of it made it ache even more.

Sullivan stared at him for a few moments and then stood up. He walked slowly until he was beside Ike's horse and then he raised the shotgun until the barrels rested beneath Ike's chin. "If you're spinning yarns right now, I can promise you... *promise you*, Ike... that I'll blow your head off and use your skull as a spittoon."

CHAPTER SEVENTEEN

Broken Stone, Wyoming

After Bonespur Bill had raced out of Broken Rock, he cut his horse away from the trail as quickly as he could. There was no question the well-worn trail was an easier journey, but Bill wanted to avoid people if possible, and though the direction he rode off in had much more difficult terrain, he thought it would be shorter in time.

And time was one thing he desperately needed more of. He had pushed his horse hard for a while, but Patches needed water and at least a short rest to catch her wind again for the rest of the ride ahead. After making their way down a sloping, rock-strewn stretch of ground, Bill reined Patches toward a thin strip of a river and got down. He stretched and twisted his aching back and pulled his canteen from the clip on the side of her saddle.

Bill took a drink, swirled it around in his mouth and spit, and then walked to the creek and crouched down beside Patches. He put the uncapped canteen into the cold water and refilled it, and from behind him a distance away, Bill heard the soft sound of weight stepping onto weeds. He yanked away from the water, tossed his canteen to the bank and reached for the Colt Walker with his right hand.

He stopped mid-motion, as his gaze took in the dozen or so Pawnee glaring at him. Most of them had bows raised with arrows notched and aimed at him, but several held large bore single-shot Enfield muskets. Bill's hand ached to fire the Colt Walker, but he knew he wasn't fast enough for all of them. The thought of Pawnee arrows sunk in his chest or taking a shot from the Enfields were both things he had no interest in.

Bill pointed to the closest brave with a rifle in his hands. "Did you make the peach jelly? You made the peach jelly, didn't you?" Bill grinned wide, baring his teeth. He yanked off his fox fur hat and tossed it to the ground. He nodded at the brave. "Damned right you made the peach jelly. But are you gonna *shaaaaare* it?"

The brave glanced at the man to his left, a confused expression on his face.

Bill unbuckled his wide leather belt and put it down. He shrugged his coat off and then put his thumbs under his suspenders and continued taking off his shirt until he was bare-chested. He laughed loudly, looked at the brave and grinned, and then made an angry face and yelled at him. "Just because you ride a horse don't make you a barber!"

He kicked off his boots and trousers until he was naked as a jaybird and then got down on the bank of ground by the water. Bill cupped a handful of the dry dirt and scrubbed it over his face and neck. He poured handfuls of dirt on top of his scalp and shook his head like a dog, watching it fly around him in a small dirt cloud.

"*Thaaaaaaat's my clemennntiiiiiiiiiiiiiine!*" Bill sang loudly, and then nodded and grinned wildly at the braves.

He reached down, cupped more dirt in his hand and shoved it into his mouth. Bill growled at the Pawnee and noticed the braves had lowered their bows and arrows as they stared at him.

One of the Pawnee nudged his horse back slightly and then another did the same. The others moved shortly after, as if they were worried they were too close and they might catch whatever ailed him. The entire group kicked into their horses and rode off toward the hillside.

"Damnation." Bill said as muddy slobber fell from his lips. His mouth was caked with mud and dry dirt and he spit, turned, and walked out into the icy water. Cupping water to his mouth, Bill rinsed it repeatedly, though the earthy taste remained. He gritted his teeth and splashed water over his face and neck, over his chest. It was like washing with chips of ice and Bill groaned through clenched teeth.

As he stamped up onto dry ground, the wind blew against his wet bare skin and a whole body shiver rippled through him. Bill unbuckled the right saddlebag on Patches and drew out the blackberry whiskey. He took a heavy drink as he stood there and the cold wind dried his skin.

Patches snorted and turned her head to look at him. Bill caught her gaze, glanced down at himself, and then looked at the horse again. "Yeah, well… it's cold out here, alright?"

Bonespur Bill took another drink and stuffed the whiskey back into the saddlebag. He walked to the pile of his things on the ground and got dressed with his back toward the judgmental horse. When he finished adjusting his belt and tucking the tomahawk beneath the worn leather, Bill saddled up and turned Patches toward Bagger's Creek.

CHAPTER EIGHTEEN
Bagger's Creek, Wyoming

Abram opened his eyes when the Marshals drove the wagon into the town of Bagger's Creek. When gold nuggets began to be discovered in the Sweetwater River, Bagger's Creek had exploded overnight, drawing people in search of hard work and the hope of discovering a fortune. But like many such towns, it was nothing but a spark in a dark landscape and burned out as fast as it had started. The gold was traced upstream and the Carissa Mine was established, but it was too far from Bagger's Creek and the town suffered for it. It had dwindled down to mostly empty buildings of sun-beaten planks, leaving only the businesses essential to keep a town's heartbeat alive.

The Marshals pulled the wagon to a stop along the boardwalk and the wounded driver set the handbrake. He let out a heavy groan as he straightened up and twisted his back, and then he climbed down to the ground. The other Marshal, still holding the Yellowboy rifle in his hands, got down on the other side. He glared at Abram and glanced at Blaine, and then turned to the other Marshal. "Go on in and let the Sheriff know."

Abram turned to the building and saw a two-foot tall wooden sign shaped like a badge with the words SHERIFF in painted letters that were chipped and peeling. The front door was off its hinges and leaned against the front of the building. The Marshal checked the bloody bandage around his arm and walked inside.

"When we get the go ahead, you all are gonna get out o' that cage and walk inside real nice and easy." The Marshal held the rifle up in front of him as if to make sure they all saw the weapon. "And if'n you don't, then there won't be much need for a trial later."

"Trial for what, Marshal?" Abram shook his head and smiled. "We ain't done a thing."

The old lawman clenched his teeth and spit on the ground as his partner stepped out of the Sheriff's office and waved him on.

After the Marshal unlocked the cage, Calhoun crawled out first and stood to the side of the wagon. Abram got out next, feeling his knees pop as his legs stretched. Blaine slowly crawled to the edge of the wagon, swung his legs over the floorboards and tried to stand up. His knees buckled almost immediately and Abram moved quickly, grabbing him with both hands.

Blaine gave him a lopsided smile. "I had it."

"I know." Abram snickered and nodded. "I know you did." Abram helped Blaine walk into the Sheriff's office and saw the open door of a jail cell waiting for them. A rotund man in a plain work shirt and a vest with a badge on it stood off to one side and watched.

The walls of the office were threaded with cracks through the horsehair plaster. The wounded Marshal gripped onto the bars of the cell and gave them a solid yank. He looked back at the older lawman. "It'll do."

The old man gestured with the barrel of the Yellowboy toward a window up high in the jail cell wall. "Check that too."

After testing the bars on the window, the younger Marshal walked out, satisfied.

Abram helped drag Blaine into the cell and eased him down to a cot speckled with bird droppings over one end. Blaine let out a heavy sigh and nodded thanks at Abram. He leaned against the wall of the cell and took shallow breaths. As he heard the cell door close and get locked, Abram turned around. "This man needs a doc, ain't no two ways about it."

The Marshal with the rifle stared at Blaine for a moment. "I'll find a doc in town." He nodded toward the younger lawman. "But he'll take care of this man's wounds first." He snickered. "See if your man can hold out on dying for just a little while longer."

"Old bastard." Calhoun muttered under his breath as he went to sit on another cot in the cell.

The overweight Sheriff sat down behind his desk with a heavy sigh, as if he had just finished exerting himself and spoke to the lawmen. "You fellers go on up to Doc Partridge. He's down the street on the left, can't miss the sign on his building. And get y'selves a hot meal and some whiskey at Dixie's. I'll be here through the night and I already told Mabel over at the boarding house, to get you some beds ready." He set out a pair of Pietta 1860 Army Sheriff revolvers on the desk in front of him. "These sons o' bitches ain't going anywhere."

"Much obliged, Sheriff Atters." The older lawman tipped his hat, gave one final glare at Abram, and the two men walked toward the door.

"Oh, Marshals?" The Sheriff called out to them and the older lawman turned. "Telegram operator said something came in for you, sent in from Broken Stone."

The Marshal give a nod and Abram watched him walk away. He turned to look at the fat man behind the desk, watched him stare at the open doorway as if he was making sure the Marshals weren't going to suddenly return. A moment later, the Sheriff pulled open a desk drawer and took out a piece of cloth and a handful of sugar cookies and began to eat them, two bites at a time. Crumbs fell from his thick-lipped mouth and caught in the fabric of his shirt. Abram turned away and leaned his head back against the wall.

Beside him, Abram could feel the fever rolling off Blaine and he looked at the bandage around the man's shoulder. It was dark with dried blood but there was nothing new and wet soaking through. He only hoped when a doc finally came to help him, that the sawbones brought some whiskey or ether to help with pain. The simple act of peeling off the bandages would be hellish enough, dried and stuck to the bullet wound. Abram sighed heavily and wondered if Bonespur Bill was on his way or if the crazy old bastard had simply taken the money and run.

Booted feet and slow heavy footsteps outside the front of the office drew Abram's attention. He only saw a shadow cast inside the building but the Sheriff's eyes went wide and he tossed the sugar cookie in his hand onto the desk, got up quickly, and headed outside.

Abram heard him talking with someone in voices too low to understand and then a long-bearded man in an oilskin duster and a black gambler's hat walked inside. The duster was trail beaten and deeply creased at the inner elbows from years of use. He looked downward slightly as he walked toward the jail cell and the brim of his hat cast his face in shadow.

The man stopped in front of the cell and lifted his face to reveal eyes the deep, frozen blue of rivers in winter. They were framed in a face with deeply set wrinkles and a crosshatching of scars along the left side. The front of his duster parted slightly and a worn silver Marshal's badge shone in the low light of the room. He gave a nod and spoke in a low voice full of road grit and gravel. "Abram."

Abram's eyes went wide as he stared at the man. His throat went dry and he swallowed hard as he eased himself up from the cot and shuffled to stand in front of the bars. His leg irons jangled against the floor. "Sir."

"There's a witness, a woman that saw you, saw *all* of you on the train. She's—"

A thin man in a bowler derby quickly stepped inside the office. He carried a wide black satchel in his left hand and after pausing to look at Blaine in the jail cell, he walked toward him.

"Give me a minute, Doc." The old lawman said to him.

The man turned and shrugged. "Now... now I came right over here after taking care of that Marshal that was all shot up. They said—"

"I *said* give me a damned minute." The Marshal's voice raised ever so slightly but it carried a harsh edge to it.

The doctor flinched and gave a curt nod. "I-I'll be uh... right outside."

"You go and add about ten or fifteen paces to that distance while you're at it." He glared at the doctor with blue chips of anger.

Giving another fast, nervous nod, the doctor quickly left the office and the Marshal turned back to Abram.

Calhoun shifted on his cot and stared. "Who the hell are *you* anyway, *lawman*?

"I'm the man who'll open this cell and gut you like a hog where you sit if you decide to open that gib-faced mouth of yours again." The threat was slow and casual, and absolutely deadly.

Calhoun seemed like he wanted to say more, but he was smart enough to keep the words in his mind instead of letting them escape his mouth.

The man turned back to Abram. "The woman's alive and being escorted to Casper by a young Marshal." The lawman sighed heavily as he stared at Abram. "She goes by the name Nadine Bartlett."

Abram felt his stomach twist. A witness coming to speak before a judge would mean a noose around their necks for sure. "Can you—"

"I'll do what I can... but it ain't gonna be much. I've got other fish frying in the skillet right now. I'll try and sic a reliable hound on the woman. It's the best I can do." The Marshal took a deep breath, sighed heavily and reached between the bars and put his hand on Abram's shoulder.

Abram nodded at the lawman's words. It was hard for him to look into the man's eyes but he forced himself to meet his gaze. "I thank you then, for what you *can* do."

The Marshal gave a slight nod of his head and walked away. He paused at the threshold of the door as if he was considering something, and then walked outside without looking back. A moment later, Abram heard the canter of a horse as it trotted away.

"Who the hell was that? Talking awful *friendly* like with a—"

"He's my father." Abram cut off Calhoun's words.

"Your… your *father* is a United States Marshal and you…" Calhoun scoffed and went on with an angry voice. "What in the hell, Abram? I've known you nigh six damned years and you ain't never, not *once*, said a—"

Abram snapped around toward Calhoun and crossed the distance quickly. He raised the handcuffs and jammed the chain across Calhoun's throat, shoving him down against the cot. Abram pressed the steel chain hard, cutting off the man's breath.

Calhoun coughed and sputtered as he tried to grab at the chain across his Adam's apple.

"*Naw*, Calhoun, I *ain't* never mentioned it, have I? And if you think on it a minute, you might come to a reckoning that I have my *reasons* for not mentioning it." Abram leaned down closer and glared at him. He gave another hard shove against Calhoun and then released him and stood up.

Calhoun lurched up to sit, coughing and spitting onto the floor as he massaged his throat and wheezed in breaths.

"I thought the man was dead." Abram looked at the open door to the street outside. "Ain't seen him in almost ten years."

Sheriff Atters waddled inside with the doctor right behind him. Abram stepped away from the bars and sat down on the cot as the lawman unlocked the cell to let the doctor come in and work on Blaine.

When the doctor pulled out a bottle of rotgut whiskey from his satchel and made Blaine drink from the dirty bottle, Abram let out a long breath. He closed his eyes and listened to Blaine whimper and groan through clenched teeth. He didn't want to watch the bandages peel off, nor watch the doc clean the bullet wound entrance and exit.

Abram sat still and thought about the reality of a witness and what that meant. For him, killing had always been killing, didn't much matter what was on the other side of the barrel.

The simple fact was that the woman, *Nadine Bartlett*, had to die.

CHAPTER NINETEEN
Bagger's Creek

Bonespur Bill rode Patches slowly into town and when he saw the first hitching post, he reined her to a stop and got down from the saddle. As he tied off the reins, Bill looked at the group of rundown structures. Farther down the street, he saw what appeared to be a saloon. Closer and on the left side of the street looked like a doctor's office and then several boarded-up buildings, and a Sheriff's office. A wagon was parked out front, and Bill studied the empty steel cage.

He gave Patches a scratch behind her ears while his gaze shifted to the door sitting on the boardwalk beside the entrance to the Sheriff's. Bill crossed the street and paused when he saw a heavyweight man inside the building and another thinner man in a derby hat. He shifted to his left until they were out of his angle of sight, but he saw the jail cell inside.

Bill recognized Blaine Gilmont, and even though he had never met the other two men in the cell, it was a safe bet they were what was left of the Pale Horse gang. He nodded and walked down the street toward the saloon. It was another safe bet was that Marshals on a break from a long journey would be itching for some whiskey.

The sign on the front presented the place as Dixie's Trough and Eatery, and Bill snorted a laugh at the description. It seemed to be taken care of more than the other buildings, but not by much. The line of the roof sagged in the middle like an old mare's back, and an upstairs window was busted free of glass. Bill adjusted his Kentucky pistol tucked beneath his belt, and then walked inside.

From the corner of his eye, Bill saw a handful of customers at tables in the room. A couple more stood by the bar and he headed there and waited for the barkeep to walk over. She was a gray-haired woman with a face weathered by time and too much sun, but Bill could tell in her younger years she must have been a beautiful woman. She slid a glass of whiskey in front of a man at the other end of the bar and shuffled along. "Hey there, stranger. What can I get for you?"

Bill smiled and gave her a quick nod. "Got any mescal?"

Her eyebrows knitted together and she looked behind her at three shelves on the wall. She reached for a short wide stoneware vessel, uncorked it and took a sniff. The woman gave the bottle a soft shake and then set it down in front of Bill. "Ain't got much call around here but you're welcome to it."

"I'm obliged, ma'am."

"Ain't no ma'ams around here. It's Dixie." She tucked a few loose strands of gray hair behind her right ear and smiled at him with a wink of her right eye.

"Dixie, then." He lifted the bottle, took a drink and savored the smoky liquor in his mouth before swallowing it.

The old barkeep wandered away, snatched a ragged towel from beneath the counter, and wiped down the bar. Bill smelled seasoned meat and roasted vegetables and he heard the sound of forks against plates. He glanced at the old ranch hands standing at the bar, minding their own business and focusing on their drinks. He turned away from the bar slowly and saw the two men eating a meal at a table against the rear wall of the saloon.

Seasoned men to be that cautious, but then, I ain't never met a Marshal who wasn't.

Their backs were against the wall and they faced the entrance. One of them had his coat off, hanging on the back of his chair. A clean piece of cloth was wrapped around one arm. The other man was older, his expression stoic even as he ate his food. He worked his knife and fork on a piece of meat on his plate and Bill saw the silver glint of a badge on his coat. Behind him, Bill saw a Yellowboy rifle leaned against the wall.

He steered his gaze elsewhere and took another drink of mescal.

That's two of the four Marshals. Now where in hell are the other two?

Bill drew a possibles bag out of his coat pocket, fished out some money and slid it on the bar top. Dixie glanced at him and he smiled and winked back at her as he took the stoneware of mescal with him and walked outside. He stole another glance at the two Marshals eating dinner and saw they were almost finished with their food.

They'll either sit and drink whiskey a while, or they'll finish that meal and come on out.

Bonespur Bill turned to his right and stopped beneath the lopsided porch roof of a rundown building. He leaned against the weathered gray clapboard in the shadows. When the men came out, Bill wasn't sure yet if he would kill them or not. Putting down a common man was one thing, but snuffing out two US Marshals was another thing entirely. Still, if he was going to get the Pale Horse gang out of jail, there was going to be some blood spilled.

He upended the stoneware and guzzled the rest of the smoky liquor. When it was empty, Bill dropped it through a hole broken in the floorboards of the porch and then he crossed his arms and waited.

It wasn't much longer before he heard booted heels against wooden planks and the two Marshals stepped out onto the porch. The older man rolled a cigarette, put it between his lips and struck a match to it.

When the two Marshals walked from the boardwalk down into the street, Bill drew his heavy-bladed Bowie knife from its sheath and quietly walked behind them, closing the distance rapidly.

CHAPTER TWENTY

West of Bagger's Creek, Wyoming

Every single jolt against the saddle sent whip cracks of pain through Ike's body and he glanced down occasionally at the bandage on his chest. It had started to bleed through almost an hour before they reached Bagger's Creek. Sullivan rode close, keeping him within eyeshot. His double-barreled shotgun was in a scabbard on the side of his horse and Ike still felt the way the cold steel shoved up beneath his chin.

The rest of Sullivan's crew rode with them and it was a hard and fast ride from their shack across the plains toward Bagger's Creek. After Gord—one of Sullivan's men—had patched Ike up, they had given him a bowl of stew but it was little more than a few bites of meat and some potatoes in a thin broth. He hadn't eaten since, and Ike's stomach growled and swirled with hunger pangs. He curled his injured arm against his chest and tried to quiet the throbbing heartbeat in his forearm.

Sullivan steered the group along the southern side of Bagger's Creek, approaching the line of haggard looking buildings from behind. They slowed their pace and Ike scanned over the row of structures. Piles of weathered and warped lumber lay discarded and scattered. A wagon with a broken axle sat behind a building without a roof. The canvas top on the wagon was wind-beaten and tattered and flapped in the soft breeze.

Behind what appeared to be an old livery stable, Sullivan reined his horse to a stop and looped its reins around a fallen roof beam, thicker than a man's waist. He pulled his shotgun from its scabbard and turned to Gord and Weathers as they got off their horses. "Okay, boys. May as well get to it."

Gord snickered as he reached into his saddlebag and pulled out four sticks of dynamite. "Won't have to wait very long."

"This is gonna be fun." Weathers eyed the sticks of

explosive and nodded. "Reckon that's too many?"

"Ain't no such thing." Gord grinned at him.

Sullivan turned to Ike. "Can you still shoot or you gonna sit around and nurse those scuffs of yours?"

Ike clenched his teeth as he got down from his horse. His missing toe screamed in agony and the wound in his chest made his breath hitch, but he wasn't about to let Sullivan see it. "I can shoot."

Sullivan gave a grunt of acknowledgement and gestured toward the rest of his men. "Tater and Buckshot, you go around to the left side. Nick and Cullen? You're on the right. Clover, you waltz on out front, sit for a spell across the street from the Sheriff's and you keep that Yellowboy cocked and ready. If any lawmen start running out the front like mice out of an outhouse, you put that rifle to use."

Clover, a thick-necked Irishmen with a red beard and mustache, gave him a nod and drew his Yellowboy from the scabbard on his palomino.

"Ike, you'll be right beside me, dead center." Sullivan gave a slight smirk and looked over his men, then his gaze landed on Gord. "Well alright then, best get to it."

The group broke apart and Ike followed Sullivan to the front of the broken-down livery. They stepped inside the ruins, behind two timbers holding up the last of the roof and several wooden planks barely hanging onto the support columns.

Weathers stepped to the right side of the building and Gord walked to the center. The structure was made of fieldstone and a simple wood and tin roof. A small window with iron bars was set up high in the stone wall of the building and Gord crouched right beneath it. Ike watched him strike a match and then a small shower of sparks erupted as the fuses were lit. He set the sticks of dynamite against the stone wall, a few feet apart.

Weathers grinned wildly as he walked around the right side of the building and put his back to the wall. Quickly,

Gord crept to the left, turned the corner of the building and cupped a hand over one ear.

Peering over the wooden planks, Ike stared at the sparkling fuse, transfixed. Sullivan reached up, grabbed his coat, and pulled him down behind the cover of the weathered boards. He glared at him like a parent would at a child doing something stupid.

Without even the soft sound of a breeze, the only noise was the sizzling fuses as they burned to their end.

Thatcher reined Ginger down the main street of Bagger's Creek and Nadine rode at his side. It was a quiet-looking town to be certain, though Thatcher thought in its short-lived heyday, it must have been quite something. His gaze ran over the line of darkened buildings and picked out the ones that still seemed alive. Thatcher glanced at the Sheriff's office, saw the jail wagon out front, and he nudged Ginger further along. He reined the horse to stop in front of a Barber shop and got down. There was a building across the street that looked like a saloon maybe. Across from that, Thatcher saw what seemed to be a boarding house. He nodded to himself and looped Ginger's reins around the hitching post.

Nadine watched his actions and repeated it with Sadie's reins.

Thatcher nodded and smiled. She was a quick learner, and that was something he appreciated. He watched as she studied the reins for a moment as if to satisfy herself, and then Nadine straightened up and turned to him.

He stared at her a moment. "That… disguise works fine at a distance, but it ain't much for up close."

"No?" Nadine put her hands on her hips. "I can't pass for a… a ranch hand?"

"Well uh… you…" Thatcher felt himself fumbling at a choice of words.

Nadine smirked slightly. "Go on."

"You're a might…" Thatcher cleared his throat. "Well you're uh…" He felt color rise in his face, knew the pink was noticeable to anyone who looked at him. He shook his head and met her gaze. "No. You can't pass for any ranch hand I ever seen in my life, ma'am."

Nadine smiled at him, full of mischief. "I told you to call me Nadine."

He looked away from her eyes and reached for her coat, pulled the edges together and buttoned a single button. Up close like that, he could smell that intoxicating smell of lilacs again.

Thatcher took a few steps backward and appraised her. If anything, tightening the coat only seemed to accentuate the curves of Nadine's body *more*.

Heat rushed through Thatcher and he felt like he'd gotten sunburned. He cleared his throat and turned to look down the street. "I'll um… we need to get a place to sleep." He walked toward the boarding house and heard Nadine's footsteps fall in line beside him.

The woman behind the counter at the boarding house looked up from the book she was reading and set it aside as she stood up. She eyed up Thatcher and gave him a smile. "Is there a music band comin' along later?"

Thatcher studied her weathered face and shook his head in confusion.

"Four of you Marshals in town," she grinned. "I reckon y'all must be having a square dance or somethin'."

He glanced down at the badge on his coat and then turned back to the woman. "Something like that. Need a room for the night."

The woman glanced toward the front door at Nadine, and then gave a slight nod as she flipped open a book and tapped her finger on the page below a list of names. "Sign in and I'll get you all set up."

Thatcher scribbled his signature and looked up at the

woman. "I'll be back later for the room, right now a hot meal is what I'm after."

The woman nodded toward the right of the building. "Dixie's ain't bad, which is good, 'cause that's the only choice you got."

"Obliged, ma'am." Thatcher tipped his hat and he and Nadine walked outside to the street again. "Come with me." He walked along the left side of the street, keeping the Sheriff's office in sight. Thatcher took off his Marshal's badge and stuffed it in his pocket. After the lady at the boarding house, it occurred to him that it might be best to avoid advertising who he was.

He walked on a little farther and then turned to look at the Sheriff's office across the street. Thatcher casually walked at an angle until he could see inside through the open front door. He waved Nadine closer to him and he pointed and whispered. "You recognize any of them?"

She looked, the brim of the hat concealing the upper half of her face, and stared at them. "Yeah, two of them. The man with the blue eyes there, and the other beside him. He was the one who… shot people along the…" Nadine, with glassy eyes, glanced at Thatcher. "I didn't see the third man in there."

"That's alright. That's enough." Thatcher put his hand against the small of her back and guided her toward the other side of the street again.

"So now what?"

"Well now…" Thatcher glanced at the Sheriff's Office to make sure they hadn't been seen. "Now we stay low, get ourselves a hot meal and a good night's sleep, and head out early, get ahead of the Marshals before they leave for Casper. Pulling that jail wagon, we'll get there long before they do."

"Are you going to find the other Marshals and let them know we're here?"

Thatcher scratched the back of his neck as he considered her question, and then shook his head. "*Naw*, I… I don't think I will. I reckon it might be best just to… keep quiet." He looked at the saloon and then turned back to Nadine. "Tuck your hair up underneath that hat a bit more."

She removed her hat, leaned forward so that her long curls of dark hair draped down, and then Nadine whipped her hair back, drew it together in one hand and twisted it up as she put the hat back in place.

"Better?"

Thatcher let out a slow breath as he watched her motions. "Better."

What he'd thought but didn't say earlier, was that she was a hell of sight curvier than any ranch hand he'd ever seen in his life. His throat was dry and he turned toward the saloon. "C'mon, let's get a hot meal."

The two of them walked down the street and Thatcher saw two men standing on the front porch of Dixie's. Both of them wore dusters and as the man on the left took a puff on his cigarette, Thatcher saw the flash of his badge.

Those are two of the Marshals.

The man took another drag of his cigarette and they stepped down to the street.

To the left of the saloon, Thatcher saw a burly man in a fox fur hat move out of the shadows of a porch roof, and fall in behind the two men. A massive Bowie knife was clutched in the man's hand and without thinking about it, Thatcher drew a Peacemaker and yelled out toward the two men in long dusters.

"*Heyyyy!*" Thatcher cocked his revolver and raised it, had time to see the two men's expressions register frightened surprise.

Then the world around Thatcher exploded into dust and grit and a locomotive of heat knocked him and Nadine from their feet.

CHAPTER TWENTY-ONE

Broken Stone, Wyoming

When the dynamite went off, Ike flinched from the ear-splitting detonation and in the time it took to blink, a short length of iron bar speared through the wooden plank in front of him. He stared at the metal spike, which could have easily impaled him. The air was thick with dust, and grit rained all around them.

Sullivan charged from around the thick board, leveled his shotgun and barreling into the cloud of smoke. Ike walked from the ruins of the livery and raised a revolver, though he wasn't sure how the hell he was supposed to try and aim.

Abram watched Sheriff Atters behind the desk and wondered to himself how a man could simply go on shoveling food in his mouth like that. When the sugar cookies were finished, the lawman produced a sandwich of some kind with slices of bread easily an inch thick. The sandwich dripped something onto the desk, and as the lawman used the sleeve of his shirt to wipe it up, the rear wall of the jail exploded in a blast of stones and dust. Abram was thrown from the cot to the floor and Blaine tumbled down beside him. Chunks of rock slammed against the bars and the cell door busted away from its top hinge.

A slab of fieldstone the size of a pie tin hurtled across the room and caught the Sheriff in the throat, cleaved down to his spine and nearly took his head off. His heavy body was thrown sideways and the chair toppled over as he slammed against the wall in a red splotch.

Abram's ears rang like church bells as the cloud of dust swirled through the jail cell. Even the sight of the dead Sheriff, only several feet away, was completely obscured. Abram coughed and sputtered and clutched the back of Blaine's shirt.

"C-Calhoun!" He called out and heard the man coughing from the other side of the jail cell.

A strong hand grabbed the back of Abram's coat and yanked him back toward the rear of the room. He let go of Blaine and twisted around, ready to swing a fist, but over the ringing bells in his head, Abram heard a rough voice growl "This way outside."

The hand let him go and Abram grabbed Blaine and heaved the man up to his feet. He saw a flash of movement and figured it was Calhoun rushing out the massive hole in the wall.

Abram stepped forward, felt rocks slide beneath his boots, and walked carefully ahead with Blaine in tow. He saw the edge of a stone foundation at his feet and he stepped over it to the ground just beyond.

A revolver cracked and a bullet ricocheted from what was left of the wall beside him. Abram pulled back inside the cell as more gunfire exploded in the cloud of dust. He saw flashes of muzzle fire to his right, and Abram jerked Blaine close to him and screamed. "Let's go!"

He charged forward, hoping like hell the gunfire wouldn't turn his way again.

The sound of men yelling came from Ike's right and he squinted his eyes against the dust. A gunshot cracked the air and Ike heard the bullet ping and ricochet off stone. He aimed in the direction the shot had come from and then saw bright flashes as Sullivan's men opened fire. The dust had only started to get blown away, and as it cleared part of the livery stable, Ike saw the man called Tater shoot his revolvers one by one. On his third shot, a bullet from somewhere caught the man in his right eye and the side of his head blew off as Tater fell to the ground.

Buckshot rose up from the dust cloud and fired a shotgun. A man screamed and Buckshot fired again.

From the rubble of the jail, Ike watched as Sullivan charged out with another man close behind him. More gunfire to the left drew Ike's attention and he saw Buckshot drop his shotgun, draw two Colt Navy revolvers and start shooting. A bullet tore through his right shoulder and then another hit the side of his throat in a burst of red mist. Buckshot opened his mouth to scream, but the sound was a wet gargle.

Ike fired his revolver in the direction he figured the shots must have come from. He walked backwards, making his way toward the end of the livery and the horses tethered to the rear of the building.

Sullivan fired behind him as he ran, stumbled on pieces of rock, and then gained his footing again. Two other men emerged from the busted stone wall and Ike recognized Abram and Blaine as they shuffled in leg chains away from the jail.

Thatcher saw the cloud of dust and grit wash over the two Marshals and knock them to the ground. The man with the Bowie knife slammed against the boardwalk in front of the saloon and then the sight of everything was cloaked in a cloud of dirt.

"Nadine!" Thatcher rolled to his side and grabbed onto her coat. He heard her coughing and sputtering. "Are you okay?"

"Fine, I'm—"

Thatcher scrambled to his knees and then yanked her up onto her feet. He pulled her along toward the boardwalk closest to them and kicked in a door to an abandoned building. Thatcher dragged her inside, cursing as the cloud of dust followed them in. "Stay here, you understand? If anything happens, no matter what, then—"

A hail of gunfire broke out across the street and Thatcher walked Nadine backward, away from the window and close to a wall. "If anything happens, you send a telegram to

Broken Rock, Sheriff Birdie Mitchell. But stay here!"

Thatcher didn't wait for a reply before he rushed outside and drew both of his Colts. He rushed toward where the two Marshals had been but they were gone. Thatcher ran toward the sound of gunfire. As he charged through a narrow alleyway, he saw the two lawmen standing at the end, shooting their revolvers. Just as Thatcher came up close, he saw the older man get shot in the chest. He slammed back against the corner of the building and a revolver flew out of his hand.

Thatcher saw the man's expression and he was dead before he hit the ground. The younger Marshal fired a shot into the dust cloud and as Thatcher approached, he snapped around with wide eyes and aimed his revolver straight at him.

"Stop! I'm—"

A bullet sliced through the air and punched into the young Marshal's right cheek, blowing a hole through the other side in a spray of blood and teeth. A warm spatter hit Thatcher's face and he flinched as the Marshal squeezed the trigger and fired his gun. The bullet passed by like an angry bumblebee, close enough to feel the heat of the lead.

The Marshal blinked at him once, then again, and his eyes rolled up into his head as he collapsed to the ground.

More gunshots cracked out and the wooden clapboard beside Thatcher blew into splinters. He thumbed the hammers back on his Peacemakers, inhaled sharply, and lunged around the corner of the building. He fired left handed and then right, aiming toward any muzzle flash he saw. He shot a man in the chest and watched him scream and fall back against a pile of old lumber. Another heavy round of gunfire broke out and Thatcher ran in a crouch.

Horses whinnied and Thatcher ran forward as he heard hooves stamp and then break into a run. Charging ahead, Thatcher went past the broken-down building and around the edge. A group of men on horseback raced away from Bagger's Creek. He clenched his teeth at the sight of them and then looked back at the destruction they had left behind.

The cloud of dust had cleared enough that he could see the rear of the Sheriff's Office and the massive hole blasted through the thick stone wall. Thatcher walked closer until he could see the empty jail cell inside. He gritted his teeth and shifted his neck until the small bones popped.

The Pale Horse gang might have busted out, and that meant Nadine was far from safe. In fact, as free men who could get their hands on weapons, it probably meant she was in more danger than she was before.

CHAPTER TWENTY-TWO
Bagger's Creek, Wyoming

Thatcher holstered his Peacemakers and walked past the ruins of the livery stable. Broken fieldstone was everywhere on the ground and the stink of dynamite and dirt was thick in the air. A gunshot cracked from the other side of the buildings toward the main street and then he heard the heavy hooves of a fast running horse. Thatcher watched as a rider cut around the row of buildings from the street and rode off in the direction of the other group. Thatcher's breath caught in his chest.

Nadine.

He ran through the rubble and cut through an alleyway between structures. When he reached the other side, Thatcher charged across the street and slammed open the door of the building he had left Nadine in. He looked around the darkened room and whispered her name.

Thatcher heard the soft scuff of boots against gritty floorboards and Nadine slowly rose up from behind a wide wooden table flipped onto its side. Her eyes were wide and scared, but when she saw him, a gasp of relief escaped her and she ran to him and threw her arms around his neck. He held her then, tightly, and put the palm of his left hand gently against the back of her head. "It's alright. You're alright, I got you."

He felt his heart racing in his chest and he softly ran his hand over her hair until he felt her breathing slow. She pulled her head back and looked up at him. Her eyes were glassy as her gaze searched his and she whispered. "What... what happened out there?"

Thatcher let out a heavy sigh as he stepped away and looked out the window. Several people walked along the street to look at the destruction. "Just... just come with me right now."

Nadine picked her hat up from the floor and put it on as

they walked outside and crossed the street. The burly man wearing a fox fur hat and holding a Bowie knife was gone. That unnerved Thatcher and he thought again to what he had been about to interrupt earlier. It sure as hell looked like he was planning on killing the Marshals.

Thatcher approached a group standing together, staring at the rear of the Sheriff's office. He turned to Nadine. "Stay close, but don't… you don't want to see these things. Once you do, you can't unsee them."

She nodded and leaned against the back of the doctor's office building and Thatcher stepped away toward the alleyway he had run through after the dynamite explosion. The two dead Marshals lay stretched out on the ground, their dusters covered in grit and dirt and blood.

He heard some men talking in low voices and when Thatcher looked up, he saw Dixie walking closer. She wiped her hands on a rag, slung it over her shoulder, and then put her hands on her hips as she studied the corpses near the edge of the livery. One of the men standing there suddenly turned away and threw up.

Thatcher walked beside Dixie and then looked at the two dead men on the ground. "Recognize any of 'em?"

Dixie cleared her throat as she studied the corpses. She pointed a finger at the body of a bald man who had been shot once in the shoulder, and again in the side of his throat. "That heavy-set one is Buckshot Pierce." Dixie turned slightly and pointed at a thinner man with his right eye and most of his face blown off. "And that'n is… I *think* that's Sweet Potato Pete. Most call him Tater." She leaned forward, wincing at the condition of the man's face. "Though I can't rightly say for certain as there ain't much left to recognize."

She swiveled around and pointed at a third man on the ground farther away by the livery. His arms were raised above his head like he was having a religious moment. "And I can't recollect that man's face at all."

Thatcher looked at the dead man, saw he wasn't wearing

a gun belt and there was no rifle or shotgun within reach of him. He was peppered with bullet holes, courtesy of a shotgun blast.

Dixie grabbed the towel from her shoulder and wiped her hands with it again, though she hadn't touched anything. "Sheriff's been killed too, sitting right there at his desk. Still had half a ham sandwich in front of him."

Thatcher clenched his teeth and shook his head in disgust at the brutality.

The woman from the boarding house stepped up among the group, glanced at the dead men scattered on the ground, and then turned to Thatcher. "Where's the other Marshal?"

"Ma'am?"

"I said you were the fourth one in town." She pointed at the two dead Marshals in the alleyway. "These two, you, and the other'n. Older man, eyes like frost on blueberries."

Dixie turned to look at him. "You're a Marshal?"

Thatcher nodded at Dixie. "Yes ma'am." He looked around at the mess as he took out his badge and pinned it in place. Thatcher turned back to the woman. "Where's the telegrapher's office?"

Both Dixie and the lady from the boarding house pointed in the same direction, but only the lady spoke. "Left side, looks abandoned, but got a little sign up on the outside. You'll see it."

"Open the door on up and go in." Dixie continued. "Sigil Ferguson might be sleeping, but he'll wake up and do what you ask."

"Obliged." Thatcher tipped his hat, glanced around at the corpses and then caught Nadine's gaze as he walked away.

"Thatcher?" She whispered as she walked beside him.

"Not just yet." He glanced at her and quickened his pace toward main street. "We're in a bad spot, and I have to get a message to Birdie."

True to Dixie's description, the man called Sigil was stretched out on a wide oak desk, arms crossed over his chest as he slept soundly. He snorted and jolted awake when Thatcher pushed the door open.

"H-how do you like your water trough, hot or cold?" Sigil stared at them with eyes glazed from sleep as he sat up and swung his legs over the side of the desk.

"Sir?" Thatcher eyed the man up.

Sigil cleared his throat, coughed loudly and ran a hand over his tired looking face. "Don't mind me, I…" He drew a pair of spectacles from his shirt pocket, fitted them on and looked at the two of them standing by the door.

"I'm afflicted by talking in my sleep, complete gibberish at the worst, and nonsense at the best." As he stood up from the desk, tufts of his fine gray hair flared out to the sides, giving him the appearance of some strange bird. "How might I help y'all today?"

Thatcher instructed Sigil what to send in the telegram and the man jotted it down dutifully.

MARSHALS DEAD, ONE MISSING. SHERIFF DEAD. PALE HORSE GANG FREE. T. EVANS

After Sigil sent the telegram, Thatcher sat down in a chair by the desk, but it was only a moment before he stood up again, anxious.

"Sometimes it uh… it might take a while to deliver the message to the recipient." Sigil nodded at him. "Or to get a reply."

"Yeah." Thatcher scratched along his neck. He tasted dust and grit in his mouth.

"What I mean to say is… maybe you could find somewhere else to wait." Sigil smiled wide.

"I'll… we'll be at Dixie's, then." Thatcher pointed at him. "You hear *anything*, you come get me right away, you hear?"

"Of course, I will." Sigil cleared his throat and sat down in a chair in front of the telegraph. "I'll be right here waiting."

Thatcher gave him a nod before he and Nadine walked out into the street again and paused. He looked at the front of the Sheriff's Office, saw fieldstones had been blown through the open front door and busted the glass clean out of the window. The empty jail wagon sat in front, though one horse had either torn away from the harnesses or was stolen. The other stamped at the ground, still clearly spooked from the explosion.

He turned and saw Nadine staring at the empty jail cage and the ruins of the building. She whispered to Thatcher. "They've escaped, haven't they? The men I saw, the Pale Horse gang… they're free."

Thatcher chewed on his bottom lip and then nodded. "That's about the size of it, yeah."

She gave a slow nod and then looked at him. "Well then."

"Let's…" Thatcher glanced down the street at the saloon. "Let's try this again. If we're waiting around, we might as well do it with a hot meal."

"I'm not quite certain that… my appetite is—"

"Don't worry, your appetite will be there once we sit down." Without thinking about it, Thatcher put his hand gently against the small of her back and guided her toward Dixie's. "Everyone's hunger dies down in the… the thick of things like this. But it returns stronger than it was before."

Nadine glanced at him with a scared expression on her face. "Let's hope the Pale Horse gang doesn't do the same."

CHAPTER TWENTY-THREE
West of Bagger's Creek, Wyoming

Abram and Blaine rode on a dead man's horse. Because of the leg chains, both of them had to ride side-saddle and the jangling links seemed to unnerve the animal. To his left, Calhoun snapped the reins on a speckled gray appaloosa, driving the thickly muscled stallion hard.

In the cloud of dust and grit, Abram hadn't seen any of the men's faces well, and he wasn't sure who exactly they were—only that it wasn't Horace Conway and his boys. He saw Ike riding along, the expression on his face full of pain each time his horse touched ground.

They weren't following any trail, only cutting their own path through the flatlands and scrub brush. The rider in the lead cut his horse to the right and the group swayed after him like a flock of snowbirds. They rode toward a stretching grove of Lodgepole pines at the base of the hills and the lead rider drove his horse into the woods. The group narrowed, following single-file, and the hoof beats of the horses muffled against the thick carpet of dead pine needles.

The woods opened up into a wide but narrow strip of flat meadow and the other men slowed their horses. Abram adjusted the holsters on his gun belt. As he had dragged Blaine from the jail, he had stopped and stolen the pair of Colt Patersons from a dead man.

Blaine groaned in pain and Abram patted the man's arm. "Easy, brother. You can rest for a short while." He held onto Blaine's ar as the man slid down from the horse and stood on solid ground. The gunshot wound might still be painful, but Blaine had color in his face again, rather than the driftwood pale tone, and that was a start in the right direction.

Abram got down, saw Calhoun get off the appaloosa and walk closer. Calhoun whispered to him. "I need some guns."

"You'll get 'em." Abram whispered back and then he turned toward the rest of the men in the group. Ike looked like hell as he stood and leaned against his horse. The man seemed more bandages than clothing.

"Well alright then, Ike."

The gruff voice drew Abram's attention, and he saw Sullivan Worth, still on his horse, and staring at Ike.

"Well I…" Ike swallowed hard as he stepped away from his horse. "I told you *I* don't have the money. Abram does."

"I don't give a damn *who* pays me, but *some*body better hand over five thousand dollars." He glared at Ike and gave a thin smirk. "I always keep my promises."

"Easy, Sullivan." Abram slowly shuffled toward the man.

"Easy?" Sullivan turned away from Ike, his eyes reddened, either from road dust or anger.

"You're wearing Nick's guns." A weathered outlaw, a grimace on his face, sat on a buckskin horse and glared at Abram.

"Nick ain't gonna be needing them anymore." Abram shook his head and smiled as he walked closer to Sullivan's horse.

Abram's words set fire to whatever kindling for anger sat inside Sullivan's mind. "Son of a bitch! Three of my crew were put down back there and you're smiling about it! I'll be damned if it was all for—"

"I'll get you your money." Abram looked up at Sullivan and smiled. And then, lightning quick, drew the man's shotgun from its leather scabbard. He thumbed the hammers back and squeezed the trigger, blasting both barrels into Sullivan Worth's chest. It blew him backward off his horse, and Abram dropped the shotgun and drew his Colt Patersons before Sullivan landed facedown against the dead wildflowers. He cocked the revolvers and aimed in the center of the group of men, as far as his handcuffs would allow.

"Sweet mother of hell!" The man who had noticed the Colts on Abram's waist yelled, and several men shifted toward their guns.

"Now now… easy now." Abram shook his head. "You boys got a choice to make." He nodded at Sullivan's corpse.

"You can all get your dander up and draw them guns... all angry and full o' hot blood 'cause I killed Sullivan Worth. Or..." He stared at the man who had yelled. "You can ride with me and I'll cut you in on what me an' my men robbed from the train down in Broken Stone."

The man sitting on the buckskin horse glanced at Ike and then turned to Abram. "Your man there—"

"He ain't my man."

"Well... whatever he is, he said he'd pay five thousand dollars if we all busted you out." The man eased his hands away from his holsters and crossed his arms over his chest.

Abram turned to Ike and snorted a soft laugh. "Is *that* what you offered them? *Hmmm...*" He nodded, looked at the group of men, and then his gaze returned to Ike. "And I offered thirteen thousand to Horace and his boys to do it." Abram shrugged and shook his head. "Eight thousand isn't a bad cut, Ike."

Ike swallowed hard, glanced at the man on the buckskin and then to Abram. "W-well, I... I was—"

Abram aimed and squeezed the trigger, smooth and easy as a river stone. The Colt Paterson thundered as the bullet caught Ike in his left cheekbone and made a perfectly round circle before a wet spray blew out from the back of his head.

"Hellfire and..." The man on the buckskin growled and clenched his teeth at the sight.

Ike took a single step, his body unaware it was dead yet, and then his knees buckled and he slammed down to the ground, spattering the weeds with blood.

Abram turned to the other men, noting their expressions of shock. "Like I was saying... Fifteen thousand split up as even as it can. I'll cut you boys in on it if you ride with me." He nodded toward Calhoun and Blaine. "With *us*."

"T-they..." The man on cleared his throat. "Everyone calls me Gord."

"Alright then, Gord." Abram nodded at him. "Seeing as you're the only one speaking, then you decide on things, yes or no?"

Gord flicked his tongue out to wet dry lips, looked to his right and then to his left at the faces of what was left of the Worth gang. He turned back to Abram. "We'll ride with you."

"Well alright then." He turned to Calhoun and gave him a nod. "Get Sullivan's gun belt and fish around for more shells for that shotgun. It'll be easier for Blaine to use."

"We... we going to get the money now?" Gord asked as he slowly uncrossed his arms.

"*Naw*, not just yet. There's..." Abram holstered his Colt Patersons and clenched his teeth as he thought of Nadine Bartlett. "I've got other fish frying in the skillet right now."

CHAPTER TWENTY-FOUR
Broken Stone, Wyoming

Bonespur Bill sat in the second floor of what he thought used to be a blacksmith's shop. The rear half of the roof had caved in and each step he took up the stairs felt like they were going to fall through, but Bill reached the top and crouched by the broken front window. He peered around the frame with his left eye, looking out at the cloud of dust and the gunshots thundering behind the Sheriff's office.

He had no idea who the man was on the street earlier, but he acted like a lawman. After the explosion, Bill had scrambled to his feet and run when the gunshots started cracking. It wasn't out of fear of a fight, but whatever was going on was no longer his concern. By his view from the second floor, Bill watched the group of outlaws ride out of Bagger's Creek. The Pale Horse gang had busted been out of jail. The two Marshals he had seen in the saloon were dead.

Bill sat down on the sagging floorboards and leaned against the wall. Right or wrong, he had made five hundred dollars for not doing much more than riding from Broken Stone to Bagger's Creek.

A few swallows of blackberry whiskey would go down right well at the moment.

Something wasn't quite right, though. Didn't fit. The first was the man that had yelled out to the two Marshals in the street, and the second was the woman he had with him, walking around in the clothes of a field hand. He peered over the window frame again and whispered to himself. "Speak of the Devil and the Devil appears."

The woman and the young man walked across the street in the direction of the telegraph office. He watched them as long as he could, how the man walked determined and with purpose. Just before the man reached the boardwalk, Bill saw the flash of a badge pinned to his coat.

He gave a soft groan and pulled back from the window.

Why the hell wouldn't a Marshal have ridden off after the Pale Horse gang and them other men?

He absently tapped the fingers of his right hand against his leg.

It's that woman, Bill nodded to himself. *I know damned well it's got something to do with that woman.*

Except for the Sheriff, no one from Bagger's Creek had been killed in the melee. The saloon wasn't somber, more what Thatcher would describe as serious. He and Nadine walked to a table near the back, up against the wall. Dixie grunted as if she expected this and told him the two Marshals had chosen the same table when they had been in for a meal. Thatcher pushed the chair back in and he stepped one table to the right and pulled out a chair for Nadine.

Dixie nodded and smiled. "I'll bring you both a hot bowl of buffalo stew. It was made fresh today, along with some corn bread."

"That sounds mighty fine, Dixie. Thank you." Thatcher nodded and when the woman turned, he called after her. "And two whiskeys please."

The woman raised a hand of acknowledgement as she walked across the saloon to gather up the meals for them. A man leaned against the bar, slid his glass on the counter and ordered a Thistle Dew as Dixie walked by.

"What are going to do now, Thatcher?"

Nadine's voice drew his attention and he put his elbows on the table and leaned closer.

"We'll see if we hear back from Sheriff Birdie." Thatcher glanced around the room and toward the front entrance. "Then we'll get you somewhere safe, far away from here as we can."

"Back to Broken Stone?"

"Maybe." Thatcher gave a slight shrug. "Probably."

"If those men are on the run, if they're not going before a judge…" Nadine leaned forward and sighed, then stared down at the table. "Then I shouldn't be in danger from them, right?"

"Logic says you're right about that, Nadine." Thatcher gave a shake of his head. "But my head and gut tell me something different. These are… they're trail hardened men, used to running from the law. It would be a risky thing to underestimate them. If you're alive, then you're still a threat."

Nadine looked up as Dixie set two steaming bowls in front of them. A moment later, she returned with a small plate filled with sliced squares of corn bread in one hand and two whiskeys in the other.

"Thank you, ma'am." Nadine smiled.

"Thanks, Dixie." Thatcher nodded at the woman, leaned over the bowl and breathed in the stew's savory smell.

"Y'all need anything else, just holler for me." Dixie trudged away to the bar again.

"I shouldn't have been on that bloody train." Nadine picked up a square of corn bread and held it in her hand.

"Maybe not, but you were." Thatcher put a spoon into the stew and watched the steam rise up. "And out of all them seats in that train car, you were the passenger in the one spot that's still alive." He put the spoon down and picked up his glass of whiskey. "So maybe… maybe you were *exactly* where you were supposed to be." Thatcher took a drink and sat the glass down on the table.

Nadine stared at him for a moment and Thatcher looked away from her steady gaze. There was an intensity in her look that he wasn't used to. It felt as if her expression laid him open and made him vulnerable. The look in her eyes softened and warmed, revealing the slightest hint of something else.

Thatcher cleared his throat and took a bite of the buffalo stew, found the meat more tender and well seasoned than he had hoped for. He took a piece of corn bread, tore it in half, then paused and stared at Nadine as she slowly stirred her spoon in her bowl.

"I'm *going* to keep you safe."

She didn't look up right away, only continued to stare at the curls of steam rising from the delicious mixture. And then she turned her gaze to meet his and gave him a soft smile. "I know you will."

He kept his eyes on hers then, and even wearing a field hand's clothes and hat, he thought once again that Nadine Bartlett was the most beautiful woman he had ever seen. A blush suddenly flooded her face and she looked down at her stew.

They enjoyed the meal, and Thatcher had been right about her appetite returning. They were both full and though Nadine winced at the first burn of whiskey, she kept sipping until the glass was empty.

CHAPTER TWENTY-FIVE
West of Bagger's Creek, Wyoming

Abram had made Calhoun blast apart the chains on his leg irons first, and after taking care of Blaine, Abram stood over Calhoun and aimed a Colt Paterson at the chain between the man's legs.

"N-now don't…" Calhoun eyed the large mouth of the gun barrel and glanced down at the chain stretched between his ankles and then at his crotch. He looked up at Abram. "Don't hit a rock or nothing. I'd really hate for a bullet to ricochet and hit me in my—"

His words were cut off by the blast of the revolver and Calhoun let out a high-pitched yip as a single link of chain busted loose. Abram smirked and a few men laughed at Calhoun's reaction, but none were mean-spirited.

"This'll have to do for now." Abram gestured with the barrel of his revolver. "We get to the next town, we'll find ourselves a blacksmith that can take these damned things off completely."

Calhoun rubbed the ankles of his boots and slightly shifted the encircling cuff of steel. "Where you reckon we're heading?"

Abram didn't answer right away as he walked to his horse and reloaded the Colt Paterson. "The woman, that my father mentioned… she's got an escort. A young Marshal with her."

Calhoun's expression twisted up as if he was in thought. "What is it?"

He turned to Abram and gestured with his hand. "Back there in Bagger's Creek, there was another man that rushed in after them two Marshals. Young feller in that alleyway."

"Yeah, I seen him. He's a real handy son of a bitch with a Peacemaker." The big Irishman named Clover spoke up and walked closer, a jug of whiskey in his right hand. He took a heavy drink and then held the jug out to Abram. "I saw him fill Nick with lead."

Gord gritted his teeth as he listened, turned his head and spit.

"He have a woman with him?" Abram asked the big Irishman.

"Didn't see one in all the excitement, but that don't mean he didn't."

Abram sighed and nodded. "You ride on back to Bagger's Creek, find a few men there… you know the type. Let them know there's a price on the woman's head. Nadine Bartlett."

Clover scratched along his neck and frowned. "Don't usually go in for killing a woman."

"Well if she ain't dead, then none of us can get to our money." Abram glared at him. "At least not without shooting our way in and out again. So where's that sit with you?"

Clover grunted and gave a nod as he went back to his horse and climbed into the saddle. He took up the reins and looked back at Abram. "What's the bounty?"

"Five thousand dollars. Not alive, only dead." Abram nodded west. "We'll ride out in just a while, head down to Southbend while things cool down a bit and we'll put out the word on the bounty to men there as well."

"I'll meet up with you all there." The Irishman glanced at Gord and the other men, then snapped the reins on his Morgan horse and rushed out of the meadow through the line of trees.

Abram turned to Blaine, sitting on the ground and drinking from a canteen. "I'm real glad Bonespur Bill is walking around with five hundred dollars from you and Luke. That crazy ol' bastard sure came in handy."

"I don't see much of Horace Conway and his crew walking around claiming victory either." Blaine smirked at him.

"I reckon you're right about that." Abram snorted a laugh.

"Southbend, huh?" Gord walked closer and picked up Clover's jug of whiskey from the ground.

"Yeah, that town is almost as far from having law as hell itself." Abram grinned at Gord. "Just the sort of place to find some guns willing to track down that woman and put her below snakes."

"Why don't we just do it ourselves and save the money?" Calhoun sighed and took a drink from Blaine's canteen.

"Well, I thought on that, but I wouldn't be surprised if the territory was crawling with Marshals and lawmen looking for us right now." Abram gestured at Gord for the jug of whiskey and the man handed it to him. "Way too dangerous and besides, we're good at killing, but ain't a damned one of us worth a pinch of shit on tracking people down."

"Fair enough." Calhoun capped the canteen and set it down beside Blaine.

"And we'll get the money after?" Gord asked.

"You and the men'll get paid. The money's down near Broken Rock and we'll have to let the dust settle over all of this for a bit, first." Abram nodded at him. "But you'll get paid for breaking us out of jail. Hell of a job, by the way, though I thought a chunk of fieldstone was gonna take the top of my head clean off."

"You see the Sheriff?" Calhoun asked through laughter.

Abram laughed along with him. "That boar hog almost had a stone in place of his whole head."

"I'll buy the man who came up with that plan a whole bottle of Thistle Dew when we get to Southbend." Calhoun stood up from the ground, grimacing at the ankle cuffs.

"You can't. Abram killed him dead." Gord turned around and walked back to his horse.

Calhoun walked closer to Abram and whispered. "You sure we can trust these fellers? Ain't still salty over you blowing Sullivan damned near in half with his own shotgun?"

"We'll trust them until we don't need to." Abram kept his expression stoic, but he knew Calhoun saw amusement in his eyes. The man gave him a tight-lipped nod in return and looked away.

"Get some rest for a couple hours and then we'll ride to Southbend." Abram addressed the group of men and he walked close to Blaine and sat down. "Looking a might better than you have been."

"Fever's going down, so I reckon things are heading in the right direction. I'll be better in no time." Blaine nodded and leaned back on the dry grasses.

"Damned right you will." Abram nodded and looked at the line of trees framing the strip of meadow. He wondered if they should completely clear out of the territory after getting the money, gather it up from the river bank at Broken Stone and just head south. Everything comes to an end eventually, and maybe their luck had finally run out.

Except that sounds like defeat, like some yellow-bellied dog running away, scared.

All over a single woman.

Calhoun stepped closer and got down to a crouch. "What'd that Mar—" He cleared his throat and looked around to see if anyone was listening before he continued in a lower voice. "What'd your father mean back at the jail? About setting a hound loose on her?"

Abram took a deep slow breath and then let it ease out of him just as slowly. "He knows people."

"*We* know people." Calhoun snorted and smirked.

"Not this kind." Abram let the three words hang in the air and Calhoun didn't reply.

CHAPTER TWENTY-FIVE
Bagger's Creek, Wyoming

When they left Dixie's after their meal, Thatcher was watchful along the street, but even the people who lived in town had gone quiet for the night. He and Nadine walked along until they got close to what was left of the Sheriff's Office and Thatcher led her up onto the boardwalk. "Stay put a minute."

He cautiously stepped inside the ruins, saw the jail cell door busted off one hinge and enough pieces of stone blown across the floor to build a new well. A large splatter of red painted the wall to the left of the Sheriff's desk. Thatcher saw the soles of two booted feet on the floor at the corner of the piece of furniture.

"Hell of a sight, ain't it?"

Thatcher's heart lurched in his chest and he snapped his head to see a short skinny man standing in the rear corner of the darkened room.

"Oh I... I didn't mean to startle you." The man stepped over several large pieces of fieldstone. "I'm the Undertaker, James Whitfield." He nodded toward the dead Sheriff. "You know him?"

"Can't say as I did."

"He was... *okay* as far as Sheriffs go. I've seen worse, but seen a lot better as well." James shook his head as he took a step farther and stared down at the corpse. "Atters never met a pie or cookie he didn't like. Gonna need six damned men just to carry him out of here."

Thatcher felt his stomach tighten. "I'm... I'm a US—"

"Marshal, yeah." James replied without looking at him. "Word travels pretty fast here."

"Well alright then." Thatcher walked toward the desk, eying up the pair of revolvers. "I'm going to uh... put these to use."

James shrugged and gestured with one hand. "Take 'em. He sure as hell ain't gonna be using them anymore. Atters had a shooter's pouch somewhere…" He pulled open a desk drawer, winced at the contents, and then shut it quickly. James opened another and drew out a buckskin bag and set it on top of the desk. "I'm sure it's a mishmash of things in there, but I'm sure something'll be handy. Probably find a few sweets in there he forgot about."

Thatcher took the Pietta Army Sheriff revolvers and tucked them behind his gun belt. He lifted the shooter's pouch—heavier than it appeared—and gave James a nod. "Good luck there."

Still studying Sheriff Atter's dead body, James held up a finger. "Hang on."

He crouched down behind the desk, and Thatcher heard a soft metallic noise. James stood up and put his foot down on the Sheriff's body as he pulled on a strap of leather.

Several strong heaves later, the belt came loose and James staggered backward a step. He grinned as he inspected the long belt dragging the floorboards and reaching to his shoulders. "Ain't got no blood on it or nothin', though I…" James grinned at Thatcher as he held out the belt and pair of holsters to him. "I expect if it's for you, you'll have to cut the length of it in half."

"Obliged." Thatcher took the belt from him and looped it several times in his hand.

James let out a heavy exhale as he stared at the corpse again and then he turned to Thatcher with a straight-mouthed expression on his face. "I'm gonna need a damned bucket to carry his head out."

Thatcher wasn't sure what the man wanted to hear as a reply, but he felt plum out of words. He turned and stepped outside by Nadine. "Come on, let's get away from here."

She walked beside him and they went to the boarding house. The woman at the desk gave them a sleepy nod and gestured upstairs. "Second door on your right up there." She leaned back in her chair, crossed her arms, and resumed her snooze.

The room was small, but functional, and from what Thatcher could see, only one corner had a cobweb. A steamer trunk sat at the foot of a bed, and a small desk and chair were on the other side of the room near the window.

"Can you shoot?"

Nadine glanced at the gun belt in Thatcher's hands and then looked up at him. "I've never shot revolvers, only shotguns."

He nodded and lay out the belt to its full length on the bed. Next, he drew his Bowie knife, sliced the belt in half, and used the tip of the blade to drill several holes in the leather. He handed it over to Nadine and she shrugged her coat off before drawing the belt around her waist.

Watching the way the cloth of the shirt tightened around her figure made Thatcher glance away for a moment. He drew the Pietta Sheriff revolvers from his belt and gave them to Nadine one by one. "Holster them up, get used to the weight."

She did as he asked and took several steps around the room, paused and nodded at him. "I'll get used to it."

"Alright then." He nodded toward the bed. "You keep them on and—"

Nadine stepped closer and slid her right hand beneath the front of Thatcher's coat. Her palm grazed over his chest and then softly pressed against his shoulder. She looked up into his eyes. "How's your shoulder?"

"It… it'll be fine." That sweet lilac smell drifted up around him and Thatcher was beginning to wonder if it was just Nadine's natural scent.

"I can feel the heat around the wound but it's…" Nadine slid her hand to the left, against his collarbone and then lower. "It's not spreading. It's staying where the wound is."

Thatcher nodded, thinking his voice might crack with a throat as dry as his.

She slid her hand free of his coat and kept her gaze on his for a moment longer. "We ride out early?"

"Yes, ma'am." Thatcher's voice was soft and low. "I'll wake you when it's time."

"Thank you." Nadine gave him a soft smile and then sat on the edge of the bed. She stared at him a moment and then lay down, turned and pulled the blanket over her.

Thatcher felt like he had been holding his breath and he sat down in the chair by the small oak desk. He turned the chair around so that it faced the door and leaned back. Not much longer, he heard Nadine's breath soften and change into a rhythm.

CHAPTER TWENTY-SIX

Bagger's Creek, Wyoming

Bonespur Bill took his hat off and tucked it under one arm before he walked into the saloon. He nodded at Dixie as walked to the bar.

"You had the last of the mescal." She smiled at him.

"*Naw,* I know, I know." Bill grinned. "You uh… got any cactus wine?"

Dixie snorted and shook her head, but she pulled out a simple brown jug from the shelf behind the bar and set it in front of him. She held onto it and gave him a hard stare. "You sure you want this? This come delivered up from Santa Fe."

Bill waved a hand and winced. "I rode with the Mescaleros down in Texas. I ain't worried about nothing from Santa Fe except burning when I pee after a visit."

That earned him a sharp cackle from Dixie, but she set a glass up and poured some for Bill.

"If I start talking about fighting animals, then you stop pouring." Bill winked at her and then lifted the glass and smelled the amber-colored liquor. He nodded and walked through the saloon to the table farthest from the front door. After sitting down, Bill put his hat on the chair beside him, out of sight.

He sat there quietly, sipped his drink and watched the handful of customers come in and out of the saloon. Dixie's wasn't what he would call a busy saloon, but it wasn't quiet either. A dusty piano with a broken key cover rested against one wall. Bill looked up and saw a small dusty chandelier of cut ruby glass.

It was easy to see the place would have been quite a saloon years ago. Everything out west seemed to age overnight or never at all. There was no in between.

A few hours had passed when a tall man walked into the saloon and looked around before going to stand at the bar beside a couple of men in filthy oilskin dusters.

Bill didn't know the man's name, but he recognized the big Irishman immediately. He had seen him with a rifle in his hands, standing across the street from the jail before it blew to pieces. The big man glanced around again nervously and then ordered three whiskeys.

Lifting the glass of cactus wine, Bill took a sip and let more of it spill into his beard. He eased the glass down and then got up on his feet. He clutched his hat, stuffed it crookedly on his head, and slowly, Bill shuffled across the floor. He bumped into empty chairs and then paused with one hand on a tabletop as if he was balancing himself. He pursed his lips and looked at the ceiling with wide eyes and a nod.

Bill sighed heavily through his nose and staggered to the bar, to the left of the big Irishman. The man glanced at him and his expression changed into a glare. Bill smiled and then turned to Dixie as the woman approached. He raised a finger and opened his mouth as if to speak, and then closed it again and ran a hand over his face.

"You alright, stranger?" Dixie slung a towel over her shoulder and stared at Bill, amused.

"*Mmmmmmhmmmmm*…. I jush… I jush need to…" Bill wiped his hand over his face again and snorted toward the door. "Damned fighting prairie dog sons o' bitches. Bunch o' furry, buck-toothed pugilists is what they are." He pursed his lips and breathed heavily through his nose. He nodded slowly and stared at the big Irishman as if he was waiting for a reply.

"Uh… yeah." The big man glanced at Dixie and then back to Bill. "Hell yeah."

"Damned right, *hell yeah!*" Bill slapped his hand down against the bar and looked around wildly. He put his head down against the counter, closed his eyes and continued to breathe loudly through his nose.

Dixie fussed about behind the bar, used the towel to clean up spills or wipe dust away. Bill listened to the big Irishman speak in a low voice to the men beside him. He snorted a few times to make his drunken ruse believable, and passed wind once just because it amused him.

As Bill listened, more pieces of the puzzle came together about the Pale Horse gang. The two men at the end of the bar finished their drinks and set the glasses down. Bill heard them walk out.

The Irishman hadn't moved and Bill continued pretending to be passed out on the bar.

"So this woman…" Dixie spoke in a low voice.

The Irishman shifted in place and Dixie continued. "Easy there big feller. This is my bar and there ain't nothing goes on I don't know about. Now get your damned hackles down before I unload the Colt Dragoon I've got beneath the bar."

Bill heard the Irishman take a deep breath and rest his arms against the bar.

"That's better, then." Dixie let out a heavy exhale. "This woman, what if I could tell you where she was? What would that information be worth to you?"

"I reckon a right fair amount."

Fingertips tapped against the counter and Dixie spoke. "Two hundred dollars."

There was a moment of quiet and the Irishman replied. "Alright then."

"Let's see the money first."

"I ain't got the damned money on me. I look like some kind of cattle baron to you?"

"No…" Dixie replied. "You smell a lot worse than a cattle baron too." She sighed heavily again as if she was trying to decide. "They're over at the boarding house."

"They're…" The Irishman scoffed. "They're still in the damned town?"

Bill listened as the sound of heavy steps raced for the door.

"You'd better come back and pay me, you son of a bitch!" Dixie yelled out after him.

Bill stayed in place a moment longer and then slowly

raised his head up from the bar. He felt the blood rush through him.

"I ain't sure whether a mug of hot Arbuckles' or another glass of cactus wine would be best for you."

"You keep the coffee." Bill slid some money on the bar top. "If'n it ain't water or liquor, I don't want no parts of it." He walked straight as an arrow out the door, and headed for the boarding house.

CHAPTER TWENTY-SEVEN

Bagger's Creek, Wyoming

Thatcher had his arms crossed and his eyes closed. He wasn't sleeping exactly—sitting in the uncomfortable wooden chair took away any possibility of true sleep—but he let himself drift slightly while he kept his ears sharp and alert. He had kept the oil lamp burning but turned the flame down low to give a little light to the room.

Nadine had fallen asleep quickly and he was glad for it. She still hadn't fully healed from her injuries and the rest would do her well. Thatcher hoped for a word from Sheriff Birdie by morning or else he would have to make plans on his own, taking the least traveled path he could find. Less people meant less danger.

His eyes snapped open at the creak of floorboards in the hallway and Thatcher felt a rush through his veins. He stared and waited for another sound.

The door slammed open and banged against the wall and the biggest Irishman Thatcher had ever seen barged inside with a Yellowboy rifle. He raised the barrel toward the sleeping figure of Nadine as Thatcher drew one of his Peacemakers.

Thatcher thumbed the hammer and squeezed the trigger in one fluid motion. The bullet hit the forestock of the man's rifle and it blew apart in splinters. The big man fired and a bullet punched into the wall above Nadine.

As Thatcher cocked his revolver, the big man raised his rifle toward Nadine. *"Naw, naw… put that shootin' iron down and the other one too. Reeeeeal easy like."*

Thatcher slowly took out his other Peacemaker and tossed them onto the bed. The dark shape of a man moved in the shadows of the hallway but Thatcher kept his gaze on the man with the rifle.

"That's right." The big man nodded and an oily grin slid onto his face. "The Pale Horse gang sends their regards." He tightened his grip on the rifle and the large shadow from the hallway lunged onto the man's back. The big Irishman spun around and slammed his back against the wall. There was a heavy groan and he twisted and grabbed the other man's coat.

Thatcher was halfway toward the bed to grab his Colts when the big Irishman growled and stepped away, swinging the rifle around the room. From the corner of Thatcher's sight, he saw Nadine sit up.

"Put down the knife, old timer."

The man who had tried to tackle the big Irishman stepped away from the wall and Thatcher recognized the fox fur hat and the large Bowie knife in his hand. He slowly put his hand down to his side.

A gunshot cracked out in the room and the Irishman gained a bullet wound on his upper right chest. Blood gushed down the front of his shirt.

Nadine was still under the blankets with a hole in the fabric leaking a curl of gun smoke.

"You bitch!"

The old man swung his knife in a hard, underhanded throw and the blade sunk deeply right beside the bullet hole in the man's chest.

The Irishmen looked down at the heavy knife sticking out of his chest and he glared at the old man. "You old—"

Quick as lightning, the man drew his Kentucky pistol and the gun's single shot thundered in the small room. The Irishman slammed back against the wall and the Yellowboy rifle clattered to the floor beside him.

Thatcher grabbed his Peacemakers from the bed, glanced at Nadine's scared expression, and then turned his guns toward the old man.

"Easy there, Lawman." He held up the long-barreled pistol in front of him. "Single shot." He tucked it back beneath his belt and walked over to the dead Irishman. The old man put one foot on the man's stomach and gripped the handle of the Bowie knife. After some wrenching back and forth, he yanked the blade free of his chest, wiped it on the man's shirt, and stuck it back into the sheath on his belt.

"Alright then, I—"

"I don't know who you are, but—"

"Well, I was *gonna* tell you." He raised his hands out and smiled. "Call me Bonespur Bill and I'm here to offer my... protective services."

"I..." Thatcher stared at him and scoffed. "I reckon we'll do just fine. Why don't you just—"

"The Pale Horse gang's loose again."

"Yeah, I... I know that." Thatcher glared at the man.

The old timer nodded toward Nadine. "Well did you know there's a bounty on her?"

Thatcher glanced at her, and then turned back to Bill.

"A bounty?" Nadine flipped the blanket away from her and Thatcher saw she still had the Pietta revolver in her hand.

"Why, yes ma'am. On your head."

"How much?" Nadine swung her legs over the side of the bed.

"Well it's... five-thousand dollars, Miss Bartlett."

Thatcher clenched his teeth. "How'd you know her—"

"Is that... considered a lot for a bounty?" Nadine swung her legs over the edge of the bed.

Thatcher and Bill stared at her, considering the question.

"Well..." Bill gave a soft shrug. "I'd say it's a sum that's hard to ignore."

Nadine nodded, stood up and slid the revolver back into her right holster. "Dead or alive?"

"Just dead."

Thatcher sighed heavily and felt a headache trying to gather storm clouds in his skull.

Bill looked at Nadine, and then he turned to Thatcher. "When word gets out, that bounty's gonna bring out every low-bellied road agent and gutless gunslinger in the territories."

When Thatcher didn't reply, Bill turned to Nadine. "I'll

protect you for six thousand."

"*Aww* hell." Thatcher shook his head. "Six thousand dollars for a—"

"It's more than she's worth dead, ain't it? And besides," Bill nodded at the dead Irishman. "I think I've already proven my worth here. You two need me. And well… bounty price got me to wondering… why the hell is the Pale Horse gang after you so badly? Who the hell are you?"

"I saw—"

"*Naw*." Thatcher cut off Nadine's words. "There's no—"

"If he wanted me kill me and collect an easy five-thousand dollars, he'd already have shot me, or used that knife to cleave me in two." Nadine's eyes hardened as she made her point.

Bill grinned and rested his hands on his hips. "A woman who understands business."

"Have you forgotten that he was about to stab two Marshals out on the street?" Thatcher felt his blood getting hot as he pointed at Bill.

The old man made a face and shook his head. "I wasn't gonna *stab* em… just… whack 'em over the head with the handle."

Thatcher slowly turned to glare at him. "Well why in the hell—

"I saw the Pale Horse gang rob the train down in Broken Stone." Nadine let out a heavy breath. "I watched them kill passengers in cold blood over and over again."

The smile faded from Bonespur Bill's face and he sighed and spoke in a low voice. "You're a witness."

Nadine met his gaze and nodded.

"Well no wonder…" Bill gestured toward the street in the direction of the ruined jail. "All of this… you're an important woman, alright." He looked at Thatcher. "More important if the Pale Horse gang gets captured again and has to go before a judge."

"Yeah," Thatcher said softly and holstered his Peacemakers.

"They're gonna want her dead either way."

Thatcher glanced at Nadine and turned to Bill without giving him a reply.

Bill smiled again and clapped his hands together. "So where we headed?"

CHAPTER TWENTY-EIGHT
Southbend, Wyoming

Southbend was a town where secrets came to die and threats lived immortal.

It was a town built for men to disappear. Few people, let alone lawmen, came through. Some had bought cheap land after the Homestead Act, but they found the ground too damned unforgiving to do much of anything with, let alone raise a crop. Most went elsewhere to earn a living, traded goods, hunted for bounty, survived somewhere in that gray area of the law or beyond. More than a few outlaws counted themselves as citizens of Southbend, not that it made any difference—none of them would ever reveal where they were from anyway. They were well-behaved in the town they sheltered in, but outside the confines, a few of them were nothing less than cold blooded killers.

Abram figured it was the perfect place to talk about the bounty he had put on Nadine Bartlett's head. He led the group of men up and over the small ridge that opened up to Southbend, and though the presentation was less than impressive, the town was still a welcome sight to Abram's eyes.

It was a single, short trail of a street, with less than a dozen buildings on either side. Except for the general goods, a boarding house and a trading post, the structures that remained were either a saloon or a brothel. If you were trail-wise, you didn't go into the brothels, as they were often referred to as the houses of plague by men who had learned their lesson the hard way.

The saloons weren't much better.

Southbend had an undertaker for a while, but the man was shot dead in the street for sleeping with another man's wife. Since then, people took care of their own, and the unknown corpses were dragged out of town to a long shallow trough in the ground and tossed aside like cord wood. The buzzards never quite stopped circling as there was always a fresh supply.

Abram reined his horse to a stop in front of the first saloon he came to.

Gord looked at the sign and shook his head.

"What is it?" Calhoun asked him as he looped his horses reins around a hitching post.

"Any saloon that is just called..." Gord nodded toward the sign with a single hand painted word. "*Saloon*... you just know is going to be a place the upper crust gather."

Abram laughed and shook his head as he watched Blaine get down slowly from his horse. "You alright?"

Blaine nodded at him and looped the reins of his horse on the post. "I could sure use a whiskey, though."

"Well now I know damned well you're feeling better. C'mon, we'll get you one." Abram gave a low laugh and turned to Gord as the man approached him. "How much money you got on you?"

Gord gave a light shake of his head. "Not much."

"Fifty bucks?"

"I-I mean I—"

"I'm good for it, Gord." Abram grinned at the man. "In the *very* near future, you're going to see more money in one place than you've ever seen in your life, and a big juicy portion of that ol' Kansas City Rib eye is going to be in your hands. So..." Abram put his hand out palm up, and gestured with his fingers. "Give me the damned fifty dollars."

Gord sighed, dug around inside his coat, and pulled out some money. He flipped through it and then handed some over as he looked around at the saloon and other buildings. A woman's laughter drifted through the warm air. "You uh... you been here in Southbend before?"

"Once or twice." Abram grinned and turned to go inside the saloon called Saloon. He shook his head and laughed as he pushed the batwing doors in front of him.

Blaine and Calhoun were already heading toward the bar, and Abram looked around at the other half a dozen men at tables. Some of them flipped cards but most just leaned over their drinks having low-voiced conversations.

Abram looked at the man behind the bar whose suspenders seemed to be fighting for their life to contain the belly of the man who wore them. Tufts of black hair stuck out on either side of his head along with a single patch on top of his skull, as if the down of a crow feather had landed there and stuck.

"Filly?" Abram said as he stopped and stared.

The big man looked up from the bar and stared at him. A big smile crossed his face.

"Filly, how drunk are you? You're in the wrong damned building." Abram gestured with his thumb across the street and the barkeep laughed as he leaned against the bar.

"Ain't stepped foot in Pap's Trough in six months." Filly grabbed three whiskey glasses from a shelf and lined them up on top of the bar. "Pap's ticker gave out and when his wife took over, I either had to quit or I was going to drag her dead body out of town."

"Sure you made the right choice?" Abram glanced around at the weathered shack of a building.

"Some days yes, others no." Filly laughed loudly as he poured whiskey into the three glasses. "It's been a while since you came through, Abram."

"Yeah, it's… it's quite a wild ride lately."

Filly leaned closer and spoke in a low voice. "Wouldn't happen to have anything to do with a wild ride on a train near Broken Stone, would it?"

Abram winked at him and picked up the whiskey glass. Dark brown flecks of something floated in the liquor and he ignored it as he took a drink.

"I knew it!" Filly whispered and laughed. "I damned well knew it." He wiped drops of whiskey from the bar and then slung the towel over his shoulder. "Well what the hell are you doing in this rubbish heap? Shouldn't you be off spending money on senoritas and mescal?"

"Well…" Abram shook his head. "Mexico may be where we end up before it's all said and done." He scratched along his neck and stared at the barkeep. "Just got a thorn in our side at the moment. Putting out a bounty… five thousand dollars."

"Five thou…" Filly's eyes widened. "Must be quite a thorn."

"Oh, it is." Abram nodded and continued talking with the barkeep in a low voice. "A woman by the name of Nadine Bartlett. Might be accompanied by a Marshal."

Filly nodded as if he was considering the details. "Need her alive?

"*Naw,* I would *much* prefer she no longer drew breath again."

The barkeep smiled. "That'll make things easier at least. A Marshal, huh?"

"*Mmmhmm.* Traveling around the territories from Bagger's Creek, maybe back on the way to Broken Stone. The bounty price takes the Marshal into consideration."

Filly nodded and exhaled heavily through his nose. "I'll let some people know."

"Well alright then." Abram raised his glass and downed the rest of the whiskey. It had an undercurrent of burnt copper but Abram forced himself to not think about it.

The big man behind the bar grabbed two whiskey bottles and clanked them together loudly. Heads turned to look at him and Filly nodded at their attention. "Let it be known there is a five-thousand-dollar bounty on a woman by the name Nadine Bartlett. Might be with a US Marshal, might not be, but best go into it thinking he's there. Probably traveling toward Broken Stone from Bagger's Creek." Filly looked over the customers. "Man that's offering is good for the money. I'll vouch for him."

Some of the men nodded their heads with interest, but most turned back to their whiskies.

"Well that's one way to spread the word." Gord stepped up to the bar.

"Someone will take the work. Five thousand is a lot of money, but worth it." Abram nodded.

Gord gave a grunt of acknowledgement as he looked around the shabby saloon. "Me and the boys are going to go off through town a bit, maybe take some comfort for a while."

Abram nodded and saw Blaine turn away from the conversation. Calhoun seemed fit to burst inside but held his composure. Abram nodded at Gord. "You boys have fun. We'll be here with whiskey in hand."

As soon as Gord and the others walked from the saloon, Calhoun and Blaine busted out laughing and Filly came walking over to pour more whiskey.

"That's wrong of you." Filly shook his head. "Them men are riding with you and you ain't going to warn 'em? That's... that's just plain *wrong*." He laughed hard enough that his belly shook.

"They'll remember the lesson this way." Abram laughed as he picked up his glass. "They get any new painted ladies with more teeth than breasts?"

"Not a damned one of 'em." Filly wiped at the corners of his eyes. "Bunch of worn out mountain witches in this damned town."

Calhoun laughed at that, and it was good to see him do it. Abram looked at Blaine and even he was looking better. The wound in his shoulder had to be healing well enough.

"The boarding house still open?" Abram asked as he stared at his glass instead of looking at the barkeep.

"If there's still a roof, then it's still open." Filly glanced at him. "I'd be careful approaching the front door though. Sofia probably ain't going to be too happy to see you after being gone six months."

"Yeah, I reckon maybe so." Abram drank the last drops of the whiskey in his glass, winced at the taste and slid his glass across the bar. He pulled out twenty dollars of the money Gord had given him and put it on the bar. "Add a bottle, a *new* bottle, of Old Crow."

Filly reached below the counter and pulled up a bottle of the whiskey.

"This is for the drinks we've had, drinks they'll still have, and the bottle. The rest is for your help on this, Filly." Abram pulled his hand from the money and Filly looked down and smiled at him.

"Thank you, Abram. And it really is good to see your gib-faced mug." He laughed and nodded toward the batwing doors. "I wasn't kidding about being careful when you go the front door. You might want to step to the side in case she's got a shotgun ready."

Abram grinned as he took the bottle of Old Crow and sang as he walked out of the saloon. "*Sofiaaa, my love, my darliiiiin', my dear, my dove my…*" He changed from singing to whistling the melody and walked down the street toward the boarding house and Sofia Ana Juarez, the mother of his son.

CHAPTER TWENTY-NINE

Bagger's Creek, Wyoming

Thatcher Evans folded the telegram paper in half and then in half again. He clenched his teeth, stuffed the paper into his coat pocket and mumbled thanks to Sigil. The telegrapher gave him a somber-faced nod and walked out of the boarding house.

He felt Nadine's gaze on him and he turned to face her. "We'll ride out directly."

"Are you going to tell me—"

"Yeah, I..." Thatcher glanced at Bonespur Bill and turned back to Nadine.

Bill was leaning back against the front of the boarding house with his arms crossed. His narrow-eyed gaze cautiously ran over the street and surrounding buildings as if he was a dutiful sentinel searching for danger.

Thatcher sighed and turned back to Nadine. "The bounty on each member of the Pale Horse gang has been raised to twelve-thousand each."

"Twelve-thousand?" Bill's attention snapped toward Thatcher. "That's a lot of paper for some outlaws."

"Yeah, well, it's with good reason."

"So what are we supposed to do now?" Nadine adjusted her hat, tucking strands of loose hair up beneath.

"We're heading back to Broken Stone." Thatcher ran a hand over his throat and scratched at the whisker stubble. "It's too dangerous to take the trail we came in on though. They'll expect us to come back that way."

"We can take the Wildtooth Trail. Ain't no way the Pale Horse gang, or anyone *else* would expect that." Bill adjusted the Kentucky pistol tucked beneath his belt and nodded toward the skyline. "If we head out now, by nightfall we could make it to a small gully along the trail, good place to break camp."

Nadine shifted her gaze between Bill and Thatcher.

"Wildtooth Trail it is." Thatcher scratched his neck again and nodded decisively. "Lead the way."

In less than ten minutes, the three of them were riding out of Bagger's Creek. When they could no longer see the buildings in the distance behind them, Bill cut his horse left through the flatlands grown thick with scrub brush. They rode in silence for a while, Bill at the lead with Thatcher bringing up the rear.

He had to admit Bill was right about the Wildtooth Trail. No one in the world would expect them to take this path. The *path*, if you could call it that, wound through terrain of wild vines that clawed at the horses and slowed their pace as if they all had leg irons. When the growth of weeds ended and the ground began sloping downward, the land was coated in a fine layer of grit and pebbles that caused the horses to slip and stumble. Rain had passed through, turning the dirt into a thin slick of mud. Thankfully the storm had missed them, but the smell of wet grass and earth was thick in the air.

Thatcher wondered about the last people to travel the Wildtooth, and if desperation was a driving factor in their decision as well. He thought of Birdie's telegram and the bounty issued on the Pale Horse gang. Twelve-thousand a piece was more than a tidy sum, and when word got around about an officially issued bounty, Thatcher hoped it would draw attention away from the bounty on Nadine. Though, he had to admit, the men who would try to kill Nadine weren't the same as bounty hunters who would go after the Pale Horse gang. Even most bounty hunters had *some* sort of morals, even driven by money.

Who the hell busted them out of that jail?

That thought worried Thatcher, and his mind chewed on the unanswered question like a mongrel with a bone. Only three of the Pale Horse gang were still alive. Three other men were killed at the jail break, and he had seen at least half a dozen charging away from Bagger's Creek. If they all banded together and came after Nadine, it would take more than bullets to stop an outright slaughter.

By the time the sun touched the horizon line, Thatcher saw the start of the gully Bill had said would be good for a camp. It was a sharp gouge cut into the earth, as wide as two Conestoga wagons set end to end. As Bill led them deeper, Thatcher looked over the rocky ground and his gut twisted. Anyone surrounding them on both sides of the gully would have the high ground. The three of them would be easy targets.

There's no reason to think anyone would find you here.

Thatcher clenched his teeth as they rode, fighting his instincts that they were riding into a pocket of death. Bill cut his horse along the left slope of the gully, reined his horse to a stop and swung down from the saddle.

"This'll do well enough for the night, I reckon." He smiled at them and nodded, pleased with himself.

Thatcher looked around at their position and saw nothing special about it at all. His confused expression must have been apparent because Bill smiled at him.

"Not out here in the open." He pointed toward the left bank and Thatcher looked closer.

A narrow cave opening, the width of a wagon wheel and twice as high, set into the rock wall, the rusty color almost faded it completely. Thatcher nodded approval and turned to Bill. "Used this spot before, have you?"

"I might have had reason for it once or twice." Bonespur Bill gave a shrug and a shy smile. "Big enough for five, maybe six men in there."

"Well then." Nadine took the reins of her horse, lifted a rock the size of a loaf of fresh bread, and tucked the leather straps beneath it. She eyed up the entrance to the cave and looked at Thatcher. "I'll bet you take all your witnesses here."

Thatcher snorted and shook his head as he walked to the cave opening and stopped. "Hey?" He called out into the darkness, listening for any shuffle of paws against dirt, but it was quiet inside.

"Let's get a fire started." Bill looked up toward the stone ridge above them. "The cave's got a natural stove pipe in there, draws the smoke right on out. It'll be warm and dry and…" He nodded at the horses. "Aside from our mounts, ain't nobody gonna know we're in there."

"If they do, we're as dead as rats in a rain barrel."

Bill barked a sharp laugh and nodded as he searched the ground and picked up some grass and rubbed it between his fingers. "Too damp." He lifted a thin branch of cottonwood and tossed it just as quickly. "That damned rain… I got the flint and steel, but I need to find us some dry tinder. I'll use some gunpowder if I need to, but we still need things to burn."

"Might I borrow the flint and steel?"

"Why sure, little lady." Bill fished them out of his possible bag and handed them over to Nadine.

As Bill walked back in the direction they had ridden from, Thatcher set his reins beneath a rock as Nadine had done and slowly walked ahead, searching for anything dry enough to start a fire.

It would be easy for a horse to break a leg out here, too easy for a man to do the same. The sky was losing sunlight quickly and that meant the night critters would be coming out. Thatcher clenched his teeth, keeping his gaze on any rocks large enough to hide the sight of a rattler behind it. He picked up twigs and thin branches, but every single one was soaked through, too wet to even shave into thin strips to use. Thatcher shook his head and gathered several thicker pieces of wood in his arms. Inside the cave, they might dry out, but it looked like it was going to be a cold night ahead of them.

"Alright then!"

Nadine called from behind him, and Thatcher saw her standing in front of the cave entrance with her hands on her hips. In the low light of dusk, he saw a smile on her face, and a thin wisp of smoke coming out of the rock wall above her, about six feet taller than Nadine.

"What the hell..." Thatcher whispered to himself and carefully walked back along the rocky basin. Nadine waited at the cave entrance as he approached.

"Welcome to Café London, please... come in, take a seat anywhere you like." She held up one arm as if she was presenting an eatery to him and Thatcher stepped into the entrance with the small pile of branches in his arms.

The space was as Bill had described it—deep and wide enough to easily sleep a half a dozen men or more. A small stone circle was in the center, and though the flames were low, Nadine had made a fire. She followed him inside, walked around and sat close to the fire. One of her saddlebags rested on the ground beside her.

"How did you... what did you find for tinder?" Thatcher set the branches down close to the fire and spread them out to dry.

Nadine grinned at him, reached into the saddlebag and pulled out a stack of banded paper as thick as a woman's hairbrush. She peeled off a sheet of the paper, crumpled it in her hand and tossed it on the flames.

Thatcher stared closer at the fire and then he slowly shifted his gaze to study what Nadine held in her hand. His mouth dropped open at the realization. "Is that... are you burning money? Are you using money for—"

"We needed a fire. I got us a fire going." She smiled at him as she peeled off more from the banded stack, tossed them into the ring of stones, and then tossed the entire stack in as well.

"How... how much is—"

"About five hundred dollars."

"Nadine..." Thatcher groaned and sat down hard on the ground. He stared at her. "Was that in your saddlebags this entire time?"

She nodded, that *pleased-with-herself* smile still on her face.

Thatcher looked up from the fire and stared at her.

"What... exactly... is in all that heavy luggage of yours?"

"I *was* coming all the way from England. I told you it was everything I could bring of my old life, to begin a new one here. Earl exchanged pounds for United States currency when we arrived in New York." She picked up one of the branches Thatcher had brought in and put it over the flames. It smoked heavily as the fire licked away the moisture.

Thatcher took his hat off, set it on the ground, and put his hand against his forehead, rubbing his temples against the headache trying to blossom.

"Well I'll be damned." Bill walked into the cave with a small pile of wood and some weeds he must have twisted into braids while he was searching. In his other hand he held two canteens from the horses. He set down his gatherings and nodded his approval. "Glad you found some—"

"Tinder, yeah." Thatcher let out a groan and waved his hand dismissively.

Bill turned to Nadine. "What's wrong with him?"

"I'm not sure, really." Nadine grinned.

They sat around the fire and added to it slowly as the gathered wood began to dry, and soon the cave grew warm and comfortable. Bill chewed on strips of beef jerky and hardtack crackers and he set out his cloth bundle for Nadine and Thatcher to share in the food.

"*Ahhhhh.*" Bill rubbed his hands together, took a drink from his canteen and capped it as he looked up at Thatcher. "You take first watch." He turned immediately and lay down, using his saddlebag as a pillow.

Bill closed his eyes and in the space of three heartbeats, the man began to snore.

Nadine's eyes grew wide as she stared at him. She glanced at Thatcher and shook her head as she whispered. "I've... I've never seen anyone go to sleep that bloody fast in my entire life. He went to sleep like a dog."

"Well... you have to admit, the resemblance between Bill and a dog is a bit uncanny."

She snickered and held her hands out toward the fire.

Thatcher watched as the humor in her face faded to a serious expression.

"These men, the Pale Horse gang... you said they had left a trail behind them."

"I'm not the only one who believes it. It just can't be proven. The people that found the remains of things the Pale Horse gang done was all *after the fact*. There ain't never been a witness before. Not *ever*."

Thatcher drank from his canteen. "People dead here and there, always an article in the newspapers, but no sign of whoever done it. And them towns on a map, all lined up one by one, leading right toward Broken Stone."

"Violent men." Nadine's eyes danced with reflections of the orange light from the fire.

"Some of the most violent I've heard of, yes. Cold blooded killers, every last one of them. The Marshals all know it, but—"

"You're a Marshal."

"I am *now*, but the men who were *already* Marshals. They know it... but knowing it and proving it are two different things."

"Which is where I come in."

"I reckon so."

Nadine used a small branch to poke at the fire, stoking the coals, and then set it on top of the flames. "They're really going to try and kill me, aren't they?"

Thatcher stared at her and when she turned to him, he gave her a soft nod.

"It's a strange feeling, someone wanting you dead." Worry crossed Nadine's face and Thatcher shifted in place and moved closer.

"I'd tell you that you get used to it, but you don't."

"This is all so..." She gave him a strained, thin-lipped smile. "A month ago, I was in London, having tea at a café on Brimdon Street and now..." Her eyes glassed with tears.

"Hey." Thatcher took both of her hands in his and looked in her eyes. "Nadine, I ain't going to let anything happen to you, alright?"

She nodded at him, put a brave expression on her face, and without thinking about it, Thatcher put his arm around her shoulders. He felt her lean into him slightly, accepting his embrace, and they sat still like that in the warmth of the fire. The sound of the crackling wood was soothing.

"What are you thinking?" Nadine asked softly.

Thatcher gave a gentle laugh. "That's the most expensive camp fire I've ever seen in my life."

Nadine released a giggle, and Thatcher reacted, laughing with her.

Their laughter combined and Nadine began to shake. She covered her mouth with her hand as she laughed and tried to remain quiet.

Bill suddenly snorted loudly, turned over on his other side, and broke wind as he settled down again.

Nadine squeezed her eyes shut and pressed her face against Thatcher's chest as another wave of laughter racked her body. She looked up at Thatcher, who had tears springing from the corner of his eyes, and clutched onto the lapel of his coat. They were both breathless, exhaling slowly, as they regained control of themselves.

"*Ohhh, ohh* my." Nadine whispered and put her arms around him.

He held her as small fits of laughter bubbled to the surface, and then she pulled back and wiped tears from her cheeks.

Thatcher stared at her and wiped one loose tear away with the thumb of his hand. He kept it there against the side of her face and spoke to her softly. "It's going to be okay. I promise."

"Alright." Nadine closed her eyes and leaned against his hand. "I believe you."

"You get some rest." Thatcher shifted and Nadine opened

her eyes as he started to move away.

"Can you... will you stay here beside me until I fall asleep?"

He nodded at her. "Of course, I will."

Thatcher waited as Nadine lay down with a saddlebag of money as her pillow. She curled onto her side against him and closed her eyes. Thatcher took out a Peacemaker and set it on his lap, wondering what tomorrow would bring, and hoping he could live up to his promise.

CHAPTER THIRTY
Southbend, Wyoming

Liam McSweeney sat in the back of the saloon at a table by himself and sipped his glass of whiskey. He had seen the group of men when they walked into the bar and watched with disinterest as some of them left not long after. But when Filly stood behind the bar and announced a bounty, *that* held McSweeney's attention good and tight, like a panner seizing his first golden nugget.

A woman named Nadine Bartlett. Five-thousand dollars. Maybe a Marshal with her.

He took a drink of the Old Crow in his glass and enjoyed the burn down his throat and stomach. It was coming on close to six years since he had turned his life away from the pulpit and become a bounty hunter, doing penance for his sins.

One of the men leaning against the bar laughed loudly with Filly—a pure, sincere sound—and McSweeney looked away from them and stared at the amber whiskey in his glass. It had been a very long time since he had laughed like that.

Yeah, close to six years, he thought.

His mind flashed back to the day he had left his church behind and ridden out of Brigand's Passing, Kansas. His homestead had been drenched in blood that day.

McSweeney shifted in his chair and adjusted the sawed-off double-barrel on the harness beneath his coat. On his gun belt, he wore a pair of Colt Navy revolvers, custom-made with slender walnut grips—much easier to hold for a man of his stature. He let out a heavy sigh, drank the rest of the whiskey in one gulp, and hopped down from his chair.

From the other side of the room, he heard a man stifle a snicker and McSweeney glared at him. The man stared back at him, and then the man next to him swatted his arm and whispered something.

"What's he gonna do," the man replied, "climb up on a chair and kick me?"

This time, the man didn't bother trying to stop himself from laughing, and the rest of the room went quiet. Filly stopped pouring whiskey behind the bar and glanced at the two men nervously.

"H-hey, now… ehh… McSweeney, Lemmy didn't mean nothin' by—"

"He's a grown man, Filly. He can answer for himself." McSweeney walked across the room toward the two men. It certainly wasn't the first time he had been laughed at for being a dwarf—that had started from the moment he was born. But each time someone poked fun at him now, he made sure it was their last.

The man scooted his chair away from the table and, still sitting, and turned to face McSweeney as he approached him.

"*Ahhh* hell." Filly mumbled from behind the bar and walked to the far wall of the room, where a mop and bucket rested.

The man at the table laughed, shook his head, and patted one leg. "You wanna come sit on Daddy's lap for a little while?"

McSweeney smiled at the man's words as if they were the funniest thing he had ever heard in his life, and then he began to laugh. Harder and harder, he laughed as he walked toward the man, who was chuckling like a fool himself.

The shotgun swung out from beneath McSweeney's coat as smooth and practiced as the axe of a lumberjack. His small pudgy hands found the forearm and trigger and he watched the man's eyes bulge wide as the sight of death stared into his face.

McSweeney squeezed the trigger and both barrels breathed fire, the sound a roaring thunder in the small saloon. The lead slugs caught the man directly in the face, blew him backward from the chair and slammed him against the floor in a bloody splotch.

Dropping the shotgun on its leather strap, McSweeney drew both Colt Navys as the second man at the table slowly put his hands up. His face was spattered with blood and he gave a slight shake of his head. "I-I ain't g-got no beef with y-you, Reverend." He nodded toward the dead man on the floor. "L-Lemmy brought it on h-himself."

McSweeney stared at him for a long moment and then looked around the room. It seemed as if everyone was holding their breath, afraid to move. He nodded, holstered his Colts and growled at the man. "I ain't a reverend no more."

He turned away and fished some money from his pocket. The room was deathly quiet as McSweeney passed the bar and tossed the coins on top. "Sorry about the mess, Filly."

"*Yeaahhh*," Filly shook his head as he dragged the mop and bucket of water across the floor toward the corpse. "That son of a bitch was always running his mouth. It was a matter of time anyway before someone put a bullet in Lemmy."

Filly paused in front of the man and studied what was left of his head. He winced and muttered under his breath.

McSweeney paused at the door and adjusted his hat. "I'll be back to collect that bounty."

He walked outside into the night air of Southbend and looked around. The saloon across the street, Pap's Trough, was loud and boisterous. Off-key piano music drifted over harsh laughter and a blue haze of cigar smoke curled out from the open front door.

McSweeney walked to his horse, a beautiful palomino he called Samson, and grabbed onto the length of knotted rope hanging from the saddle horn. A short moment later, McSweeney climbed up and settled himself in place. He sat there, reloaded his shotgun and let it fall back into place on the leather harness.

He urged Samson down the street and toward the flatlands beyond. McSweeney had gotten his fill of Southbend for a while, and besides, he had a bounty to track down.

CHAPTER THIRTY-ONE
Southbend, Wyoming

Abram took a healthy drink from his bottle of Old Crow, took a deep breath and then walked into the boarding house. Sofia stood behind the counter and she looked up at him, her eyes full of poison, and then turned back to the ledger she was writing in. "If you're looking for a room stranger, we're full up."

He snickered and walked closer. Abram set the bottle of whiskey on the counter and leaned against it. "I know it's been—"

"It hasn't been a *while*, Abram!" Sofia hissed her words as she spun toward him. "It hasn't been a short time! It's been half a year!"

"Look, I know, alright?" Abram reached out toward her arm and she flinched away from him.

"Don't you even *think* about touching me right now." She pointed toward a closed door to her right. "Your son hasn't even *seen* you!"

Abram nodded and tried to look properly sad and disappointed in himself. "You're right." He shrugged and shook his head. "A short while turned into something else, something longer, *too* long." Abram nodded again as he spoke gently to her. "Did you name him Carlos like we talked about?"

She glared at him, clenched her teeth and then let out a long breath.

"Carlos Manuel Juarez, yes." Sofia's long curls of crow-black hair flowed down past her shoulders and she reached up to tuck loose strands angrily behind her ear. "You'd have *known* that if you weren't off tending to your other women."

"*Naw*, now Sofia…" Abram put his hand out, not quite touching her. "Now you know better than that." He softened his expression and his voice even more. "There ain't never been another woman, even *on my mind*, since I first laid eyes on you."

"So *you* say." Her brown eyes were dark and fierce. "For all *I* know, you've got a dozen other women, a dozen other *children* somewhere, too."

"*Naw, naw.*" Abram took a short step closer, reached out to brush hair away from the side of her face. "You *know* better than that. Things took some bad turns, yeah…" Abram sighed heavily. "And right now, the gang and I are—"

"Your *gang*, the *gang* and I, always the *gang*…" Sofia muttered something in Spanish and took a step back. "Always highest on the totem pole compared to your son and I."

"As I was *saying*…" Abram put his hand up dismissively. "The gang and I have done our last job."

Sofia stared at him as if she was considering his words and Abram went on, hammering it home.

"There's some things going on, yeah. But they'll be over with soon, and then I was thinking it might be time to light out of here." Abram nodded toward the closed door. "You, me and Carlos. We'll go to Mexico, like you wanted."

She shook her head with an expression of disbelief. "You hate Mexico."

"I… I don't hate it. I just…" Abram sighed. "I don't think I ever really gave it a chance. But when this is all over, let's go. We'll go down there and live high on the hog."

"Oh? And how's that?" Sofia crossed her arms and stared at him. "You plan on selling your bullshit down there too?"

Abram let out a short laugh at her verbal jab, and shook his head. "*Naw,* I'm being honest here. A week or so and we'll have more money than we know what to do with for the rest of our lives."

"Let me guess… some new bank?" Sofia scoffed and shook her head. "And what if you get killed during the—"

"It's already done."

She stopped and stared at him.

"Ain't no new job…" Abram smiled. "It's already done and over with. Money's hidden down in a river bank in Broken Stone."

"So why not just go now? Let's get it and leave." She shrugged and held her hands out.

"Can't do that just yet." Abram inhaled sharply and let his breath out slowly. He stared at the counter as if he was deep in thought. "Some loose ends have got to be snipped off before we can leave clean. But not long."

Sofia wagged a finger at him. "That's what you said last time, and it's been half a year, you son of a—"

She raised her right palm and swung it toward Abram. He caught her wrist mid-swing, yanked her toward him close, and whispered as he stared down into her eyes.

"You are strong and fierce, Miss Juarez... oh yes you are. It's what drew you to me in the first place." He let his gaze travel down her cleavage and the front of her dress. "Along with... your other assets."

Abram smiled and met her gaze again. "But don't go fooling yourself that you're stronger than me. You've had your little temper tantrum... and things are the way they are right now."

He held onto her wrist a moment more. Sofia yanked her arm away from him but didn't step back. "A week?"

Abram shrugged. "Maybe a little longer, maybe a little less, but pretty much a week, yeah."

She sighed as she stared at him. "More money than we'll know what to do with?"

"*Thasss* right." Abram smiled and leaned down to kiss her.

Sofia turned at the last moment and Abram kissed her cheek. His smile turned into a grin as he pulled back. She looked into his eyes and he leaned down again. A second time she turned her head away in the other direction, and a second time Abram felt his lips on the soft skin of her face.

He slid his hand along the nape of her neck and his fingers into the thick curls of her hair. Abram tightened a fistful in his hand and held her firmly in place as he leaned down to kiss her mouth.

An urgent breath escaped her lips as he felt her tongue

against his, and then her hands slid up the small of his back and pulled him close against her. Abram held her hair and then grabbed her waist with his other hand. Sofia let out a low moan and whispered in his ear before she quickly led him away into the second room—her bedroom— at the rear of the building.

And then, there was nothing but raw hunger and angry passion.

CHAPTER THIRTY-TWO

West of Bagger's Creek, Wyoming

A single beam of silver-blue light shone into the cave and when Thatcher opened his tired eyes, he saw movement along the ground. He stared for a moment as his eyes adjusted to the low light, and as Thatcher realized what he was watching, his guts turned to ice.

He sat up slowly, felt Nadine shift in her sleep, and Thatcher inhaled sharply. Resting a hand on her shoulder, he gave her a gentle shake.

"What is it?" She replied sleepily.

"Stay very, very still." Thatcher whispered his reply as he eased his hand away and reached for the small pile of kindling that remained. He drew out a branch as long as his arm, cautiously poked the hot coals in the fire, and watched them glow orange. Then Thatcher began flipping the embers out onto the dirt.

He heard a rattler shake its tail near the left of the cave entrance and Thatcher saw it's serpentine shape coiled in half-shadow, half-moonlight. He swallowed hard and flipped more glowing coals from the fire. Half a dozen snakes, the length of his forearm, all slithered away from the intense heat.

Bonespur Bill snorted in his sleep and made a sound like a bulldog lapping from a water dish. He groaned, sat up quickly and stared at Porter with squinted eyes. "The hell's going on?"

"Bill…" Thatcher whispered through clenched his teeth. "There's rattlesnakes in here. A *lot… of damned… rattlesnakes*."

"*Awww* is that all you're…" Bill ran a hand over his face and back up over his head as if he was trying to wake up. He threw back the blanket of his bedroll and cleared his throat before getting to his feet.

"Bill!" Thatcher growl-whispered, but the old man ignored him.

"They're just looking to get warm." Bonespur Bill picked up his fox fur hat and waved it at the shapes moving along the ground. "*Shoo*." He waved the hat again, letting the bushy tail swing in their direction. "Go on now. Go on."

Thatcher watched, stunned, as the young rattlers scurried away from the motion and headed toward the exit of the cave. All except one, to the left of the opening, and it stiffened up and slowly weaved its head in the moonlight.

Bill walked just out of striking range, crouched down to one knee and stared at the snake. "I know you're all out of sorts because you come in here for a warm spot to sleep. I reckon I would be too." Bill shook a finger toward the serpent. "But I can't have you in here acting the fool." He waved his hat toward the door and the rattler struck out, fast as lightning, and returned to its tightly coiled position.

"What did I *just* tell you?" Bill settled the hat on his head and continued glaring at the rattlesnake. He eased himself up to stand and pointed toward the front of the cave. "Go on now."

Another two warning shakes and the rattler shifted, moving quickly through the dry grit and out through the entrance. The light streaming through was getting brighter as dawn approached.

Nadine sat up slowly and looked around the cave. She glanced from Thatcher to Bill and then all around the ground. "How… did you just do that?"

"I was married once." Bill smiled and then snort-laughed at his own joke. He turned away and started tidying up his bedroll.

Thatcher realized he was still holding the kindling branch and he tossed it onto the fire. He wasn't sure what in the hell he had just witnessed Bonespur do, but he was glad the man did whatever it was. The thought of getting repeatedly bitten by a hatch of young rattlers wasn't something he wanted to entertain.

"Let's start packing up. We've still got a long ride ahead

of us." Thatcher gathered his bedroll together.

Nadine let out a yawn. "What happens when we get back to Broken Stone?"

Thatcher tied the small straps around his bundle of blankets, stared at them for a moment and then met Nadine's eyes. "In all truth, Nadine... I don't rightly know. But we'll find out, and you'll be kept safe, I know that much."

She nodded and sat up and when she was done with her bedroll, she slung the saddlebag of money over her shoulder.

Bill let out a grunt of surprise and took a quick step away from the wall of the cave. He swiped quickly with his right hand and when he held it up, Thatcher saw he held a young rattlesnake just behind its head. Bill grinned. "There's always one that don't listen, ain't it?"

"*Aww* hell." Thatcher looked around and then stepped backward toward the cave entrance. Every twig or small piece of kindling made him strain his eyes to be sure. He kept taking one cautious step at a time, until he reached the front of the cave and walked outside into the early morning light.

"Well, howdy Mister."

Thatcher dropped everything in his arms as he spun around and drew one of his Peacemakers, thumbing the hammer back and aiming at the figure on horseback. A heavy groan escaped Thatcher as he forced his hand to aim away from the young boy sitting on the saddle of a blue roan.

Thatcher holstered his revolver, leaned forward and put his hands on his knees. "Son, you..." He shook his head and let out a long heavy sigh.

"You're a might high strung this early in the mornin', ain't ya?" The boy smiled and turned to watch Nadine and Bill walk out of the cave. "Mornin' to you both."

"Cheerio to you." Nadine smiled and nodded as she walked on to her horse.

Bill looked at both directions of the gully and then stared at the boy. "You out here alone?"

"Yes sir, I am." The boy's eyes narrowed and he casually

eased his coat away to show the two revolvers on a gun belt. "But that don't mean I'm easy prey."

Bill stared in surprise for a moment and then he bellowed laughter that echoed from the rocky sides of the gully. He shook his head, still laughing as he walked toward Patches. "*Naw,* I reckon you ain't."

Thatcher caught his breath as his heart began to slow and he looked up at the kid. "What're you doing out here?"

"Good hunting down here. Animals get down in the gully and there's only one way to run." The boy glanced at the three of them and returned to Thatcher. "What're *you* three doing down here? There are lots easier trails to ride than through the gully."

"Well, that's kind of the point." Thatcher picked up his bedroll and went to Ginger to tie it up behind her saddle.

"*Awww...*" The boy's tone sounded almost reverent. "Running from the law? What'd you all do, rob a bank?"

"No we didn't..." Thatcher turned back toward the boy. "We ain't running from the law, we *are* the law."

The boy looked at Nadine and then studied Bonespur Bill before his gaze returned to Thatcher. "Whatever you say, Mister."

Clearing his throat, Thatcher peeled back his coat as he walked toward the kid to show the Marshal's badge. "Okay, maybe not these two, but *I'm* the law."

"Wow." The boy nodded. "A real life Marshal. I ain't never met one of 'em."

Thatcher got the impression that the kid was studying him, giving him a once over and was none too impressed at the first sight of a Marshal. "What's your name anyway, kid?"

"Montgomery Thurmont, but most people call me Monty."

"You live around here?"

The boy's expression changed and he narrowed his eyes. "Are you touched in the head, Mister? Ain't *nobody* lives around here."

"Listen here, you little smarta—"

"I believe," Nadine walked up, right close to the boy and smiled up at him. "What the Marshal would like to know is if there's anyone around here that would pose a danger."

"*Awww…*" Monty looked at Thatcher. "You should've just said that."

Thatcher grit his teeth, put his hands on his hips and let out a long breath as the boy continued talking to Nadine.

"You ain't from around here."

"I came from London, but I suppose you could say I'm from here now." She smiled at the boy. "I'm Nadine Bartlett."

"Pleased to meet you, ma'am." Monty replied as polite and gentlemanly as someone years older. "And *naw*, there's a few homesteads a lot farther west of here, but ain't none to fret about."

"And your folks?"

Monty looked away from her and stared ahead at the length of the gully. "Ain't got no folks anymore. Ma passed last winter, and my Pa in spring. The consumption eat 'em up, right down to the bones."

"Oh, I'm… I'm so sorry." Nadine reached a comforting hand out and Monty urged his horse slightly, just out of her reach. "And you're out here all by yourself?"

"Yes ma'am, same as I told the burly one over there." Monty smiled and glanced at Bonespur Bill. "Been on my own ever since Pa died."

Thatcher caught Nadine's gaze and he looked around the ridge of the gully. He knew damned well what the Wyoming wilderness was like, and a boy of eleven or twelve living out on his own in the middle of it all was far from believable.

"Well…" Thatcher climbed up on Ginger's saddle and watched as Bill and Nadine got on their own horses. "It was nice meeting you… *Monty*. But we'd best get on with it. We've got a long ride left."

"It was nice meeting you." Nadine smiled and Monty

gave her a nod and returned the smile.

Bill grumbled as he settled onto his saddle and urged Patches ahead.

"Where y'all heading to?" Monty turned to Thatcher.

"*Ohhhh…* west a good ways." Thatcher hesitated to tell the boy their true destination. Something about all of this just didn't set well at all. Nadine guided her horse forward and Thatcher remained for a moment longer.

"I wish you a safe journey, then." Monty cut his blue roan around toward the direction they had come from.

Ginger snorted and shook her head and Thatcher gave her a good pat on the neck.

"You all be watchful, now. The Pale Horses are only the start."

Monty's words made Thatcher bristle and a frosty trail tracked along his spine. "What the hell'd you…" He snapped around to address the boy directly, but the gully was empty except for the three of them. No sign of Monty or his horse at all.

"What in the hell…" Thatcher glanced at the opening to the cave, but it was to his right, close by. And there was no way the kid and the horse could have fit inside. That icy feeling on spread out and the hair went up on the back of Thatcher's neck.

A cool wind blew down the gully, curled around him and passed over him like a warning of winter. Thatcher tightened his hold on the reins and urged Ginger quickly ahead to catch up to Nadine and Bill. He glanced behind him several times, but there was still no sign of the boy.

Only the sound of the wind blowing over the dry weeds and stones with a sound like the dead, whispering.

CHAPTER THIRTY-THREE
Southbend, Wyoming

"My skull feels like it's been turned inside out." Calhoun reached for the cup of Arbuckles' coffee on the top of the bar.

Blaine stared at the steaming brew and then turned to look at the shelves on the wall behind the bar. "Hey Filly, pour me a double shot of Old Crow. I think the hair of the dog might be fitting for *me* this morning."

Calhoun groaned at the sight of Filly pouring whiskey into a glass. "Damn, Blaine. I don't know how you can even *smell* whiskey after last night."

"My Ma didn't raise no quitters." Blaine smiled as he slid the glass closer to him.

"Your Ma didn't raise *anyone*, Blaine." Abram said as he walked into the saloon.

"That's… that's cold, Abram." Blaine turned toward him. "That's some cold, heartless commentary, right there." He took a drink of whiskey, licked his lips and glanced at Calhoun. "My Ma died when I was four."

Abram got a cup of coffee from Filly and went to sit at a table by himself.

Calhoun snickered and spoke in a low voice. "He does have a way of finding just the right string of words with sharp teeth, don't he?"

Blaine nodded with a sigh and shook his head. He turned from the bar toward Abram. "We staying in Southbend and getting drunk again today?"

Abram stared out the window and took a drink of the steaming brew. "I thought on it for a long while last night."

Gord and some of the other men walked inside the saloon, all of them looking pale and rough around the edges. Filly laughed and started sitting out a row of coffee mugs on the bar.

"And what did your thoughts lead you to?" Gord asked Abram and then leaned against the bar as he took a mug of coffee with a nod of thanks to Filly.

"We ain't in jail no more, and I'm positive that woman's heading back to Broken Stone." Abram nodded and stood up from the table with his coffee. "I'm sure of it. Ain't no reason for her to wait around there. We'll ride to Broken Stone, see if we can save ourselves some bounty money and put a bullet in her ourselves."

Gord chewed on his bottom lip and sighed. "You sure you want to do that? Be out in the open? Y'all are wanted men. Bounty hunters and Marshals alike will be trying to draw a bead on you."

"You ain't wrong, Gord." Abram downed the rest of his coffee and set the mug on top of the bar. "But we've got to go there anyway. That's where the money is." He adjusted his coat and his gun belt. "Anything that comes within twenty feet of us, put 'em down for good."

"Well, alright then." Blaine nodded and glanced back at the rest of the men by the bar. He drank the rest of the whiskey in his glass and set it down. "You heard the man. Let's ride."

A man standing at the end of the bar shifted as if he was uncomfortable, and then scratched at the front of his trousers.

"You alright, Wilson?" Gord emptied his mug and watched the man, amused.

The man shook his head, glanced toward the front door, and then turned back to Gord. "Nothing some turpentine and a smooth shave with a straight razor won't take care of."

Bennett, the man standing beside Wilson took a step away from him, eying him up as if he might catch something. "Ain't no way a straight razor's getting anywhere near my nether regions."

"Not sure what you're worried about, Bennett." Wilson snickered. "Ain't nothing to cut off down there anyway."

"Go piss up a rope, you bootlicker." Bennett laughed and finished the coffee Filly had poured for him.

Wilson laughed along with him, and then the humor

left his expression as he scratched at his trousers again. He muttered under his breath and then looked around. "Let's get the hell out of this town. Bunch o' damned diseased cows."

"At least mine was pretty enough." Gord replied as the group of men left the saloon and went to their horses.

"*Pretty enough* is just fine when the lamps are turned down." Bennett laughed as he climbed up in the saddle of his horse. "Besides, you was drunk enough last night that a bunghole on a whiskey barrel would've been all the same."

Gord let out a sharp bark of laughter and shook his head as he saddled up. "I ain't never went to bed with an ugly woman, but I sure woke up with a few." He watched as Blaine, Calhoun, and Abram got on their horses. Wilson saddled up and then scratched again.

Gord shook his head. "Time will tell if I get the firecrotch or not, though I reckon from the looks of you, my chances of escape aren't good."

A woman stepped out from one of the buildings and leaned against the front. She wore a dirty dress over her rotund figure, wide-hipped and thick-shouldered. Her chestnut colored hair was a bird's nest around her wide face, and her eyes weren't quite aligned as they looked at the group of men and settled on Gord. The woman smiled wide with thick wet lips and revealed a smile missing her front teeth. She kissed the palm of her hand and blew Gord a kiss.

Gord's expression lost every ounce of amusement and he looked to his left and then right before returning the woman's gaze. He pointed to himself and mouthed the question. "Me?"

She nodded and licked her lips. "Thanks for last night, cowboy. I'll think of you in my dreams later."

Abram snickered and tightened the grip on his reins.

Gord turned toward him, a look of horror on his face. "Not a damned word." He kicked into his horse and trotted off down the street.

Abram burst into laughter.

Blaine rode up close. "Did he *really?*"

"*Naww, naw.*" Abram shook his head, still laughing. "That's the butcher's daughter. I paid her a dollar to come outside and say that. I figured Gord wouldn't remember last night."

Blaine and Calhoun joined in the laughter, and Bennet and a few other men joined in as they cut their horses down the street in the direction Gord had ridden.

Sofia held Carlos in her arms and stood in front of the boarding house. Abram rode close and reined his horse to a stop. She stepped to him and smiled. "You said a week."

"I said abouts a week, maybe a bit more, maybe a bit less." Abram grinned as he leaned down and kissed her. He ran a hand over the baby's head and straightened up in the saddle. "You start thinking of the kind of house you want… the sorts of dresses you want to wear down in Mexico."

Sofia's smile widened and she nodded. "Hurry back, okay?"

Abram urged his horse ahead and when they were out of earshot, Blaine spoke to him in a low voice. "Mexico?"

"There ain't no way in hell I'm going to Mexico." Abram laughed and kicked into his horse as they raced out of Southbend.

CHAPTER THIRTY-FOUR
Wildtooth Trail, Wyoming

"What's it like in London?" Thatcher guided Ginger through a thick patch of honeysuckle vines. They had ridden out of the gully across a stretch of dry flatlands and Bill directed them to follow along a thin creek he said met up with the Longblood River.

"It's…" Nadine thought and then turned to him with a smile. "Not like this."

She laughed and shook her head. "It has good and bad like everywhere, I suppose. But people seem more *confined* there."

"Is that right?" Thatcher glanced at the creek, which had been steadily growing wider the longer they followed along beside it. The dry grasses had given way to lots of greenery. "Confined by what?"

Nadine shrugged and shook her head. "Themselves, I suppose. Their own ideas of what should and shouldn't be."

"Don't sound like much freedom to me."

She smiled at him again. "Like I said, not like here."

Bill led them through a dense patch of ferns along the side of the creek and then he reined Patches to stop. "Here we go." He looked upstream and then down again, and nodded. "Yeah, I think we're alright."

The creek ran directly into a fast-flowing river about twenty feet wide. Bill let out a heavy sigh and grinned at them. "This is the Longblood River. We'll follow this for *ohhh*… half a day's ride maybe, and then we'll see the mountains. Cobbler's Den is on the other side of that."

Thatcher nodded, considering Bill's words. "I ain't looking forward to the mountains."

"*Awww*, they ain't much more than a big hill. We'll be just fine." Bill urged his horse forward and Patches walked into the river. The water reached mid-foreleg and churned around it. The mare snorted, took a drink, and then walked on into the current.

The burbling sound of the water and the cool air was

soothing. Nadine took her hat off and closed her eyes for a moment as the breeze drifted against her face.

Thatcher was struck again at the woman's beauty and wondered what it might be like walking down the cobblestone streets of London with her arm in his.

I'd probably look like a bull walking into a tailor's shop.

He stifled a laugh at himself as the three of them walked down river. Birds called out here and there, but it was peaceful with the sound of the water. Up ahead, Bill slowed and then stopped. He looked back at Thatcher with a grave expression on his face and waved him closer.

Along the left side of the river, not far ahead, Thatcher saw a series of small huts, about half the size of a covered wagon, constructed of thin woven branches and mud. The ground on the river bank was worn down smooth to the bare dirt, like an animal trail. It didn't look like any Indian camp he had ever seen before.

Bill leaned closer and whispered. "We've got to get the hell out of here as fast as we can."

"What is it?" Thatcher continued studying the group of shelters.

"It's the Pattee Clan. I was hoping we…" Bill shook his head. "We've got to *goooo*."

Thatcher saw several small fire pits and frames of branches to dry out pelts, signs of the huts being lived in, but he still couldn't see what was getting Bill so unsettled.

"You see that deer carcass?" Bonespur pointed toward the hut farthest away. "It *ain't* a deer."

Thatcher strained his eyes, saw the skinned out bloody carcass hanging upside down. What he had previously thought was venison, he could now see the rib cage, the thick spine and the hips. Thatcher swallowed hard and his gaze shifted to the ground below the hanging meat, at the still wet and gleaming human skull.

It felt like he had been punched in the gut and his breath escaped him in a fast rush. As Thatcher turned toward Nadine, that's when the first stone came from the dense woods, missing Thatcher's face by inches.

The serene sounds erupted into sharp woops and yelps from both sides of the river.

"*Ride!*" Thatcher bellowed at Nadine and her eyes went wide as she snapped Sadie's reins.

"Sons o' bitches!" Bill screamed as a volley of rocks crossed through the air.

It felt like a sledgehammer hit Thatcher's left ribs and he fell sideways off the saddle and plunged into the water. Immediately, he saw a man-shaped thing charge from the riverbank toward him, screaming loudly. It was caked and slathered with mud and its clothes were damp patches of leather.

As it ran through the water, Thatcher heard Nadine scream and saw that she had fallen from Sadie. A filthy woman leaped into the water from the other side of the river, lunging toward Nadine on all fours.

Thatcher turned and saw the man, wild-eyed and feral. He jumped on Thatcher as he fumbled to draw his Peacemaker.

The man pulled up a fist-sized river rock and swung it down, intent on crushing Thatcher's skull. He dodged to the left and the rock plunged into the river water. Thatcher felt the Peacemaker slide free of its holster and as he thumbed the hammer back, Thatcher drove it straight up and shoved the barrel into the man's mouth.

The man garbled in pain, and bits of broken teeth sprayed from between its liver-colored lips. Thatcher squeezed the trigger and the back of the man's head blew off in a red spray on the river water. It fell heavily to its side and yanked the lodged Peacemaker away from him.

Nadine screamed and struggled against the woman on top of her.

Down river, Bill tried to aim a Colt Walker in his hand, but it was too dangerous to shoot for fear of hitting Nadine. He bellowed out a war cry of rage and frustration.

Rolling over on his side, Thatcher pulled the Peacemaker

from his left holster and fired. The bullet caught the filthy river woman in her left armpit, almost blowing the limb clean off her body. She threw her head back, screaming, and then she charged toward Thatcher as her bloody arm dangled loosely.

Thatcher cocked his revolver as he grabbed hold of Ginger's stirrup. *"Heyahhh!"*

The mare jolted ahead, dragging Thatcher through the river, and he fired his Peacemaker, shooting the woman in the throat. She took one more leaping bound and fell face first into the river.

To his left, Thatcher saw a skinny man, just as filthy as the other two, climbing up the side of Bill's horse.

"Get the hell off me!" Bill pulled his Kentucky pistol from his waistband, shoved the barrel tip against the center of the man's chest and fired. The spray from the man's back sounded like hailstones against the water and he fell, damned near torn in half.

Thatcher got to his feet and ran toward Nadine. She looked around, bewildered, and her gaze fell on the dead woman in the river. "Thatcher? What in the bloody hell was—"

"Come on… come on now." He grabbed her hand, pulled her to her feet, and then helped her get back up on Sadie.

Thatcher walked back to the man's corpse, put a foot on the dead man's chest, and gripped his Peacemaker. He yanked it free of the man's mouth in a spray of blood. Thatcher swirled the barrel into the river water and shoved it back into his holster. When he climbed up onto Ginger's saddle, Thatcher turned to Bill. "You and I are going to have a talk about what the hell these things were."

"Well since we don't know if there's more'n these three, maybe we should move the hell on." Bill adjusted his fox fur hat and urged Patches down river.

Thatcher looked back at the mangled corpses and thought about their feral expressions of hunger as they attacked. His gaze landed on the human, strung up like a deer after being gutted, and he turned away, sick to his stomach.

Broken Stone seemed far *far* away from here.

CHAPTER THIRTY-FIVE
Wildtooth Trail, Wyoming

McSweeney reined Samson to a stop and the big palomino flicked his tail and snorted at the sight of the terrain looming in front of him. The mountains were a craggy, uneven quilt of rock and patches of old growth Lodgepole pines and cedar. McSweeney's gaze traced over the sight of it all, trying to find the easiest path to take.

He felt certain that the woman, Nadine Bartlett, and a single Marshal would take one of the most, or *the* most difficult trail back to Broken Stone. Maybe with a *few* lawmen, they would've simply trotted along the easy path without a care in the world, but a *single* Marshal would have to be more than careful, choosing a path that might make others give up the chase.

McSweeney nodded at the mountain in front of him and muttered softly. "Though the path before us be not easy, thou shall take strength where I offer."

Samson snorted again, gave a slight shake of his head and then started forward. A hawk screeched as it sliced across the clear sky in search of prey. He hoped both he and the hawk would find what they were after very soon.

An hour into the ascent, McSweeney felt eyes watching him from the dense patches of cedar trees. He reined Samson to stop and put his arms out to his sides. It had been a long while since he had spoken the Crow language, but McSweeney called out to them in their native tongue, telling them to come forth.

One by one, Crow braves stepped into sight until at least half a dozen circled McSweeney and Samson. Their faces were painted in patchwork, and in the shadows and low light of the forest, McSweeney was certain they would blend in and fade away. He kept his hands out to his sides, watching as they stepped closer. Their bows and arrows were down at their sides.

The closest brave studied McSweeney and then relaxed his weapon and growled Crow in a low voice to the others. All of them eased and straightened where they stood.

Slowly, McSweeney reached into his right saddlebag and drew out a half-full bottle of Thistle Dew. He tossed it to the closest brave, who caught it on reflex, stared at the bottle of liquor and nodded.

McSweeney had never met an Indian that didn't seem unsettled by looking at him. But that wasn't exactly a complete explanation—it wasn't that they found him grotesque, more like he was something unique and not to be touched.

He had never seen a dwarf Indian, but McSweeney found it hard to believe there wasn't at least a few here and there among the many tribes. He pointed toward the valley near the top of the mountain ridge, patted his chest and then pointed again.

For a moment, the Crow brave stared at him as if he was some sort of rare flower in the wild. Then the brave who caught the whiskey bottle gave a grunt and nodded.

McSweeney nodded in return and urged Samson past them and up the hillside. There wasn't an ounce of fear in his veins and that only made him more certain he was on the right path.

CHAPTER THIRTY-SIX
Wildtooth Trail, Wyoming

For a long distance, the Longblood River widened and narrowed in a rhythm, and then it veered south. Bill led them out of the water into the woods with a thick carpet of dead pine needles and blackened trees, their trunks and branches burned. The dead forest continued and without even the sound of birds in the trees, it was an eerie desolate feeling.

A sharp invisible line separated the old burned growth from an explosion of greenery, honeysuckle vines and wild raspberry bushes, red cedar and Lodgepole pines. Only moments before, there was neither cover nor concealment for quite a ways. Now, it was dense enough that ten feet into the woods, someone could vanish from sight.

Thatcher kept glancing at Nadine, who had been quiet since the attack at the river. He couldn't blame her, it had been on his mind for a lot of the ride as well. The *Pattee Clan*, Bill had called them.

What in the hell would make people eat their own?

The thought of ending up strung and tied like the other corpse made Thatcher's guts clench. He hoped Nadine hadn't seen the grisly sight of the bloody remains, but the attack was bad enough.

The sound of a snapping branch came from their left along with an angry low whisper. "*Welllll, shitpickles!*"

Bill stopped Patches and stared in the direction of the sound. He looked down at his horse for a moment, sighed heavily and then returned his gaze to the woods. "Tootie? That you and Doyle out there?"

It was quiet for a moment and then a man's voice replied. "Bill, is that you?"

Bonespur shook his head and sighed again. "It's me."

"*Awwww* hell." Disappointment was evident in the man's voice.

"We... we've been friends a long while now, Doyle."

"Yeah, we sure have." From behind the cover of the woods, a man cleared his throat. "But an awful lot of money is on the line, Bill."

"I reckon it is, but... can't you set this one aside? I'm caught up in the middle of it all."

"'Fraid not. This..." The man cleared his throat again. "This life ain't got much more left in it for me. Might be my last bounty and I've got to make it a good one, provide for my kin when I'm gone."

Nadine whispered. "What if we paid the five thousand to him?"

"Oh, I don't know... Doyle, he's—"

"It worked on you." Nadine stared at Bill and shrugged.

"Hey Doyle! What if we was to pay you the five-thousand bounty and have you and Tootie just... run on out o' here?"

Nadine reached into her saddle bag and gathered banded stacks of money until she had five thousand in her grasp.

"If you're walking about with seventy-five hundred dollars in your pocket, then you've been on quite a streak of bounty money." Doyle laughed from the woods, but it was sincere and full of good humor.

"I thought..." Bill glanced at Thatcher and then back to the woods. "Thought it was five thousand for the woman."

"It *is*, but we'll take another twenty-five hundred for the Marshal."

That was a woman's voice—Tootie, Doyle's long-time bounty hunting partner and wife.

Nadine let out a short gasp and dug into the saddlebag again. There was only half a bundle of money remaining and she stared at it as she drew it free. She looked up at Bill and shook her head as she whispered. "I don't have that much. I *did*, but—"

"Well what did you do with it? We ain't been nowhere to *spend* it. Where's the rest of—"

"It kept us warm last night." Thatcher interjected as he casually eased his hand down by his side.

Bill groaned as realization hit him. "How short are you?"

Nadine quickly rifled through the money and then looked up at him. "Maybe eight-hundred dollars."

Wincing, Bill called out to the woods. "We're shy about eight hundred, Doyle. That good enough for today? For an old friend?"

It was quiet for a moment, and Doyle yelled out. "Eight hundred's quite a bit short, Bill."

"Goddamnit, you stubborn ol' mule! You're gonna go toe to toe over eight hundred dollars? We used to wipe our *asses* with that kind o' bounty money years ago!"

"Yes we did, Bill." Doyle laughed from the woods." Had ourselves a grand ol' time doing it, too. But I'm an ol' man now. Getting eaten up from the inside. Ain't but a few months left maybe."

Bonespur Bill put his head down, deep in thought.

Thatcher eased his Peacemaker from his holster and held it down at his side.

"Well… I reckon I'll see you on the other side, Doyle." Bill sniffled and wiped his nose with the sleeve of his coat. "I'm pretty sure it's your turn to buy whiskey."

The man laughed again from the cover of the forest, but when he spoke, there was a tired sadness in his voice. "By my recollection, I think you're right about that, ol' friend."

"Well, alright then." Bill nodded. "Hey Tootie?"

"I hear you, Bill."

Bonespur slowly reached back and pulled out his Springfield rifle. "I'm real sorry about this, Tootie."

"Don't be sorry for anything yet. Both of you are still above snakes." The woman let out a short laugh. "You know… don't matter if Doyle's sick or not, if you put him down, … I ain't gonna stop."

Bill nodded. "I know, Tootie. That's the kind of love I'd expect from a wife and you're living up to it."

"Hey Bill?" Doyle called out to him again.

"Yeah?"

"We're burning daylight."

A gunshot cracked from the thick greenery and the bullet sliced past Thatcher's face close enough to feel the heat. He fired blindly into the spot he thought the voices came from and drew his other Peacemaker.

"Damn you, Doyle!" Bill screamed as he fired his Kentucky pistol and it boomed and released a cloud of blue smoke.

Thatcher saw Nadine draw a pistol and he growled at her. "Get down from the horse, get down and get to cover!"

A rifle shot thundered and Bill fell backwards from Patches. As he fell, Bill clawed at the stock of his Springfield rifle and drew it from the scabbard before he slammed to the ground. Blood leaked from his right forearm and Bill crawled into the weeds.

Thatcher raised both Peacemakers and fired one after the other into the brush. He saw a flash of movement to the left and fired again, trying to track the motion. From the spot he had just been aiming, another shot thundered and Thatcher felt a hot blazing streak across the top of his right shoulder. He screamed in pain and dropped to one knee.

A man as big around as a whiskey barrel walked from the heavy growth and aimed a Spencer rifle at Thatcher. To his right, a woman crept beside him, a pair of Colt Dragoons up and ready to fire.

His wiry gray hair hung halfway down his chest and Thatcher saw he wore a bone-tube necklace around his throat. His doe-skin jacket was fringed and weathered, the bead work missing parts here and there. A large pouch hung from his side, close to a massive Bowie knife in a beaded sheath. His expression didn't carry any anger at all, in fact, Thatcher thought he seemed stoic and absent of emotion at all.

Thatcher clenched his teeth and glared at the man. "You don't have to do this."

"Yeah…" Doyle gave a slight shake of his head. "'Fraid

I do, lawman. But I'll make it quick."

The woman stopped right by the man's side, keeping her revolvers in front of her, one trained on Thatcher and the other on Nadine.

"Doyle?"

The big man flinched at the sound of Bill's voice and looked toward the brush where Bonespur Bill had crawled. "Yeah?"

"I'm sorry."

Thatcher heard the snap of a musket hammer and then it sounded as if lightning cracked nearby. There was no other way to describe it—the ammunition bag on Doyle's hip exploded into a ball of fire and shrapnel. Tootie's right side shredded as bullets punctured through her ribs and the side of her face. She fired both revolvers before she died on the way to the dirt.

Pieces of meat and gristle rained down against the ferns and weeds and the bloody mist in the air smelled like copper.

Doyle was slammed away so quickly, the Spencer rifle in his hands landed flat on the ground as it was ripped out of his hands. He fell to the ground, his eyes open wide, and stared lifelessly. The side of his body where his ammunition bag had rested was nothing but a bloody crater of shredded meat and bone.

Crawling slowly out of the weeds, Bill put the stock of the Springfield against the ground and used it to push himself up to stand. "Damn you, Doyle," he growled as he went to Patches and slid the rifle into the scabbard again.

Thatcher stared at the carnage in front of him. He heard Nadine come closer to stand behind him. It seemed as if there wasn't a single green leaf that wasn't spattered with drops of red. The rusty-colored pine needles on the ground around their bodies glistened darkly, soaked with their blood.

"Bill?" Thatcher turned to look at the old man. "What was in that Springfield of yours?"

"Gardner's explosive rounds." He patted the scabbard.

"It's all I ever shoot in this."

Thatcher pushed himself off the ground and holstered his Peacemakers.

"That was a bloody bomb." Nadine looked paler than she had back at the river.

"Well…" Bill drank from his canteen. "It is when you shoot another man's ammunition bag." He nodded toward his saddle bag. "I got about a hundred more of 'em in there."

"Where in the blue hell did you get that many of them?" Thatcher took his canteen from Ginger and took several deep drinks.

Bill shrugged. "People left all sorts of things behind during the war."

"How many of those do you have?" Nadine took the canteen from Thatcher when he offered it.

"Oh I… I don't know. A few." Bill screwed the cap back on.

"Few *hundred*?" Thatcher stared at him.

"*Naw*." Bill shook his head and glanced at the bullet wound in his forearm. "Few *crates*. Maybe… fifteen-hundred in each crate."

"Sweet bloomin' Jesus." Thatcher let out a heavy sigh and stared at the corpses. "These were friends of yours?"

"For the better part of thirty years." Bill pulled on his bison teeth and turquoise necklace until the leather cord snapped behind his neck. He walked over to Doyle's corpse, crouched and put the necklace on the man's chest. Bill gave it a gentle pat, whispered something, and stood up again.

"I'm sorry." Nadine picked up her Pietta revolver from the ground and returned it to its holster. "This is my fault."

"*Naw* it ain't." Bill shook his head at her. "It ain't. Doyle and Tootie chose that life, chose this here today, too. Ain't your fault."

"I'm still sorry." Nadine said in a soft voice.

Bill grunted acknowledgement and turned toward the direction they had been riding in. "Cobbler's Den is a few hours from here, maybe a little less. I reckon we might bed down there for the night.

"I've heard of it, but never been through." Thatcher studied the graze wound on his shoulder and clenched his teeth at the pain. It wasn't a bad wound, but bad enough to hold his attention.

"Ain't much of a town, handful of buildings. No one ever *goes* there, you *end* up there." Bill climbed up into Patches' saddle and took up the reins.

"I never thought I'd say this," Thatcher got up onto Ginger. "But I'm glad you're with us, Bill."

"Then it's a good day indeed, ain't it?" Bill grinned and cut his horse around, leading them farther along the trail toward Cobbler's Den.

CHAPTER THIRTY-SEVEN
Crow's Call Trail, Wyoming

It had been almost a week since the ambush of the Marshals and the buzzards still circled the skies. Abram had led the crew across the flatlands from Southbend until they reached the Crow's Call Trail that the Marshals had taken with the jail wagon. When the group reached the narrow pinch along the rocky path, Abram reined his horse to a stop and stared at what was left of the dead men. Only three of the corpses remained, the others probably dragged away by coyotes.

"Damn they stink to high heaven." Gord made an expression of disgust and looked at the corpse of a dead Marshal, the man's silver badge still pinned to his coat. His face had been gnawed down to the skull and threads of his hair fluttered in the soft breeze.

"There ain't no heaven where these men went." Abram spat on the ground and looked at the surroundings.

Behind a boulder, the rotting carcass of Horace Conway was covered in a quilt of blowflies that shifted each time the buzzard beside him pecked and pulled away strings of meat.

"Poor bastards." Blaine put an arm up to cover his nose and mouth.

"I reckon." Abram adjusted the brim of his hat against the sun and eyed the trail in front of them. It sloped upward to a ridge and then it wasn't far on the flatlands until they reached Broken Stone. "Come on, let the dead be dead."

Abram took the lead, with Blaine and Calhoun not far behind him. Gord, Wilson, and Bennett brought up the end of the group. When they crested the ridge, Abram saw a funeral coach up ahead. The vehicle was tilted at an odd angle, and he figured a wheel had come off or worse, an axle had busted. He eased his coat away from his Colt Patersons as they rode closer. Abram relaxed slightly when he saw the driver sitting on the bench in shadow beneath the overhang. The sides of the funeral coach were painted black and carved with ornate designs of hanging curtains and veils with flowers. Abram could see clear through the windows of the coach and saw no one hiding inside. He reined his horse to a stop and the other men did the same.

The woman smiled and nodded at Abram and he saw she wasn't old—she was ancient.

She wore a black dress buttoned up to her neck and her gray hair was pulled back in a ponytail that lay over her shoulder and hung down to her waist. One eye was milky-blue with a cataract, while the other was clear and dark and sharp as a hawk's. Both of them were set in a weathered face as lined and wrinkled as a patch of drought-cracked ground.

Abram eyed up the rear right wheel of the coach, saw that it had fallen at an angle because of a missing pin along the axle arm. He turned to the old woman. "I reckon you ain't going to get to where you're going, missing one wheel."

The burlap face of the woman widened in a toothless smile and she let out a short cackle. "*Ohhhh*, I'm right where I'm supposed to be."

Abram snorted a laugh and got down from his horse. He stopped and looked at the rest of the men. "What're you all waiting on? Let's help this lady get her coach fixed."

Blaine shook his head as he got down. "You're an unpredictable cuss, you know that, Abram?"

"That's what I've heard." Abram took his canteen and walked to the front of the coach as the other men went to work on the wheel. He held it out to the woman and she nodded thanks as she held it and took a long drink. She cleared her throat of phlegm, spit over the side of the bench seat, then handed the canteen back to him.

As Abram took it from the old woman, he felt her fingertips brush over the back of his hand, a sensation like cold cobwebs brushing against his flesh. It made him flinch and he stared at her as he put the cap back onto the canteen.

"*Ohhhh* dearie, dear…" The woman let out another short

cackle and she rocked back and forth slightly.

The corner of the wagon lifted as the men raised it for Blaine and Calhoun to fit the wheel back onto the axle. Abram watched as the men eased the weight of the coach back in place and Blaine picked up the loose pin from the ground.

"You take this now… take it." The old woman whispered.

Abram held his hand out reflexively and the old woman dropped what was in her hand. It was a lock of combed black horsehair, bound together at the top with a strip of tanned leather, sewn and wrapped with glass trade beads.

The old woman tilted her head forward and stared at Abram with her good eye. "You keep that close to you, now. It'll keep the shadows away."

"What…" Abram glanced at the talisman and then looked back to her. "What shadows?"

She laughed and rocked against the bench seat again. "You know the ones…" She lowered her voice to a gravelly whisper. "Them shadows hunting after you, clawing and hungry."

A twist of ice ran through Abram's stomach and he swallowed hard. He couldn't shake the feeling that the old woman's cataract-covered eye somehow saw more than the clear one.

"There we are." Blaine shoved the pin back in place until it secured the wheel. He looked up at Abram and gave him a nod. "It's ready to go."

Quick as a prairie rattler, the old woman snatched her hand out, grabbed onto Abram's wrist and yanked him closer. She whispered in his ear and the sound was rustling leaves in a fall wind. Just as quickly, the old woman let him ago and sat back. She laughed and clapped several times as Abram took a step backward.

That twist of ice grew and grew inside him. "Go on and get."

The old woman laughed harder as she took up the reins in her hands.

"Go on, you crazy ol' woman! Get the hell out of here!"

Abram stepped farther away from her as she snapped the reins and the horses pulled the coach along the trail.

Blaine walked up beside him as the coach left a small cloud of dust in its wake. "What the hell'd that old woman whisper in your ear?"

Abram glanced at him and then watched the coach rumble away along the trail. "She... she said death rides a pale horse, too." He stared at the horsehair talisman in his hand. "She said we'd all be seeing him soon."

"What in the hell..." Calhoun scoffed and stared off in the direction she had driven the coach. "You want us to run after her? Put a bullet in her?"

"*Naw*, I..." Abram shook his head, gritted his teeth, and threw the talisman, watched it twirl through the air and vanish into the weeds. "Let's get to Broken Stone, get the money and..." He watched as the funeral coach disappeared over the ridge and drove downhill. The skin of his hand still felt chilled where the old woman had touched him. Abram turned away and headed for his horse. "Let's ride."

CHAPTER THIRTY-EIGHT
Cobbler's Den, Wyoming

"There she is, in all her glory." Bonespur Bill reined Patches to a stop as Thatcher and Nadine rode up beside him. In the footprint of the mountains ahead, there were two groups of buildings clustered together, three on one side and four on the other of a wide street. Even from a distance, the town seemed taken care of and not some ramshackle group of structures left to fall apart. Two people walked along the street and then crossed from one side to the next.

"People out walking around." Bill stared at them as they walked and he shook his head. "Damn, I hate crowds."

"Charming." Nadine looked at the town and then smiled at Thatcher before she urged her horse across the plains.

Cobbler's Den, close-up, was unusually well taken care of. The buildings were painted in varying shades of white or dark brown, and most of the cleanly-swept porches had railings and spindles painted to match. Even the posts on the porches had simple but pretty designs down their length. Each sign on the buildings had been created with a skilled hand, the letters chiseled into the wooden planks and then painted over to make them pleasing to the eye.

"*Ohhhhh…*" Nadine adjusted her hat and smiled as she looked over the buildings. "It really *is* charming."

"There's what I was looking for." Bill reined Patches toward a hitching post in front of a dark brown building with a sign on front that read Cobbler's Den Saloon in a curled script painted black and red. Bill gathered reins in his hands and gave a grunt of amusement at the row of black and red diamonds painted on the hitching post. He turned to Nadine and smiled. "Fancy."

"I reckon I could use a whiskey, myself." Nadine said, imitating a western drawl as she got down from Sadie.

"*Ohhh,*" Thatcher laughed at her as he tethered Ginger to the post. "You'll fit in just fine." He glanced around the still empty street and the town seemed about as calm and safe as the front pew in a church. Thatcher gave a nod of approval and then turned and followed Bill and Nadine into the saloon.

It was quiet inside, but as clean and tidy as the out. A skinny railroad spike of a man wearing a white pin-striped shirt and a pair of black suspenders, stood behind the bar. He looked up at the three of them and smiled sincerely. "I'm Henry. You folks come on in and have a seat."

Thatcher glanced around the room, saw a man by himself at a table in the far corner of the room and a couple sitting across from each other at another table near a front window. Thatcher saw a closed door set in the rear wall of the saloon and made note of it. He glanced at the front again and then sat down at a table and put his back to the wall. Nadine sat down and slid her chair slightly closer to him. Bill moved to sit down and froze when the man in the corner spoke.

"My day was going *jusssst* fine and then I see you're still walking around, breathing."

As Thatcher turned toward the deep voice, Bill drew one of his Colt Walkers and spun around with it aimed steady and true. Thatcher pulled a Peacemaker and aimed from beneath the table, waiting on Bill's next move.

Henry, the barkeep, stopped dead in his tracks halfway across the room. The color leeched from his face and his gaze kept flitting from one man to the next. The couple sitting near the window shifted in their chairs and the woman clutched onto the man's hand.

Bill spoke in a casual easy tone. "Word travels fast among brigands and cutthroats."

The man lifted his head slightly, his bright gray eyes glanced at Thatcher and his attention lingered on Nadine for a moment, before he turned back to Bill. "I figured you'd be on the run for this bounty."

"I *was*." Bill nodded. "But as things worked out, it's better the other way."

The man grunted and reached for a glass of whiskey on the table in front of him. Bill followed his movement with the barrel of his Colt Walker. The man slowed his movement as he put his hand around the glass and took a drink.

"Bill, you and I've run in the same circles for quite a while."

"I reckon we have. Ain't never had no quarrel with you, neither, Tom." Bill nodded toward the table beside him. "But I can't let you take the woman down. The Marshal neither."

Tom stared at Bill and then his expression lightened. He laughed and shook his head and put the glass of whiskey down. "I ain't taking nothin' down."

For the first time, Thatcher noticed the man had a blanket over his lap and he showed the palm of his hand out as if to show it was empty. Tom slowly lifted the thick cloth away and revealed both legs were amputated from the knees down. The chair he sat in was an invalid's chair with wheels at the base of each leg. "My gunning and running days are long behind me, ol' Hoss."

Bill let out a soft groan and pointed his Walker at the ceiling as he eased the hammer back in place. "*Aww* hell. I'm…" He holstered his revolver and shook his head. "Tom, this way of living makes a man not trust much of anyone."

"I reckon it does." The man nodded at him. "Well if'n you ain't going to kill me, why don't the three of you join me? Been a while since I had any company 'cept for Henry there."

The barkeep was still frozen in place and Bill laughed. "You can take a breath, Henry. Everything's alright, but I would greatly appreciate a bottle of whiskey for the table."

Henry uttered a high-pitched yip and hurried off to the bar.

"It's alright folks, you go on and enjoy yourselves." Bill spoke to the couple, and they both visibly relaxed. He turned away from them.

"Thatcher, Nadine, this is Tom Pennington, one of the

orneriest damned bounty hunters I've ever had the pleasure of knowing." Bill gestured for them to join him as he walked over and sat down beside the man.

Releasing a sigh of relief, Thatcher holstered his Peacemaker as he stood up. "Hell of an introduction, Tom."

"Pleased to meet both of you." The man laughed and lifted his glass of whiskey in a cheers gesture before he took another drink.

"We came along the Wildtooth Trail." Bill smiled as Henry sat three glasses and a bottle of Thistle Dew on the table.

Tom snickered. "You see the kid?"

Everyone's attention snapped up directly to Tom and the old man laughed. "I reckon I'll take that as a yes."

"I ain't never had a *grown* man get under my skin like that boy did." Thatcher took the glass of whiskey Bill had poured for him.

"He seemed polite enough." Nadine sipped from her glass and gave Thatcher a smile.

"He was to *you*."

"Yeah." Tom nodded and let out a soft laugh. "He got to me like that too. When he spoke, it felt like a splinter I couldn't quite get rid of. Must've been... *ohhh*..." Tom looked into his glass of whiskey and swirled it around slightly. "Close to fifteen years ago I seen him. I bet he would have been quite a man."

Nadine held her glass with both hands and stared at Tom. "Fifteen years ago? The boy we met was... maybe eleven or twelve at most."

"And carried a pair of revolvers with confidence." Bill drank two heavy swallows of whiskey and released a satisfied sigh.

"*Mmmmhmm*." Tom laughed and leaned against the table. He poured more whiskey into his glass. "That's Montgomery Thurmont, alright."

Thatcher felt the same chill up his spine that he had felt

in the gully when the boy and the horse had vanished in the blink of an eye.

"The Thurmont family came out to Wyoming from Virginia, I believe." Tom let out a soft belch and patted his stomach. "Came out here in search of better things, but better things ain't what found 'em. Wasn't more than a year when Rose Thurmont got the consumption. Can't remember the father's name, but not long after, the sickness took 'em both."

"Monty said as much, but—"

"*Ohhh.*" Tom's gaze turned to Nadine. "Oh, he must've *really* liked you to talk that much." The corners of his gray eyes wrinkled as he smiled. "Pretty girl like you, ain't much of a wonder, though."

Nadine smiled and glanced away.

"Montgomery was left on his own, and out here... well..." Tom shrugged and turned to Thatcher. "A fur trader come through the gully along Wildtooth Trail, not long after spring thaw, and found the boy half buried in the snow. He had been mauled all to hell, him and his horse."

"He..." Thatcher paused with his whiskey glass halfway toward his mouth. "You saying that boy... the one we talked to..."

Tom put his hands up and shook his head. "I ain't saying nothin' at all. Just... tellin' you what I've heard." He looked at Nadine. "He only said a few words, and it took me a long, *lonnnnng* while to make any sort of peace with them. But I reckon sometimes the true meaning of things takes quite some time to make any sense at all."

"What... what did Monty say to you?" Nadine set her glass down on the table, hanging on Tom's every word.

The man took a deep inhale and let it out slowly. "He said life would force me to slow down, but it would keep me alive longer." Tom shook his head and adjusted the blanket over his amputated legs. "And well, here we are."

"Bloody hell." Nadine whispered and turned to Thatcher as she reached for her glass. "Did he say anything quite so prophetic to you?"

Thatcher gave a slight shake of his head and took a drink of Thistle Dew. He didn't much feel like talking about the kid any longer, but the boy's words had hung with him ever since the gully. *You all be watchful, now. The Pale Horses are only the start.*

"Well." Bill let out a sharp laugh. "It's a might early in the day to sit around telling spooky stories." He took off his fox fur hat and set it down on the floor beside his chair, then turned to Tom. "You mentioned that you figured I'd be running for this bounty. Where'd you heard about it?"

"*Mmmmm.*" Tom nodded and tapped his fingertips against the table top. "Doyle and Tootie come rolling through Cobbler's Den late last night. We shared a few whiskeys and... well, you know how Tootie can get when she gets a snort of liquor. She said they had come through Bagger's Creek and—"

"Dixie." Bill muttered and clenched his teeth.

"The woman from the bar?" Nadine stiffened in her chair. "That bloody wench."

"*Thass* exactly right." Tom raised his glass toward Nadine and laughed.

Bill leaned back in his chair and crossed his arms. "Doyle and Tootie won't be coming through again."

Tom stared at him for a moment and then looked into his glass of whiskey again. "Sorry about that, Bill. You and them, hell, all of us have known each other a long while."

"Cut our teeth together as bounty hunters, chasing after..." Bill laughed and shook his head. "You remember that skinny little bastard we used to call Stringbean Sam?"

"He the cattle rustler?"

"*Naw,* that was... that was uh..." Bill waved his hand. "It don't matter. Stringbean Sam was the one that kept stealing sheep and—"

"*Awww* hell, Bill." Tom rocked back in his chair, laughed and made a pained expression on his face. "I'd done put that fella out of my mind and for *damned* good reasons."

Bill laughed along with him and then nodded. "The years go by fast."

"That they do, ol' friend." Tom took a big swallow of whiskey and nodded. "That they do."

"If those people, Doyle and Tootie, I mean, if they heard about the bounty, it stands to reason others have too." Thatcher had hoped taking the rough trail of Wildtooth would have provided a path others would hesitate to follow, but it sure didn't seem that way.

"I'd stand to agree with you." Tom nodded.

"You can't stand *at all*." Bill added.

Slowly, Tom turned toward Bill, stared at him, and then started laughing. "You're the same ol' bootlicker, you know that?"

Bill clapped the man on his shoulder and poured some more whiskey into his glass. "Who else you figure would come on after this bounty? Ones to worry about, I mean."

"Well, there's still a few running around Wyoming, but most of the heavy gunners shifted south, leaving these winters behind so their old bones won't ache as much. Hell, as much as I love Wyoming, I've been considering it myself. But as for who'd come a running for a bounty this size?" Tom nodded and sighed. "When Tootie mentioned it, *you* came to mind easily enough. Weasel Hudson was—"

"Weasel's been dead for few years now."

"What?" Tom stared at Bill. "How?"

"He was in Abilene, messin' around where he shouldn't have been messin' around."

"Card tables or a married woman's bedroom?"

"Knowing Weasel, it was probably both." Bill snickered. "But someone shot him in the back, dragged him into an alley. Happened during the winter and the poor bastard wasn't found for damned near a month."

"Shame." Tom let out a heavy sigh and shook his head.

Thatcher didn't recognize any of the men's names, but he

wasn't surprised. Back in Broken Stone, it was rare to have bounty hunters bring their captures into town, preferring to go on to a bigger city so they could spend their earnings after.

"The only other name that come to mind is one you ain't gonna like much." Tom glanced at Bill and then took a drink of whiskey. "The reverend."

"*Naw*." Bill shook his head. "That little runt's dead too."

"Unless something happened in the last few weeks, McSweeney's alive and as well as can be. Seen him myself." The expression on Tom's face grew serious.

Thatcher took a drink of whiskey and listened, hoping beyond hope, that there was more than one McSweeney in the world who hunted bounty.

Bill groaned. "I thought he died in Old Mexico, going after Mescal Mitchum?"

"He was there alright, but it went the other way around. McSweeney took down Mitchum." Tom shook his head.

"The hell you say. Mitchum's three hundred pounds and four foot taller than—"

"He did." Tom raised a hand up in protest. "I was there when McSweeney collected the bounty payment."

"Now I know you're full of it." Bill narrowed his eyes and shook his head. "Ain't no way McSweeney could get Mitchum's big ol' buffalo ass up on a horse by himself."

"You're right," Tom nodded. "He couldn't. McSweeney cut off Mitchum's head and brought it back to prove the bounty. A hell of a lot easier coming back from Old Mexico that way."

"Are you men…" Thatcher cleared his throat, asking the question he already knew the answer to deep in his gut. "You wouldn't happen to be talking about…*Reverend* Liam McSweeney?"

"You know any other McSweeneys?" Tom asked and Thatcher shook his head. "Then it's the one you know about."

Thatcher leaned back in his chair and let out a groan of dismay.

"A reverend?" Nadine's gaze shifted among the men. She had a slightly amused expression on her face.

"He *used* to be, ain't anymore, but the title sure stuck." Tom took a drink of whiskey and set his glass down and turned to Bill. "If McSweeney's heard a single word about any of this, then you can bet your ass he's coming after her."

CHAPTER THIRTY-NINE

East of Broken Stone, Wyoming

McSweeney and Samson walked along the mountain until he saw what seemed to be a barely tread path leading up toward a dip between two hills.

That's the trail. That's where they'll cross through.

He urged Samson through a grove of cedar trees about twenty feet away from the seldom-traveled trail. McSweeney got down, looped Samson's reins around a tree trunk, and got to work.

The sky had been a chalky gray all day and weather was rolling in. The breeze was getting stronger and carried a chill along with it. McSweeney gathered a pile of cedar branches and it didn't take him long to make a small lean-to shelter, low enough to the ground for him to lie down beneath. He spread out his bedroll on the carpet of dead needles and lay prone facing the trail.

Snowflakes began to fall, a sudden bright burst of activity, and then they slowed. McSweeney let out a heavy sigh and pulled the collar of his coat up against the cold wind.

It was all a matter of time now. Patience was a virtue McSweeney had plenty of. When this was over, he had thought about taking the bounty money and heading back to Old Mexico. No one seemed to care how tall he was down there. Maybe penance for his sins would finally be paid.

He shifted against his bedroll and drew his custom Colt Navys. McSweeney lay them in front of him close by. He closed his eyes, propped his chin on his hands, and let his mind drift.

Cobbler's Den, Wyoming

About five o'clock, a beautiful Mexican woman Tom

introduced as Rosa came into the saloon. She leaned down and kissed him on the cheek, exchanged pleasantries, and then wheeled Tom's invalid chair out of the saloon. He winked at Bill as he passed by and wished him luck.

After a few moments of quiet, Nadine was the first to speak. "So... McSween—"

"I knew it." Thatcher leaned forward and shook his head. "I just *knew* you were going to bring him up."

She stifled a laugh. "In the past few days, I've seen you in shoot outs, watched you as... whatever the bloody hell those mud-people were tried to attack us and..." Nadine let the rest of her thoughts on the Pattee Clan fade. "My point is, I've never seen you rattled, not once, until his name was mentioned." She raised her glass, took a drink of whiskey and pointed at Thatcher. "Why?"

Thatcher glanced at Bill and then cleared his throat. "McSweeney—"

"You heard he used to be a reverend..." Bill interjected. "He was a damned good one, had the gift of inspiration from what I've heard. Had a specially built pulpit and everything."

"Had himself a beautiful young wife, too." Thatcher poured a splash of whiskey for himself.

"Yeah," Bill nodded. "Story goes that one Sunday, the Reverend's wife pleaded ill and remained at their homestead while McSweeney went to church, delivering a sermon to beat all sermons. Now normally, after church, he would stay around and do all the handshaking and departing words and take care of church things for a while. But that day, for whatever reason, McSweeney left early."

Thatcher took a drink and nodded. "And when he got back to the homestead, he caught his wife and the town blacksmith."

"Oh *myyyyy*." Nadine's eyes went wide. "Quite the scandal."

Thatcher and Bill replied at the same time.

"Welllllllll—"

"That's not—"

Thatcher pointed at Bill. "You go ahead."

"McSweeney flew into a rage. That Irish temper of his blacked out everything else." Bill shook his head. "He killed both of 'em, his wife and the blacksmith, right there in bed. Rode out that very day, left the church behind along with the two corpses."

"How horrid." Nadine shook her head and then turned to Bill. "You mentioned he had a special pulpit... what was special about it?"

"Well, Mcsweeney uh... he's..."

Thatcher gave a sharp shake of his head, and Nadine noticed. She leaned on the table and focused on him. "What is it?"

"He's..." Thatcher ran a hand over his face and let out a heavy sigh. "McSweeney... he's a short person."

Confusion clouded Nadine's face. "How short?"

Thatcher cleared his throat, shook his head noncommittally and pointed to a spot on Nadine's arm about the middle of her bicep. He mumbled something incoherently.

"Pardon?" Nadine smiled with amusement and surprise.

"McSweeney's about that tall on you." Thatcher repeated his words more clearly.

Nadine looked from Thatcher to Bill and back again. "Are you telling me... that McSweeney is... a little *wee* man?" An amused smile crept onto her face. "And he's *Irish*?"

As Thatcher met Bill's gaze, Nadine erupted into laughter.

Thatcher met Bill's gaze. "She's not taking this seriously."

"*Naw*, not at all."

"But he's..." Nadine wiped at her eyes. "He's still a wee *little* man, right?"

Before either Thatcher or Bill could reply, Nadine burst into breathless laughter, stood up from her chair and waved her hands as if she was trying to fan away the flames of humor. She walked across the room and leaned against the bar as Henry watched, confused but amused at her outburst.

Thatcher turned to Bill. "I heard McSweeney never takes the first shot at a bounty."

"Heard the same." Bonespur nodded, glanced at Nadine still laughing at the bar, and then he drank from his glass. "Someone told me he does it to see if he's still loved and protected by God."

"Well that's just..." Thatcher scoffed and shook his head. "That's an entirely new river of—"

"Crazy, yeah." Bill sighed heavily. "We ain't got much farther. Let's skin on out of here at first light and get over the mountain. Once the hard part's over with, it'll be an easy stretch to Broken Stone."

Thatcher nodded and crossed his arms. He wondered if any lawmen were closing in on Abram and his crew. For all he knew, the men could have been captured all over again and waiting in some jail.

But I know better.

The Pale Horse gang—*at least what remained of them*—would play things smart and hide the best they could. Thatcher stared at his glass of whiskey and he thought about the train wreck back in Broken Stone.

Marshals caught up to the outlaws not long after and had a shoot out in Crimson Creek before they were captured.

What the hell did they rob? Ain't a single lawman said a word about recovering stolen goods from the train.

Thatcher shook his head and drank the last of his whiskey.

It's still in Broken Stone. Whatever loot they robbed is still by that river.

Rose's was the only boarding house in Cobbler's Den and it was as clean and well taken care of as everything else in town, right down to clean bed linens.

Bill had staggered into a room and Thatcher could hear

him already snoring behind the closed door. Nadine walked inside their room and Thatcher paused in the hallway, looked over the stair railing downstairs and then through the window to the main street. He nodded approval and went into the room with Nadine.

She had taken her hat off and her hair was down and Nadine let out a soft, tired groan as she lay back on the soft-looking bed. Thatcher closed the door and cleared his throat as he glanced at the small chair by the window. "You uh... get some rest and I'll just..."

Nadine sat up and turned to him. "Do you *really* think anyone will try to get me here in this little town?"

"Well... Tom said that Doyle and Tootie came through just last night." Thatcher shrugged. "Hard to say who else has heard about things and is trying to track you... *us*, down."

"Valid point, but still." She smiled at him. "You need sleep too. At least one good night."

Nadine stared at him a moment and then held her hand out to him.

Thatcher stared at her hand and felt his heartbeat quicken as he took it in his. He walked closer and sat down on the edge of the bed beside her. She stared into his eyes and shifted, tilted her head slightly.

"You..." Thatcher let out a soft breath. "Nadine, you just might be..." He shook his head slightly and then looked into her eyes. "No, not *might be*... you *are* the most beautiful woman I've ever known. You're kind and brave and... everything and more a man could want and wish for."

"Including you?" Nadine's expression softened and she smiled softly.

"Most *definitely* including me." Thatcher sighed. "But right now, we've got to keep focused on what needs done, on the things we need to do to keep us alive."

Nadine shifted her gaze from his, considering his words. She nodded and looked back at him. "Yes. Okay."

"Okay?" Thatcher was surprised at her reply.

She nodded. "You're right."

He turned away with a slight shake of his head.

"What's wrong?"

"I just… I reckon that might be the first time a woman's told me I'm right about something."

Nadine laughed and laid her hand against Thatcher's arm. "When you're right, you're right, and I have no issue saying such a thing. We focus on what needs doing until I'm… *we* are all safe in Broken Stone."

"Right."

She stared into his eyes and a slight smile crossed her lips. "But one thing… because if I don't… it'll absolutely become the *only* thing I'll be able to focus on."

Thatcher felt her hand slide up along his arm and his heart raced faster. "Oh, well… in *that* case, by all means. I… I wouldn't want your mind occupied by other things."

Her smile widened. "I hoped you'd agree."

Nadine moved her hand up against the back of his neck.

"Well, when you're right, you're right." Thatcher whispered.

She kissed him, and Thatcher felt her lips against his. He moved his hand around her waist to the small of her back and Nadine let out a small groan. The world faded completely until it was only the two of them in this moment and it took every ounce of strength in Thatcher to pull away.

"Whew… I… *whewwww.*" Thatcher felt light headed and he swallowed hard.

Nadine smiled and exhaled slowly as she gently pulled him to lie down on the bed. She turned onto her side and lay against his chest as he put his arm around her. "How much farther until we get to Broken Stone?"

Thatcher wondered if she could feel the way his heart seemed ready to thump right on out of his chest. "We'll be there by nightfall tomorrow."

Even though he couldn't see her face, Thatcher heard the smile in her tone as she whispered to him in the darkness. "Good."

CHAPTER FORTY

Broken Stone, Wyoming

Abram saw the sign outside Macie's Saloon and reined his horse in front of a hitching post. The rest of the men followed suit and when they all got down from their saddles, he spoke to them.

"Mark my words, fellas. You'd best behave yourselves." Abram snickered and shrugged as if he was addressing mischievous boys. "Within reason. Keep them damned revolvers holstered." He looked them over and met each of their gazes as he did. "We don't want to draw any undue attention to ourselves, am I clear?"

The men nodded their heads in understanding.

"Alright then." Abram turned and marched inside Macie's. A piano player was just sitting down behind the instrument and a handful of customers were inside. He caught the gaze of the woman behind the bar. "Whiskey, Thistle Dew if you got it."

"I'll bring over a few bottles." Her gaze ran over the crew of men and she nodded at Abram as he, Blaine and Calhoun found a table.

"Don't seem like a bad town." Wilson hitched up the back of his pants.

"Well, you just got here, so I'm sure it'll go to hell soon."

"Shut up, Bennett." Wilson winced and scratched the front of his trousers as the two of them walked to a table.

Gord snickered. "You might want to get that taken care of before you go rompin' through town."

"I'm just fine, thanks." Wilson took the bottle of whiskey from Macie as she arrived, uncorked it with flourish and poured into a glass. He took a drink and sat it down, appearing to be happy as a pig in mud.

Gord studied him for a moment, and then Wilson's face broke out in red splotches as if he was exerting a lot of effort to restraining himself.

Wilson growled and scratched his crotch, then let out a groan of relief. "Damned mountain witches, every one of 'em."

Gord busted out laughing, along with Bennett, and then the rest of the men joined in.

"Go on, laugh it up, chuckleheads." Wilson nodded and stood up, drank the rest of the whiskey he had poured and then yelled. "Hey barkeep? Where's your mercantile at?"

Macie gestured with her thumb. "Two doors down."

He nodded and turned to Gord. "I'll be back. Gonna get some damned turpentine and a straight razor." Wilson marched across the saloon.

"Might want some new clothes too. Burn the ones you got on." Abram laughed as the man walked out of the saloon. The piano player started a tune, and Abram watched as a few dancing girls begin working the room. A blonde-haired, blue-eyed woman tilted her head and winked at him. Abram winked back and then turned to Blaine and Calhoun. "Some places just... have a better class of *everything*, don't they?"

"They damned sure do." Blaine nodded as his gaze ran over the blue-eyed beauty.

Now sitting by himself, Bennett shifted his chair to join the other men at their table and Gord crossed the room to stand at the bar and flirt with Macie.

Calhoun took a drink of whiskey, and with the men out of earshot, he leaned closer and spoke in a low voice. "Speaking of higher class, I've been wanting to ask. Are we *really* going to split up the money with these other men?"

Abram smiled and raised an eyebrow.

"That's what I thought." Blaine nodded and swatted Calhoun's arm. "I told you."

"After the Bartlett woman's been taken care of, but not before. We may need them against the Marshal." Abram sighed and drank some Thistle Dew. "After that... well, I reckon it'll be time to part ways and get things back to normal again."

A heavyset man with a round-brimmed hat walked into the saloon, looked around and then stared at the bar. He nodded and smiled wide. "Gord!"

Turning away from Macie, Gord eyed the man up and down. "Maybe."

The other man's smile widened and he shook a finger at Gord as if a joke was being pulled on him. "*Nawww*, it's you. Gord Blanchford." He put his arms out to his sides as if to present himself. "Don't you remember me? Hank Kilmont."

Abram watched the way Hank stood, the way his expression on his face didn't quite fit with his friendly, *good buddy* words.

Gord took a sip of whiskey and studied him for a moment before he shook his head. "I'm sorry, ol' cuss. I reckon it's probably been a while and I usually remember a face, but I... can't quite recollect—"

"Well *naw*, I..." Hank shook his head. "I reckon I ain't quite being fair to you. We ain't never actually *seen* each other. I just figured out of some kind of curiosity maybe, that you'd know who the husband of the woman you was sleeping with."

"*Awww helllll*." Abram growled under his breath.

The smile left Hank's face and he glared at Gord. "Shannon Kilmont. Long red hair, green eyes that shone like emeralds in the sun." Hatred glowed in Hank's eyes like molten iron.

"*Mmmmm*." Gord sighed, took another drink of whiskey and slowly nodded as if his memory was coming back. "I do recall her... o' course... I saw her mostly from behind."

"Damn!" Abram shoved his chair away from the table and stood up, but it was far too late to make any difference.

"You son of a bitch!" Hank swung a ham-handed fist and punched Gord on the side of his face.

Gord's head snapped to the side and he brought his glass up and smashed it against Hank's face. Whiskey splashed over his face and shards of glass stuck out from Hank's bloody skin. He staggered a step backward and pulled a belly-popper derringer from his coat pocket. His thick-fingered hand struggled to cock the hammer and that was the only hesitation Gord needed.

Quick as lightning, Gord drew a revolver, cocked and shot Hank in the center of his chest. The bullet passed through his back and a blood sprayed against the dirty saloon floorboards. A trickle of blood fell from the entrance wound, but Hank fell face forward and slammed against the floor, dead before he landed.

Gord holstered his revolver and turned toward Macie. "I'll need another glass."

"I don't reckon you'll be needing one at all."

An older man with a Sheriff's badge stood just inside the front door. He looked at Hank's body and then glared at Gord.

Abram turned to Blaine and Calhoun and growled in a low voice. "No undue attention."

CHAPTER FORTY-ONE

West of Cobbler's Den, Wyoming

As they rode out of Cobbler's Den and across the flatlands, the air turned bitter and the sky changed to a mottled gray. Ahead of them, the tops of the mountains were shrouded in a gray mist. The wind against their backs was brutal and cold, blowing from east to the west and it felt like a storm was brewing.

They rode on, bracing against the chill until they reached the base of the mountains and stopped. Snow began to fall like down feathers from a busted pillow. The sun had become a ball of light hidden behind a gray veil.

The horses breathed plumes of steam and Ginger flicked her tail at the sight of the terrain ahead.

"That looks none too promising." Bill pulled the collar of his coat up around his neck. "But we'd best get to it." He urged Patches ahead and they started up the trail with Thatcher at the end.

The farther they traveled, the heavier the snow fell and Thatcher saw drifts begin, swirling up along the base of the cedar trees. He glanced down at the tracks of the horses and watched it continue to deepen as they climbed. The horses stepped cautiously, but even so, one or another would slip against the snow-covered ground.

Thatcher glanced behind him and felt the full brunt of the wind against his face. The base of the mountain and the flatlands were gone, lost in a blizzard of white.

❖ ❖ ❖

Broken Stone, Wyoming

"So what in the Sam Hill is this all about?" Sheriff Birdie crossed his arms and leaned back against his desk. He stared at Gord and Abram spoke up.

"It… it was all over something that happened long ago." Abram gestured to Gord. "He was trying to remain civil but that other man, Hank, drew a gun on him. It was self defense."

Birdie turned to Abram. "And who the hell are you again?"

"*Me*?" Abram pointed at his chest. "I'm just… I'm nobody. Just a citizen who just happened to witness this *terrible* event."

"Uh huh." Birdie narrowed his eyes.

Williams, who had been standing in front of the jail cell, walked over and stood beside Birdie. "What's this about messing around with the man's wife? I reckon I might be hunting some blood m'self over something like that."

Williams crossed his arms and leaned back against the desk like Birdie.

"She was a red head." Abram snickered and shook his head. "A finer passion, there is none, and prone to driving men half crazy." He slowly crossed the room and pointed back at Gord. "But that aside, viewing this man for anything else other than self-def—"

Abram turned quickly, drew the knife from the sheath at his side as he did, and plunged it into William's stomach. As he yanked the blade free, Abram heard the sound of Gord cocking the hammers on his revolvers.

Williams stared at the bloody wound on his stomach and then his eyes rolled back to show the whites as he fell forward against the floorboards.

Birdie's face flushed red and his hands twitched at his side. He glared at the barrels of Gord's revolvers and hissed through clenched teeth.

"Now then," Abram turned away from the deputy and looked at the Sheriff. "Ease those Peacemakers from your holsters, put 'em on the floor and kick 'em over."

Birdie did as he was told and one of the revolvers slid through a puddle of Williams' blood on the floor, dragging a red streak over the worn wood.

"That's a good boy." Abram picked them up from the floor and held them out, admiring the guns. He gave a nod of approval and then quickly closed the distance and slammed a barrel against the side of Birdie's face.

The Sheriff yelled and Abram jammed the barrel of the revolver just below Birdie's rib cage. The old lawman wheezed for breath and Abram shoved him back down flat against the desk.

Blood flowed from the gash on Birdie's face and he clutched his chest and gasped for air.

"You and I are going to have a little conversation." Abram leaned closer and tapped the barrel of the Peacemaker against the lawman's kneecap. "Every time you give me an answer that's not to my liking, I'm going to get angry... and I'm going to hurt you. Badly."

Abram smiled at Birdie and tapped the Peacemaker against his leg again. "The first bullet is going to go in that kneecap of yours."

Birdie glared at him with red eyes. Blood dripped along the side of his face to the top of his desk.

CHAPTER FORTY-TWO

East of Broken Stone, Wyoming

Thatcher could no longer see Bill at the front of their group and could barely see Nadine and Sadie in front of him. The wind gusted against his back, hard enough at times that Thatcher held onto the saddle horn to keep his balance.

Ginger began to slip more frequently and when Thatcher looked at Sadie's tracks in front of him, he saw the snow was at least a foot deep, if not more. It was a churning chaos of white and gray and the snowdrifts rose on either side of the trail.

They rode in silence, the whispering sound of snow against the trees the only noise, and then the blizzard began to slow as they neared the top of the mountain ridge. Overhead, the sky brightened and Thatcher squinted his eyes against the abrupt change in light. The snowflakes slowed and Nadine reined her horse to a stop.

Thatcher reined Ginger to stop and looked ahead of them.

Bill's voice growling up ahead. "Come on, you big bastard!"

Thatcher called out. "Bill, you alright?"

For a moment, there was no reply and then Thatcher heard the sound of Bill grunting with effort and then the sound of snapping branches.

"*Hahaaaa!*" Bill yelled and as the wind died down, Thatcher could see the burly man standing beside the thick trunk of a fallen tree.

"See? Nothing to worry about!" Bill laughed and climbed back up onto Patches while Nadine and Thatcher rode up close to him on the crest of the mountain.

Ahead of them, the forest of cedar trees was blanketed by snow, bright and pure and stretching on forever. White mist cloaked what lay ahead, making the whole region dreamlike and surreal.

Nadine stared out at the sight with an expression of awe.

"Don't have anything like this in London, huh?" Thatcher smiled at her.

"No," Nadine looked around and smiled back at him. "Nothing even close."

Thatcher looked back the way they had come and then up at the mountain ridge. A massive bulkhead of snow had built up from the swirling wind. The size of a Conestoga wagon, the drift was long smooth curves as beautiful as a marble sculpture.

"Well, it might be pretty, but it damned sure ain't where we need to be." Bill took his hat off and slapped it on his leg, knocking the snow off. "If another snow squall like that one snaps up, we'll be sleeping on this damned mountain."

He stuffed his hat back on his head and started down the other side.

"Broken Stone and a hot bath await." Thatcher said.

"And continued conversation." Nadine smiled at him as she urged Sadie ahead after Bill.

"*Aww,* I…" Thatcher smiled back at her. "I ain't forgot about that."

He waited for a moment to get some distance between Ginger and Sadie, and then Thatcher urged his horse ahead. The trail here was a steeper slope than the ascent, a narrow deep cut into the ground book ended by dense cedar tree growth on either side.

"Hey Bill?" Thatcher called out. "What're you going to do after all this is settled?"

"*Ohhh* well…" Bill coughed and spit on the side of the trail. "Maybe Tom was onto something about all them heavy gunners going south to get away from these winters."

"If you go south," Nadine spoke up, "you might have to give up that fox fur hat."

Bill raised one hand in the air defiantly. "I'll give up my fox fur hat when they pry it out of my cold, dead han—"

A gunshot cracked from the woods and parted the top of Bill's hat. A second shot followed and Patches whinnied in pain. The mare bucked down the sharp slope and Thatcher saw a length of rope rise out of the fallen snow across the path. He opened his mouth to yell but it was too late. The rope caught the horse's legs and she fell forward, throwing Bill from the saddle along the side of the trail.

Sadie, right behind Patches, spooked and slid, tripped on the rope and fell on her side. Nadine screamed as her leg became pinned beneath the horse.

Thatcher jumped down from Ginger as he drew a Peacemaker and eyed the left side of the trail. He ran toward Nadine as Sadie thrashed against the snow and got to her feet, Thatcher yanked Nadine away from the trail and shoved her behind a cedar tree.

"You okay?" He whispered to Nadine.

She nodded at him, wide-eyed and scared.

Thatcher crouched low. "Get your guns and don't shoot until you're sure of who it is."

He took a deep breath and charged toward another cedar tree to his right. A gunshot cracked and bark blasted from the tree trunk and Thatcher dove down onto his stomach. He crawled behind a thick, snow-covered tree trunk and inched forward.

Bill started shooting his Colt Walkers, one after another.

Thatcher drew his other Peacemaker, intent on joining Bill. He peered around the side and ducked back again as he saw a flash of movement. The side of the tree exploded as the bullet punched through the rotten wood. Thatcher felt a searing heat as hot lead grazed his right cheekbone and he growled in pain between clenched teeth.

Behind him, Nadine shot and Thatcher spun around to see her duck back behind the tree trunk. Her breath made plumes of steam as she sunk down against the snow.

Muffled footsteps ran through the snow farther up along the trail.

Thatcher cocked the hammers on his revolvers and charged out from cover.

CHAPTER FORTY-THREE
Broken Stone, Wyoming

"Can't we just kill him and be done with it?" Gord leaned closer to study Sheriff Birdie.

The man's left eye was swelled almost entirely shut, puffed taut to a shiny black and purple. Blood leaked from his right nostril and clotted along his upper lip. A cloth gag had been tied around his mouth and Birdie glared at the men with his one good eye.

Gord winced and shook his head. "The world will be much better off without one more lawman."

Abram stared at Deputy Williams face down on the floor. "I ain't disagreeing with you, but *nawww*, not just yet." He scratched at the whiskers along his neck and nodded at the Sheriff. "I can't put my finger on it just yet, but something tells me that *fat boy* might still be of use."

"So what're we going to do, babysit him until someone comes into the Sheriff's office and finds us here?" Gord scoffed and pointed against one wall. "I reckon we could just stack up the bodies like wood over there."

"*Naw*, that's…" Abram shook his head. "I think I've got a better idea."

He walked to Birdie and tapped the barrel of a Peacemaker against Birdie's forehead. "Where's your homestead, Sheriff?" Abram smiled and leaned closer. "*Hmmm*? Tell me where you hang your hat at the end of the day."

Less than an hour later, Abram and Gord had taken horse blankets from the back room and wrapped the old lawman, tying it tightly with twine. They struggled and grunted with effort as they carried him through the back door and tossed him in the back of the wagon there.

"Damn." Abram breathed heavily, leaned forward and put his hands on his knees. "If we was carrying gold, we'd be wealthy men."

"Too bad it's just a worthless sack of pig shit." Gord

snickered. "You sure being at the Sheriff's house is a good idea?"

"Only thing I'm sure of right now is where I hid the money from the train robbery." Abram grinned and stood up straight. "But I reckon using the lawman's house as a hideout for a day or two will suit us all *jussst* fine."

Abram looked at the blanket-wrapped shape in the wagon. He reached his hand out and slapped at what he figured was the Sheriff's rump. "*Whewwwheee*! Gonna have us a hog killing good time!"

CHAPTER FORTY-FOUR
East of Broken Stone, Wyoming

Thatcher felt his heart hammering in his chest as he charged across the trail into the woods. The wound on his face burned and bled down his cheek. He ran between the trees in the direction he had heard the running footsteps and stopped behind a massive cedar.

He listened and looked around the woods, but there was nothing, not even the sight of tracks through the fallen snow.

There.

A flicker of movement to his left, uphill, and Thatcher ran ahead. This way and that, the figure moved, somehow always keeping a tree between them. A shot cracked, the bullet so close Thatcher felt it buzz past him like an angry bumblebee. He clenched his teeth and shot back in the direction he thought it came from.

Drawing me out away from the others. Clever little bastard.

A clutch of fallen trees lay on the mountain, and Thatcher watched as the short figure ran beneath, moving and dodging, fast as a prairie dog. Thatcher jumped over a log and saw a line of fresh tracks in the snow. The sight of them made his heart lurch with excitement and Thatcher barreled through the fallen debris, seeing dark flashes of a wool coat moving through the woods.

A shot blasted and a bullet blew a chunk of wood from the tree Thatcher had just moved away from. He growled and fired back twice as he ran ahead, stumbled, and his right arm caught on a tree branch. The Peacemaker fell from his hand and as Thatcher reached for it, he froze and stared at the downed tree in front of him. His ears rang from the dead quiet in the woods and the blood pulsing in his ears.

McSweeney leaped from behind the tree and Thatcher dove forward in the snow and grabbed onto the man's right ankle. McSweeney let out a sharp yelp of surprise and then brought the heel of his other boot down, grinding it over Thatcher's fingers.

Thatcher screamed and pulled his hand back, and McSweeney crawled on top of the fallen tree. As the man raised his Colt Navy revolvers, Thatcher scrambled to his knees with everything he had and punched McSweeney squarely in the face.

The little man flew backward from the log and fell directly into the snowdrift behind it. Thatcher clawed at the tree, pulling himself upright, and then swung his arm to knock away the drift of snow. He glared over the top of the log but there was nothing but a few drops of blood on the pile of white.

In the middle of the snow, a pair of eyes flicked open and Thatcher saw the end of a double-barreled shotgun raise and aim at him. In such close distance, the sound of the shotgun thundered and as Thatcher ducked down, he felt the lead shot pepper his right shoulder. The log in front of him exploded into splinters of cedar and rained down on Thatcher.

McSweeney turned and ran and Thatcher pushed himself to his knees again. The snow beneath him was speckled with blood and the wound on his shoulder burned like a thousand hornet stings. He growled in rage, grabbed his Peacemaker from the snow and quickly crawled over the cedar tree, studying McSweeney's tracks.

Thatcher barreled through the woods, crossing patches of snow and areas of bare ground, protected by the canopy of trees. He paused behind a cedar, gripped his Peacemakers tightly, and listened. His labored breath escaped him in plumes of steam. Thatcher aimed his revolvers in front of him, looking for any flash of movement.

"I reckon I should've been using something smaller for target practice with you being all... *tiny*." Thatcher spoke in a loud voice, knowing McSweeney was within easy hearing range.

"Just keep talkin', Marshal."

Bastard!

As Thatcher turned his head in the direction of McSweeney's voice, a shot cracked and he felt a sledgehammer hit him low and to the side. He grunted with shock and spun around behind the tree. Thatcher looked down and saw the bullet wound in his lower right abdomen. He clenched his teeth and shook his head. It was a numb, heavy sensation, but the pain would come soon and try to swallow him whole like some great beast. Thatcher put his back against the tree and reloaded his Peacemakers. When he was finished, he spun around from behind the tree and fired, one revolver after the next, and saw McSweeney run away from his position.

Fast little bastard for someone with such short little legs.

Rage flowed through Thatcher as he ran through the wood and chased after him. He fired again, hoping to get a lucky bullet, but McSweeney somehow always dodged behind a tree, keeping cover between him and Thatcher's Peacemakers.

The canopy of trees ahead started to thin and Thatcher realized they were getting close to the trail again. A thunderous shot boomed and from his right, Thatcher heard a short, muffled, huffing sound. Through the branches of the cedar trees, he saw the bulkhead of snow crack in half.

As he ran into the middle of the trail, McSweeney turned backwards and raised his Colt Navys out in front of him toward Thatcher.

The snow barreled down the narrow channel of the trail like a massive white locomotive. Snow dust blew around it like the steam from an engine and it gathered everything in its path. McSweeney's eyes went wide as the avalanche descended, a churning pile of chaos. He had time to scream and then the snow swallowed him and the muzzle flashes of his Colt Navys whole.

Thatcher reached the edge of the trail and saw the horses buck and scramble out of the way. Bill leaped aside as the snow charged past him and Nadine watched from behind the tree he had left her. The avalanche roared down the hillside, and as the trail narrowed, the mass picked up speed and gathered snapped branches and debris.

He walked across the trail, now a hard-packed channel of snow. Thatcher pulled his coat tight against his side as he walked to Nadine. "You alright?"

She slowly stood up and though her expression was terrified, Nadine nodded. "I'm okay." Her eyes focused on his bleeding cheek. "Thatcher—"

"Get…" Thatcher said breathlessly and gestured toward Sadie. "Get on your horse."

Her gaze fell on the lead shot wounds on his shoulder and her eyes went wide. "You've been shot! Thatcher, you—"

"Get… on your horse." Thatcher repeated as he turned away and walked toward Bill. The pain had arrived, burning scalding hot like a second sun had built a nest in his side. "Bill, you okay?"

Bonespur shoved his rifle into the leather scabbard on Patches and leaned closer to look at the bullet wound on her left haunch. The grazing bullet had left a deep groove in her hide and it bled, but it would heal quickly. Bill turned to Thatcher. "I reckon I'll stay above snakes for a little while longer."

Thatcher nodded at him and Bill's expression changed. His gaze flicked down to Thatcher's side and he gave Bill a nod and pulled his coat aside to show the bloody patch.

Bill let out a low groan and he met Thatcher's gaze and spoke in a low voice. "Can you ride?"

"I can ride." Thatcher nodded.

"Then let's get the hell off this damned mountain."

CHAPTER FORTY-FIVE
Broken Stone, Wyoming

Sheriff Birdie believed in community. It was one of the reasons that drove him to become Sheriff in the first place, along with a strong sense of justice. He served the people of Broken Stone and did the best he could to uphold the law. Birdie enjoyed knowing people's names along with their faces, took pride in handling each situation with as much understanding and, if *possible*, leniency as he could. Broken Stone wasn't a town of outlaws, just people being people, and they sometimes made mistakes—often ones they regretted as soon as the action was done.

But his deep belief in community is why he made his home right in town, in the thick of things. It was a simple two-story house painted a soft gray with darker trim around the windows and door.

Abram and Gord brought the wagon to a stop behind Birdie's house. Gord kicked open the back door and the two men carried the Sheriff inside and dropped him on the floor of the living room near the fireplace hearth.

"Cut the twine off him before he suffocates in there." Abram nodded to Gord and the man knelt down with his knife and sliced the thin rope wrapped around the horse blankets. After he exposed Birdie, Gord tied the twine around Birdie's wrists, cinching it tightly.

Birdie was red-faced and soaked with sweat. The gash above his battered eye leaked blood and had turned an angry purple, dark as an eggplant.

Snickering, Abram stared at Birdie and shook his head. "Not a bad little shack you got here, lawman." He nodded and looked around. "Yeah, I reckon this'll do just fine, right in town so we can't miss a thing."

"Reckon he's got any liquor in here?" Gord left Birdie on the floor, walked to the kitchen and started opening cabinets.

"He's a *lawman*, of course there's liquor in here."

Abram laughed and walked to a dark mahogany table beside the fireplace. A row of framed tintypes was lined up and Abram leaned down to look at them. Some of the men bore a resemblance to Birdie and Abram nodded. There was a photo of a woman, maybe in her twenties, dark brunette curls cascaded mid-way down her back and she held fire in her eyes. Abram picked it up and walked toward Birdie on the floor. He held it out toward the lawman. "Your Ma?"

Birdie glared at him with his one open eye and breathed heavily through his nose.

Abram laughed and tapped the picture. "*Whewwweee*... she *is* a beauty. I'd have taken over as your daddy without another thought."

Birdie said something behind the cloth gag in his mouth and though Abram couldn't understand the words, he understood the angry tone and laughed as he tossed the frame onto the lawman's chest.

"Hot damn!" Gord pulled down two jugs of whiskey from a kitchen cabinet and held them up proudly.

"I told you so!" Abram smiled and nodded. "Go and tell the other fellers over at Macie's where we're holing up at."

Gord nodded as he took a drink from one of the jugs and hissed a breath. "I'll bring back some more whiskey too. This tastes like rotgut rye."

"There's just no accounting for good taste." Abram laughed and looked down at Birdie. Without any warning and just as much thought, Abram kicked the Sheriff in the ribs. The man's breath rushed out of him and he choked behind the gag and rolled onto his side.

"I'll be back in a bit." Gord let out a low gravelly laugh as he opened the front door. "Try to keep him alive while I'm gone."

"I'll see." Abram laughed and sat down on a small couch. It was quiet except for the lawman's labored breathing and occasional sounds from main street. He drank from a jug of whiskey, grimaced as the harsh taste flooded his mouth, but swallowed it anyway.

"Sweet holy hell, lawman." Abram looked at the jug. "Gord's an idiot, but he ain't wrong. This tastes like bull piss." He put the liquor down on the floor, leaned forward and glared at the Sheriff.

"Nadine Bartlett and that Marshal had better be back in Broken Stone awful soon. Can't be more than a day." Abram sighed and leaned back again. "Hell, we stopped in Southbend for the night and I reckon they'd do the same somewhere."

The hair on Birdie's head was damp with sweat. He leaned his head against the floorboard and breathed slowly.

Abram moved closer and crouched down. He opened his mouth to speak and then shook his head and groaned. "You stink of piss, you know that? Sweet mother, I'll have to get a bucket of water to throw on you like a muddy hog."

He stood up and stared at Birdie. "If I found out you've been lying to me... *whewww... ohhhh* Sheriff." Abram took off his hat and tossed it to the couch. "I'll give you the ol' Apache treatment. Find a spot way out yonder and bury you up to your neck. I'll put a little honey on you, not a *lot* mind you, just enough."

Abram snickered and continued. "Couple hours and every ant in the territory will be crawling on that pretty ol' head of yours, eating away at that honey. And when that's gone..." Abram smiled. "They'll start on your eyes, wriggle up your nose and ears, trying to find out what's inside and if it's worth eating or not."

Birdie glared at him and the red color in his face bleached white.

Abram nodded. "That's alright. You don't have to say nothing. Yet."

CHAPTER FORTY-SIX

East of Broken Stone, Wyoming

At the bottom of the trail, the avalanche lay in a massive pile that spilled out onto the frozen pond of spring-fed water. Twists of tree limbs and jagged broken branches stuck out at all angles like the quills of a porcupine.

The trail had become a smooth, hard-packed trench of snow and the horses moved slowly, choosing their steps. Each time Ginger's footing slipped, the jostle made an explosion of agony in Thatcher's side. He clenched his teeth, pressed his hand against his abdomen and kept his sights ahead of him on Nadine.

On either side of the trail, snow was piled four-foot high, remnants left behind from the massive pile plunging down the path. A hundred feet down, the base of the trail cut hard to the left and ran along the edge of the spring-fed pond. Ginger slipped and Thatcher groaned with the pain. The waist of his trousers was soaked in blood and he pressed his hand tightly over his coat against the wound.

The pile of snow to their right exploded and McSweeney, red-faced and screaming, leaped from the top toward Nadine. He fired his two Colt Navys in mid-air.

Thatcher saw one bullet catch a loose lock of Nadine's hair. The second clipped the side of her arm and she screamed as McSweeney tackled her from the horse. They slammed down against the hard-packed snow and Nadine swung her arm, elbowing McSweeney's face.

She clawed at the snow, got to her feet, and raced past Bill as he drew his Colt Walkers and aimed at McSweeney. The little man jumped beneath Sadie and crawled through the other side as Bill shot and missed.

Thatcher jumped down from Ginger, grunted in pain as he landed, and charged down the trail.

Bill shot again and McSweeney screamed as the bullet caught his right shoulder. He drew back beneath the horse as

Thatcher aimed at the empty patch of snow where he had been.

Mcsweeney got to his feet and Thatcher ran around and lunged at him, dragging him to the ground. Their weight and motion propelled them along the smoothly packed channel and they began sliding downhill. McSweeney clawed at Thatcher's face. Twisting against the snow, Thatcher jammed his right thumb into McSweeney's eye and the man screamed.

A jagged rock in the trail caught Thatcher's right ribs and as he slammed against the side of the trail, he felt McSweeney flying out of his grasp. The breath left his lungs, and black spots danced in the corners of his vision. The snow around Thatcher was spattered in his blood. He gritted his teeth against the pain, pushed himself up off the ground, and charged after McSweeney.

Thatcher reached down for his Peacemakers, but his holsters were empty, lost in the slide downhill. He growled his rage and watched Nadine, at the base of the trail, stumble and fall at the side of the massive mound of snow. She crawled onto the frozen pond and Thatcher's heart lurched in his chest.

No, don't... don't go out on the ice.

McSweeney had reached the base of the hill and pushed himself to his feet. He turned to look at Thatcher and then pulled a sawed-off shotgun from beneath his coat. Casually, he broke the barrel, dropped the spent shells, and reloaded it fresh. McSweeney smiled before he turned his back on Thatcher and took a cautious step onto the frozen pond. And then another.

You son of a bitch!

Nadine glanced back at him and clawed her way past the middle of the pond. The bullet wound on her arm left a trail of blood over the milky-colored ice.

On the side of the trail ahead of him, Thatcher saw one of McSweeney's fallen Colt Navy revolvers. He leaned and stumbled as he snatched the gun from the ground, thumbed the hammer and kept running downhill.

Thatcher aimed at McSweeney's back and squeezed the trigger. The Navy dry-fired and Thatcher screamed as he ran the last few feet to the edge of the pond.

"*Patience*... is better than pride." McSweeney leveled the shotgun out in front of him, aimed right at Nadine's back.

Thatcher threw the Colt Navy as hard as he could, watched as it sailed through the air and landed right behind McSweeney's right boot. The ice made a dull cracking noise and then, as quick as the trapdoor on a hangman's gallows, the ice gave way beneath McSweeney's feet. He fired his shotgun skyward before he plunged straight down into the black waters.

There were several frantic thumps from beneath the ice, an awful scraping sound, and then it was quiet. Thatcher watched as a short thick shadow moved under the ice, headed toward the open end of the pond.

Bill reached the bottom of the trail with Ginger and Sadie behind him.

Thatcher glanced at him and then stared at Nadine. He raised a hand up to her. "N-now Nadine... easy. You just... just take it slow."

"Stand up." Bill shook his head and laughed.

"Bill!" Thatcher snapped his attention around. "What the hell are you—"

"Just... stand up." Bill nodded at Nadine.

She looked at Bill with an expression of confusion on her face, then yelped as the ice cracked directly beneath her.

"Nadine!" Thatcher yelled, ready to plunge after her.

Nadine fell into the water, coughed and sputtered, and then stood up in the frigid waters, which reached just beneath her shoulder.

Bill laughed and nodded toward the opening that fed the downhill stream. Thatcher watched as McSweeney's body floated from beneath the ice and flowed along the current.

"Being short must be a real pain in the ass." Bill laughed loudly as he got down from Patches and then turned to

Nadine. "Come on out o' there, little miss. I'll get a fire going."

Thatcher kicked and broke the ice along the edge of the pond as he walked out in the water up to his knees. Nadine's teeth chattered as she reached him and she shook as he put his arm around her. Thatcher crouched slightly, put his other arm at the back of her knees, and lifted her from the icy waters. She looked up into his eyes and Thatcher could tell it reminded Nadine of when he had carried her out of the river in Broken Stone.

"I got you." Thatcher took her up onto the trail as water fell from her soaked clothes. A few feet off the path, Bill knelt down by a small fire and added thin branches to it. He had taken the three bedrolls from their horses and had the blankets grouped together. Bill looked up as Thatcher set Nadine down to her feet.

"Ain't got time for modesty today, ma'am, but I assure you I'll avert my weary old eyes." Bill looked at Thatcher. "Get her out of them clothes and wrap her up in them bedroll blankets. We've got to get her warmed up."

Nadine turned away and Thatcher helped her from her soaked wool coat. He tossed that aside and held up a blanket as she finished undressing. Nadine hissed and trembled as the cold wind blew against her and chattered curses beneath her breath.

When she was done, Thatcher quickly draped the blanket over her back and then grabbed another. He wrapped it around her and led her close to the fire.

Nadine sat down and pulled the blankets tight around her. Her teeth chattered as she spoke. "B-bloody h-h-hell."

"Here," Bill looked at her and rubbed his big gnarled hand over his heart. "Like this, in a circle. Warm your heart up and the blood'll warm after."

Nadine nodded and shook beneath the blankets. Thatcher hung her clothes on twists of branches by the fire and groaned as he sat down heavily.

"How's that doing?" Bill met his gaze and then glanced down at the bloody patch.

"One more bullet and I'll be just fine." Thatcher groaned and lay down. "You wouldn't happen to have any whiskey along with you, would you, Bi—"

"Th-Thatcher!" Nadine chattered his name as she saw the bullet wound in his side. "Y-you're s-shot!"

Thatcher groaned. "More than a few times, yeah."

"*Naw, naw.*" Bill added a thicker chunk of wood to the fire, wiped his hands together and stood up. He walked over and crouched beside Thatcher, peeled the bloody shirt away from the wound to take a closer look. Bill sniffled and nodded to himself, then he went to Patches and pulled out a jug from the saddlebag.

"The last of my blackberry whiskey, but I reckon under the circumstances…" He knelt down and spilled some over the entrance wound and Thatcher clenched his hands into fists and growled behind a closed mouth.

After washing the exit wound, Bill nodded and handed the jug to Thatcher. "Go on and drink the rest. I'll be back." He drew his Bowie knife and walked off into the woods.

Thatcher opened his eyes and stared at Nadine. She had pulled her shoulders up so the blankets were around her neck. "You warmin' up?"

She nodded at him and he saw worry in her eyes.

Bill came back, holding his Bowie knife out with a thick gob of cedar tree sap on the blade. He held it out over the flame of the fire.

Nadine's gaze went to the bloody wound on Thatcher's cheek.

He gave her a weak smile. "I won't win anymore beauty contests, but it'll heal."

Nadine's eyes softened. "How many have you won in the past?"

"A few." Thatcher smiled and turned as Bill walked closer and crouched down beside him again.

"This ain't going to feel good." Bill didn't hesitate after that, only flipped the blade over and smeared a thick gob of softened sap over the entrance wound.

Thatcher clenched his teeth and growled in pain as the scalding putty hit the wound.

"Now the other side." Bill repeated the procedure on Thatcher's back.

It felt like a branding iron had pressed Thatcher's flesh and he arched his back and clenched his hands into fists.

"There we are." Bill appraised his patch-up work and nodded. "That'll hold until we get to Broken Stone and a real doc. Lucky shot though. Looks clean to me. At least I think so."

"Yep, that's how I feel." Thatcher put an arm over his forehead. "Mighty lucky."

Bill laughed, moved away and sat down on the other side of the fire. "That uh… that whole thing about McSweeney not firing the first shot—"

"Was a bunch o' horseshit." Thatcher growled.

"Yeah, *mmhmmm*." Bill nodded and rubbed his hands together close to the flame. "Sure was."

They sat there in the quiet for a moment, save for the popping sound of burning cedar wood.

Nadine softly cleared her throat. "That was the angriest leprechaun in history."

Bill snorted and looked at Thatcher, who let out a short bark of laughter.

And that was the plug in the dam that gave way.

They burst into laughter pure and sincere and honest, and it echoed off the mountain rocks around them like the sweetest sound of normalcy.

When the laughter died down, and the random snickering dried up, Bill stretched out flat on the ground and crossed his arms over his barrel chest. "When them clothes dry, we'll ride out of here and we ain't stopping for a single damned thing."

Expectedly, Bill began to snore in the next few moments.

Thatcher turned to Nadine. "Chill wearing off?"

"Almost." Nadine smiled and scooted closer to him. "Better now."

Thatcher noticed her teeth weren't chattering anymore and that was a good sign.

"We'll still get to Broken Stone by tonight, won't we?" She whispered.

He reached out and cradled the side of her face. "Damned right, we will."

CHAPTER FORTY-SEVEN
East of Broken Stone, Wyoming

Thatcher brought up the end of the group as they rode down the last of the trail at the base of the mountain. He kept thinking he saw flickers of movement along the trees to his left and it unsettled him. Thatcher turned and stared into the thicket of cedar trees.

As it turned out, what he was looking for was already ahead of them, across the trail.

"*Whoaa, whoa.*"

Thatcher turned to see Bill and Nadine stopping their horses, and the group of Crow warriors not much farther.

They had arrows notched in their bows, held down at their sides.

Bill stuttered and stopped as he tried to remember how to speak in Crow. The braves didn't flinch, only stared at him with faces made of stone. Bill looked back at Thatcher and Nadine. "Either of you two speak Crow?"

They both shook their head and Bill sighed and turned around. He held up both hands to show he was unarmed and took off his hat and held it up in the air as an offering.

One warrior urged his horse forward and when he got close, Bill tossed it at him. The Crow brave caught it, turned it over one way and the other, then brought it closer to his face and sniffed. He shook his head with a disgusted face and tossed it back to Bill.

"Well fine, fine." Bill shook his head. "No appreciation for…" He licked his lips nervously. "Alright then… uh…" Leaning back, Bill undid a saddlebag and pulled out a small cloth bundle. He opened it up to reveal some hardtack crackers and held them out toward the Crow.

With his free hand, Bill mimed eating them, and then tapped his fingers against his lips.

The Indian looked at him and then cautiously took one the crackers. He smelled it, glanced at Bill, and then took a bite. The Crow chewed once, twice, and then turned and spit it out onto the ground.

Immediately, the rest of the group raised their bows and arrows.

"*Waiiit*! Wait!" Bill dropped the rest of the crackers and pointed angrily at the group. "Wait a damned minute! I'm the Buffalo walker among the Crow!"

Bill yelled and pointed at his throat. "Your damned medicine man gave me this necklace as…" His words faded off as he looked down at the empty spot where his turquoise and buffalo teeth necklace had been. "*Welllllll*, shitpickles."

The sound of many stretching bow strings made Bill snap his attention back up. "Wait, wait!" His eyes widened and he turned to the Crow close to him. Bill held up a finger to the man. "Okay, alright." Bill slowly reached down to his side and drew out his Bowie knife. He stared at it for a moment and sighed, then held it out so the Brave could grab the handle.

The Crow brave gave a soft grunt as he tilted the thick-bladed Bowie one way and the other, and then he nodded and gave a grunt of approval. He glanced back at the rest of the braves and they lowered their bows and arrows and urged their horses up among the cedar trees. A moment later, there was no sign of them, ghosts among the wood.

Thatcher eased his hand off of his revolver and let out a heavy sigh of relief. He looked ahead and saw Nadine staring back at him.

She shook her head and whispered. "There's no bloody Crow in London, either." Nadine turned around as Bill urged his horse forward, and they reached the base of the mountain.

Thatcher turned to look up at the sloping hillside and the patches of cedars leading up to the craggy rocks. He figured he should take a good look, since there was no way he was ever coming back.

❖ ❖ ❖

Broken Stone, Wyoming

Abram laughed as Calhoun poured what was left in the jug of whiskey over Sheriff Birdie's face. The man groaned behind the cloth gag around his mouth and shook his head, slinging drops of liquor to the floor.

"His taste in whiskey must be improving." Gord laughed, took a drink from the bottle of Thistle Dew in his hands, and then passed it to Bennett.

The inside of the Sheriff's house had been rifled through, framed photos thrown to the floor, books tossed from their shelves, cabinets torn open. Men sat on the couch and at the kitchen table, all of them drinking whiskey and laughing at the lawman's expense. Wilson had opened a can of peaches and pulled the slices of fruit from the can with his fingers. Syrup dripped down his chin as he smiled. Bennett watched him in disgust, turned his entire chair away from him, and took a drink of whiskey.

The front door swung open and Calhoun barged inside and shut the door quickly behind him. He looked at Abram. "I just saw Bonespur Bill riding in on the east side of town."

"Was he alone?" Abram set down the whiskey glass in his hand.

Calhoun smiled and shook his head. "Got a lawman with him. And a woman."

"Split up!" Abram pointed toward the front door. "Gord, you and your boys get over in them alleyways across the street." He turned to Calhoun. "You plant yourself right there by that front window so you can see them as they come by."

Abram stepped back toward the staircase. "Blaine, you're upstairs in the other bedroom." He paused and looked at the men. "Don't a damned one of you shoot until I do. Nadine Bartlett is mine."

"Feels a little strange being back." Thatcher looked around at the townspeople. "Like the town got smaller somehow."

Nadine smiled. "Long journeys tend to do such a thing."

"I reckon so." Thatcher smiled back, feeling the weariness settling into his bones. "Well, best get to Sheriff Birdie's office and—"

"The Sheriff?" Bill's attention snapped to Thatcher.

"Yeah." Thatcher looked at him curiously. "Hopefully he'll have some sort of good news. Who knows, maybe Marshals caught up with the Pale Horse gang already."

"Oh, I… I don't reckon I'll uh…" Bill shook his head and seemed nervous all of a sudden. "You two go on. I'll… I'll be over at Macie's saloon. It ain't like I can add anything official anyway." Bill shrugged and his expression was anxious. He tipped his hat and guided Patches to the front of Macie's.

"What do you suppose *that* was all about?" Nadine turned to watch Bill tether the horse to the hitching post. "He seemed a bit nervous."

"Hard to say with him." Thatcher laughed as they rode on. Several townspeople waved and he nodded and smiled in return.

Nadine sighed and took off her hat. Her hair fell down along her back and she shook her head to loosen it up. "Part of me wishes they *are* captured already, and yet another part isn't ready for another long ride so soon to be a witness."

Thatcher watched the loose strands of her hair fall to the sides of her face. "Oh, I reckon there's time for a bit of rest no matter what."

Sheriff Birdie knew it was now or never. He eased onto his side behind his sofa, and moved toward the tintypes on the floor. Far across the room, the man named Calhoun stared nervously out the window, all of his attention focused outside.

Birdie reached the photo of his dear mother, tossed to the floor with a butcher knife stabbed through the tin. With his hands tied with twine, Birdie grabbed the knife, wiggled the blade free, and turned it in his hands to slice at the twine around his wrists.

He cut through the twine and Birdie pulled his hands apart and quietly crawled along the floor, glancing at Calhoun to make sure the man didn't notice. Birdie's side ached and he thought his ribs were cracked, but he continued on until he reached the bottom of the stairs. He put a hand against the wall and forced himself to stand up. Then, Birdie crept step by step upstairs with the butcher knife gripped in his hand.

He went slowly until he reached the top of the stairs. In the second bedroom, Blaine crouched down by the window and stared outside, as nervously as Calhoun. Birdie looked into his bedroom and saw Abram, standing off to the side of the window.

A single step inside, and a floorboard creaked.

As Abram turned, Birdie charged him, holding the knife high overhead.

Abram yelled and tried to turn the Yellowboy rifle in his hands, but Birdie was already there. He plunged the knife down into Abram's shoulder.

The outlaw screamed and squeezed the trigger. The shot thundered in the room and it unleashed hell as gunfire erupted everywhere outside.

CHAPTER FORTY-EIGHT

A dark shape moved in front of an open upstairs window of Birdie's house and Thatcher's eyes went wide as a rifle barrel poked through. He raised the leather reins in his hand and swung them down hard on Ginger's rump. The horse lurched forward and raced ahead with Nadine holding on tightly.

Thatcher heard the sound of a gunshot, muffled from inside the upstairs of Birdie's house. A flurry of bullets passed through the air where Nadine had been a moment ago. Thatcher drew a Peacemaker and shot at the figure in the upstairs window. The glass shattered and he saw a spray of blood over the sill and a man slumped down against the sill.

Townspeople screamed and ran for cover. A shot came from the ground floor of Birdie's house and Thatcher felt the hot lead punch into his left shoulder. Ginger whinnied loudly as Thatcher fell and slammed to the ground. His left arm went numb from the shoulder down and his blood spilled onto the dirt.

Movement from the narrow alleyway across the street drew his attention and Thatcher raised his Peacemaker and fired. A bullet blasted a hunk of weathered wood siding and when Thatcher shot again, a man screamed and clutched the side of his face as blood spurted through his fingers.

Gunfire from Birdie's house made Thatcher roll onto his side, and from beneath Ginger's legs, he fired twice through the window on the first floor. He heard a man shriek loudly and the rifle withdrew from the window.

"You sons o' bitches!" Bonespur Bill screamed as he came running up the middle of the street and a rifle shot cracked through the air. The bullet found Bill's left upper arm and a burst of blood erupted from it. He howled as he saw the wound and Bill's eyes went wild and he screamed at the men in the alleyway. "You *shot* me! You think this is the first time I've been shot, you mangy sons o'bitches!"

Bill raised his Springfield rifle and fired into the alleyway.

When the exploding round hit the side of the building beside the men's heads, it blew a shower of splinters around them. Before they had all reached the ground Bill pulled his pair of Colt Walkers and charged, firing one revolver after the next. One man's chest took two bullets and he slammed backward into the man behind him. Thatcher fired and saw his bullet hit the man in the face and they both went down to the ground.

The front door of Birdie's house swung open and Thatcher saw a man charge outside. His left ear had been blown off his head and blood soaked the side of his face and neck. He held a pair of revolvers and when his gaze fell on Thatcher, he raised them both and began to shoot. The bullets punched into the ground on either side of Thatcher, and he scrambled forward behind a watering trough near the boardwalk.

As Thatcher found cover, he aimed beneath the watering trough and shot at the man's left boot. The Peacemaker's bullet blew a hole through the man's ankle and Thatcher heard him scream in agony before he fell to the wooden planks. Now completely in his sights, Thatcher fired again and the bullet hit the center of the man's chest. He let out a surprised groan and slumped dead where he lay.

Abram held the rifle in both hands and shoved it toward Birdie's face. The Sheriff yanked the knife from his shoulder and sliced the blade over the knuckles on Abram's left hand.

The outlaw screamed in pain and rage as he dropped the rifle. Abram grabbed the lawman's shirt, yanked him forward, and head butted him.

Sheriff Birdie groaned and the knife fell from his hands. His world swam and black dots danced in front of him. The lawman bellowed in rage and he grabbed Abram's arms and shoved him forward with all the strength he had left.

When they hit the window, Birdie heard the frame snap

and the glass shatter as the two of them tumbled over the windowsill. They smashed down onto the tin porch roof and then rolled over the edge until they fell and slammed onto the dirt.

Abram raised up first and a fire storm of bullets exploded around him. A bullet caught him in the outer thigh and he screamed and limped away from the Sheriff, back toward the house. Birdie tried to roll onto his side, away from the flurry of bullets. His broken ribs shifted against each other and then a great ball of pain crashed into him.

Birdie's world faded to darkness.

CHAPTER FORTY-NINE

As soon as the flurry of gunfire began, the people started screaming and Sadie reared up on her hind legs. Nadine held onto the reins and leaned forward as far as she could, her legs stiff in the stirrups. When Sadie came down, Nadine yanked the reins hard and turned the mare's head.

Nadine swung her leg out of the saddle and when she got down, she quickly tethered the reins around the hitching post. She turned to Sadie and gave her a fast pat on the neck, though the mare looked around, wide-eyed and scared.

Turning toward the gunfire, Nadine saw two men burst out of an upstairs window and fall against the porch roof. They fell again, slamming against the dirt, and more gunfire erupted. She took aim with her Pietta revolver as the man ran back into the house. Nadine fired and hit the door frame as the rushed inside. She saw his face when the shot missed. He looked at her and Nadine recognized him from the Pale Horse gang.

She holstered her revolver, took the saddlebag from Sadie, and marched up the street.

Abram looked around inside Birdie's house and picked up Calhoun's Henry rifle. He crossed the room to the far side, hid behind the couch, and lay the rifle barrel against the back. Heavy footsteps rushed from the rear of the house and Abram spun the rifle toward the sound. He growled and aimed the rifle away from Gord as the man ran into the room.

"That's a good way to get yourself killed!" He growled at Gord.

"Well, I reckon we might end up dead by the time it's through anyway." Gord looked out the broken front windows and clenched his teeth. "We've got to get the hell out of—"

Gord stopped talking as a loud clear voice yelled outside—a woman's voice.

Abram turned and saw the Bartlett woman holding up a saddlebag in front of her.

"You kill me, and you'll never find your bloody money, you hear?" Nadine's eyes were full of fire as she marched ahead. "I swear to you, I hid it *realllll* good. I took a little though, or maybe... maybe I took a *lot*."

Nadine held a revolver down at her side and continued yelling. "That's right, Mr. Outlaw, I was laying in that river for a mighty long while... watching..." Nadine glared at the front of Birdie's house. "I saw just where you hid the money. But guess what, big man? It bloody well ain't there now!"

Nadine unbuckled the saddlebag in her hand. "In fact, it got a little cold for my tastes a few nights ago and I burned some to stay warm. Makes a *reallll* nice fire." She held up her hand with the stacks of cash in it. "Longer this goes on, the more I'll burn. It's up to you just how much."

"You dumb son of a bitch." Gord growled as he glared at Abram.

"She's... she's lying." Abram shook his head and felt his guts twist inside. He turned to Gord. "She's lying."

Gord aimed a revolver at Abram's face. "She's holding up the damned stacks of money in her hands!"

"That..." Abram glanced at the Bartlett woman and when he looked back at Gord, he saw the man's head explode as a gun fired from the darkened hallway.

As Gord fell, he squeezed the trigger on his revolver and the bullet punched into the sofa.

The big figure emerged from the hallway and Abram saw the Marshal standing there holding a Peacemaker with smoke curling from the barrel.

Thatcher turned away from watching Nadine to look at Bill and Bill shrugged, his face a mask of confusion. Thatcher gripped one of his Peacemakers and turned toward Birdie's house.

Damned crazy woman. I hope you're good at bluffing because that story is a whopper.

He clawed to his feet, one arm dangling uselessly, and Thatcher charged the front door of Sheriff Birdie's house.

Abram watched as his father marched into the room.

"Why didn't you just kill that bitch out front? The lawman too!"

The Marshal clenched his teeth and stepped face to face. "Because the more dead *lawman* are put down, the higher *your* bounty goes. Dead lawmen make the newspapers and that draws attention." He narrowed his eyes. "Keep on going, and they'll *never* stop chasing you. Right now, you still got a chance."

Abram glanced outside. It sure as hell didn't feel like he stood a snowball's chance in hell.

"Any men of yours are already dead, they just don't know it yet. You want to join 'em?" The Marshal pointed to the back door. "There's a horse in the back, saddled and waiting. Ride the hell out of here and don't look back."

Abram hesitated for a single moment, and then he ran down the hallway toward the back door. As he stepped outside, Abram heard the front door of the Sheriff's house slam open.

Thatcher aimed a Peacemaker in front of him as he kicked open the front door and rushed inside. At the end of the hallway in front of him, he saw the back door of the house close and cut off the sunlight. Thatcher charged ahead and the figure of a big, tall man stepped out of the shadows right in front of him and aimed a revolver in his face.

"Drop the iron, lawman." His voice was low and full of trail dust and gravel.

Thatcher clenched his teeth and braced for the gunshot. He slowly hissed a breath before he dropped his revolver to the floor.

The big man kept his revolver aimed at Thatcher and slowly walked backwards down the hallway. "Don't follow me or I'll add to the bullet wounds you already got."

The man turned, ran outside and slammed the door closed behind him.

Thatcher grabbed his Peacemaker from the floor and charged down the hallway. As soon as he kicked the door open, a bullet blew apart the door frame above his head and rained splinters of wood around him. Thatcher pulled back inside, gritted his teeth and then screamed as he charged outside and looked for anything that moved. His numb left arm hung useless at his side.

Thatcher ran down the alley and saw a flash of movement ahead of him. He squeezed the trigger and the hammer fell on a spent round. Thatcher bellowed in rage, holstered his gun and drew the Peacemaker in his left holster with his right hand.

He ran down the alley until he saw a narrow passage on his left between two buildings. The silhouette of the big man rushed down the alleyway and Thatcher ran after him and fired. A pink spray flew out from the man's shoulder, he stumbled, and then reached the opening to the main street.

Thatcher barreled down the passage until he saw splashes of blood on the ground. Just beyond, he rushed out of the narrow opening and saw more blood trailing into the street. Thatcher ran ahead and saw the blood trail end as a two-horse team pulled a wagon along the muddy tracks.

"No!" Thatcher looked around at the townspeople walking around, riding their horses through the street. He saw no one that looked like the man he had been chasing. Even his blood had been swallowed up whole.

CHAPTER FIFTY

Thatcher walked along the street until he saw Bill, sitting on the edge of the boardwalk in front of Sheriff Birdie's house. He had taken his coat off and the sleeve of his shirt was soaked with blood. Nadine stood beside him, holding the saddlebag in one hand.

Bill looked up at Thatcher as he walked closer, and his expression was solemn as he glanced toward the street.

Turning away, Thatcher walked to where Birdie lay and crouched down on one knee. "Oh, come on, hoss. I'm sure it's been a hell of a beating, but you're just sleeping on the job." He put a hand on the Sheriff's shoulder and gently rolled him over.

A single bullet wound was in the center of Birdie's chest.

CHAPTER FIFTY-ONE

When Thatcher found Williams, the man was still breathing—barely. When they got him to Doc McKenzie, the old sawbones told them that Williams was as close to death as he had ever seen a man, but the young deputy still had fight left in him. It took the better part of a week, but the Deputy was still alive and finally opened his eyes.

Doc McKenzie nodded as he led Thatcher and Nadine to the Deputy's bedside. "He's been in a lot of pain so I... took care of that."

Williams smirked and pointed a finger at the doc and winked. "You damned sure did."

"He lost quite a bit of blood, but he's got the good stuff, thick blood." Doc nodded.

"That's 'cause I..." Williams nodded and stared at them with eyes like an owl. "I eat my beets twice a week since I was in cradle school." He turned to look at Nadine and he smiled. "You're *purdy*. Awful *purdy* lady."

Nadine smiled and snickered at him. "You get some rest, but thank you, Deputy. You've been very brave." She leaned down and kissed Williams' forehead.

"*Awwhawwww*... that's..." Williams laughed and shook his head, smiling wide. "*Mmmm*...that's just as nice as cotton candy at the fair." He stopped and nodded to himself. "*Ohhh, I could really eat some cotton candy right now.*" The Deputy grinned and stared at his hand as he wiggled his fingers in front of his face. "I *feel* like cotton candy right now, all... floaty like."

Thatcher patted his shoulder gently. "You get some rest, friend."

Doc McKenzie walked out with them. "How's the arm? And... the rest of you?"

"It'll heal alright. At least I can move it." Thatcher gave him a nod. "Thank you for taking care of me, and for Williams."

"It's why I became a doc." McKenzie smiled and closed the door behind them as they walked outside.

They stood there watching Broken Stone's people going about their business as if the slaughter had never happened only a few days ago.

Thatcher sighed, but he knew he couldn't blame them. They had to go on. Everyone did.

The two of them walked arm in arm down the street toward Sheriff Birdie's office. It felt wrong to be in here, empty and hollow without the man's contagious laugh and warm smile. Thatcher let out a heavy sigh and tapped a hand against the desk.

"So now what?" Nadine looked at him and gave a soft smile.

"Well…" Thatcher held his hands out and she took them in his. He brought her close and took her in his arms. "I reckon we'll go on, too."

She smiled as he kissed her and leaned into his embrace.

PROLOGUE
Three months later

"You don't wait for the market in business. You bloody well create one." Nadine smiled at Thatcher as she looked at the plans for the hotel she was going to build right in Broken Stone.

"I never claimed to have a mind for business, but…" Thatcher tapped the architect plans. "Seems quite a risk for a place that big in this little town."

"If I can build a hotel large enough to support lots of people, well then, the infrastructure's already in place." Nadine smiled at him. "The market will come to *us*. Besides, I sent a telegram to my father. He's got the ear of the railroads and they're listening."

"Of *course* he does." Thatcher nodded slowly. "Was he happy to hear we retrieved all the hotel funding?"

"He was very happy to hear that." Nadine laughed and nodded. "Thank you again for riding out and getting the luggage."

"Well I reckon it would have been a shame to leave all that money out there for the prairie dogs to chew on." Thatcher shook his head, smiled at her, and then sounded out each syllable of the word she had used. "*In-fra-struc-ture…* yeah." Thatcher nodded. "You've got entirely too many smarts to have a face that pretty."

"Oh!" Nadine's eyes sparkled at his comment.

"*You're so purdy…*" Thatcher imitated Deputy Williams.

Nadine laughed loudly and threw her arms around his neck. "You are bloody *awful* at mimicry, you know that?"

"I guess I reckon that's because deep down, I only want to be me."

"Well…" Nadine acted shocked at his words. "That's a very… centered outlook."

"*Naw,* it ain't nothing to do with that." Thatcher shook his head. "It's cause I'm the only one who gets to do this."

He pulled her against him for a kiss.

The door to the Sheriff's office swung open and the man who stepped inside cleared his throat. A second man followed right behind the first.

Nadine stepped away quickly, blushing, and smiled. "Gentlemen."

Thatcher laughed at Nadine and then he glanced at the two Marshal badges on the men's coats. "Come on in, Marshals. Have a seat."

"Yes, well I... I have to um..." Nadine cleared her throat and grabbed the roll of floor plans. She glanced at Thatcher, stifled an embarrassed smile and stepped toward the door.

"Don't forget, Williams is coming for dinner!" Thatcher called to her.

Nadine turned around to face him, and she smiled. "I know, I talked to the young lady he's bringing with him."

Thatcher glanced at the two Marshals and then looked back to Nadine. "He's bringing a lady friend to dinner?"

"Macie from the saloon? Her sister, Laura." Nadine smiled.

"Didn't even know Macie *had* a sister." Thatcher shook his head.

"Laura's lived here *all* her life. How did you not know—"

"Yeah, I know they're both coming for dinner. Just wanted to remind you." Thatcher grinned and winked at her.

She narrowed her sparkling eyes and shook her head as she smiled at him. Nadine turned to the Marshals. "Good luck, he's absolutely *full* of mischief today."

"That's my wife to be." Thatcher nodded as Nadine closed the door on her way out.

"Nadine Bartlett, yes, and you're Thatcher Evans." One man sat down and the other took a seat. "I'm Marshal Cooper. This is Marshal Noble."

Thatcher nodded as he eyed the men up. "I'm usually pretty good at remembering a man's face, but... have we met before?"

"*Naw*, ain't never met, but we know…" Cooper glanced at the other Marshal, "quite a bit about everything that happened with the Pale Horse gang."

"Alright then." Thatcher leaned forward in his chair. "What can I help you men out with?"

Marshal Noble spoke up next. "We were coming through the territory and wanted to stop in, see if you had heard or seen anything about Abram Foster."

"Not hide nor hair." Thatcher tapped his fingertips against his desk. "I reckon after everything, he skinned out of here, rode off to Mexico maybe."

"Maybe, or maybe he's dead in a ditch somewhere. One can hope." Cooper leaned back in his chair. "So what's next for Broken Stone?"

Thatcher gave a light shrug. "I reckon I'll stay on as town Marshal as long as the people want me to be. I ain't got any aspirations of riding hell over yonder as a roaming Marshal. Broken Stone's big enough for me."

"I was sorry to hear about the Sheriff." Cooper shook his head. "Birdie Mitchell was a good man."

"He was," Thatcher nodded. "He's sorely missed by many."

"Well," Noble leaned forward as if to stand up from his chair. "Keep a watch out. Might want to add another deputy or two, just in case."

"I'm sorry," Thatcher laughed. "*Two* new deputies? Just for Abram Foster?"

Noble glanced at Cooper and then stared at Thatcher. When he spoke, his words were as if he was talking to himself. "You don't know."

Marshal Cooper turned to Noble and spoke in a low voice. "Were any of the papers sent down here as soon when we found out about the Bartlett woman?"

"I…" Noble gave a light shrug and shook his head. "It happened so fast, I don't think so." He nodded toward Thatcher as he continued talking to his fellow lawman. "He became a

Marshal so fast that I reckon no one thought of it after."

Noble's face flushed red and his eyes blazed with anger. "Three months, James. *Three months* this man's been going around not having any damned clue that—"

"You want to fill me in on what I'm missing?" Thatcher smiled and tapped against the desk. "I mean, I'm… right here. May as well not go over it once for him and once for me."

Cooper let out a heavy sigh as if he was embarrassed. "Marshals have been working with the Pinkertons for the past few years, building as much information as we can about the Pale Horse gang. Any known associates, family if they exist, anything that might help us track them down. The Pinkertons have started doing that with outlaws like the Pale Horse gang."

Thatcher listened intently and cleared his throat. "*Yeahhhh*, that information would've been mighty handy a few months back."

"Apologies about that. "Noble nodded, anger still on his face, and glanced at Cooper. "I promise you, someone's getting a hunk taken out of their ass when I get back."

"Well, what's done is done, I reckon." Thatcher shrugged. "Don't much matter now, but I still ain't sure why I should be looking for a couple deputies. I reckon the one I already have ought to be enough."

Noble scoffed, leaned forward in his chair and steepled his hands together. "The Pale Horse gang, except Abram *maybe*, they're all dead."

"Right." Thatcher shook his head slightly, confused. "That's sort of my point."

"Abram Foster has a twin brother." Cooper ran a hand over his face as if stress was chewing on him. "From what I hear, they hated each other, bad as Cain and Abel. Couldn't even be in the same gang together."

"But kin is kin," Noble added as he stood up from his chair. "He ain't going to take you killing his brother none too kindly."

Thatcher scratched at the back of his neck and considered the new information.

"Alright then." Thatcher rose to his feet as Cooper stood up. "Well, what's his brother's name? I reckon I don't scare easily from a single man."

"Abram was bad," Cooper said as he walked toward the door, "but his brother is the worse of the two."

"His name is Randall Foster." Noble stared at Thatcher, studying his face. "Runs a gang called the Black Hand. You uh... might've heard of them."

Thatcher's stomach twisted inside and it must have shown on his face.

Noble nodded as if he expected Thatcher's reaction. "Still don't think you scare easily?" The Marshal gave him a thin smile and tipped his hat as he and Cooper left.

Thatcher hadn't told Nadine everything the Marshals had said on their visit. He didn't reckon it was a direct lie, but it was in a gray part of the truth to be certain. He also reckoned he'd tell her when and *if* he needed to.

The Black Hand was a gang of legend, and the only quality that surpassed the bold nature of their crimes and the outright luck of their getaways was the gang's brutality. No one was safe—man, woman or child. New graveyards were made for their victims alone.

Maybe I should round up another couple of deputies. Can't hurt for a while, at least.

Thatcher lay in the darkness beside Nadine as thoughts swirled through his mind.

Bonespur ought to be coming through town soon, maybe I'll offer him a job.

Nadine curled up against him in her sleep and he drew the blanket up over her and held her close. After Birdie's funeral, Thatcher had talked with the Broken Stone bank about the Sheriff's house, and since there was no next of kin and they liked that he was staying on as Marshal, they were all too happy to work things out for he and Nadine to live there.

They had settled in as best they could and Nadine made the place her own. She even kept and fixed Birdie's framed tintype photos and displayed them on the fireplace mantel.

It seemed a quiet life. A *nice* life.

And mostly, Thatcher thought, *it is*.

He thought of being along the Wildtooth Trail and hearing Montgomery Thurmont softly whisper that *The Pale Horses are only the start*. He thought about Nadine and Bill and of sitting beside Sheriff Birdie on the front porch during so many warm evenings, sipping whiskey and nodding as the townspeople walked by.

But one single thought kept returning back to him late at night, after Nadine had settled into sleep and Thatcher lay awake, staring through the window at the night sky. In the darkened hallway of Birdie's house, the man who had stepped from the shadows into a single band of light, barely enough to reveal anything, but for the blink of an eye, it shone light on a strip of the man's face. In that brief flash of light, Thatcher couldn't shake the thought that there was something familiar there—the lines of the man's face, the shape of his eyes, *something*.

Thatcher couldn't quite get a hold of it, no matter how hard he tried.

THE END

Thank you for reading
THEY RODE PALE HORSES
by Gideon Stone

If you could take a moment to rate and/or write even a
quick review on the book page on Amazon, it would be
greatly appreciated!

Look for more upcoming old west tales from Gideon Stone,
and the next book in the *Thatcher Evans* series,
THE THREE WISE MEN

Printed in Great Britain
by Amazon